DAISY'S DILEMMA

"You have come to ask me to marry you, Lord Kincade," Daisy said, astonished. "Why?"

"You can ask me that after last night?" Kincade said, equally amazed.

"It was all foolishness," Daisy declared.

"Miss Morrison," Kincade said. "Will you consider what was observed last night? You and I were alone in very close embrace."

Daisy flushed. "Nonsense. You were not really kissing me."

"I was holding your body to mine and had your mouth covered with my own," he said bluntly. "In the vocabulary of most people, that constitutes a kiss."

Thus Miss Daisy Morrison was faced with a most perplexing problem. How could she make the most attractive lord in England take no for an answer. . . . ?

MARY BALOGH, who won the *Romantic Times* Award for Best New Regency Writer in 1985, has since become one of the genre's most popular and bestselling authors. She also won the Waldenbooks Award for Best-selling Short Historical in 1986, for THE FIRST SNOWDROP.

Lady with the Black Umbrella

Mary Balogh

A SIGNET BOOK

NEW AMERICAN LIBRARY

A DIVISION OF PENGUIN BOOKS USA INC.

Copyright © 1989 by Mary Balogh

SIGNET TRADEMARK REG. U.S.PAT. OFF. AND FOREIGN COUNTRIES
REGISTERED TRADEMARK—MARCA REGISTRADA
HECHO EN DRESDEN. TN. U.S.A.

SIGNET, SIGNET CLASSIC, MENTOR, ONYX, PLUME, MERIDIAN
and NAL BOOKS are published by New American Library,
a division of Penguin Books USA Inc., 1633 Broadway,
New York, New York 10019

First Printing, September, 1989

1 2 3 4 5 6 7 8 9

PRINTED IN THE UNITED STATES OF AMERICA

To Moira Dearnley, my sister
who has always encouraged me
to write humor

And to the memory of my father,
another gentle Arthur

1

The cobbled stableyard of the Golden Eagle Inn, thirty miles from London on the main road to Bath, was alive with activity despite the early hour. A stagecoach proceeding west had just resumed its journey, having disgorged its passengers half an hour earlier for breakfast and swallowed them up again a mere twenty-five minutes later. Stable lads were forking manure and old straw from the stalls. Two ostlers, one whistling cheerfully, were grooming horses. A third was harnessing the Viscount Kincade's team to his sporting curricle.

The viscount himself stood silently close to the door from which he had just emerged, watching the activity. He appeared to be the typical fashionable man-about-town from the crown of his beaver hat, past the ten capes of his heavy greatcoat, to the tips of his shining Hessian boots. The expression of studied indolence on his handsome face confirmed the impression. His eyes were heavy-lidded, his face impassive, and his lips curled into what might have been a sneer. It was true that his tall figure and perfect posture might indicate that the indolence was a pose. But it was impossible to know for sure what was the general condition of his physique beneath the long, heavy coat.

Lord Kincade was tapping a riding whip absentmindedly against his boots, the only outward sign of his impatience to be gone. He ran keen eyes over his team, noting that they had indeed been well-cared-for. The ostler who was hitching them to his curricle cast him a nervous glance and bent to his task

7

again. He was certainly taking his time, the viscount thought, hiding a yawn behind one tan leather glove.

It was a quite unholy hour to be beginning a journey. It must be barely six o'clock. His intention of making an early start had originally focused on the hour of nine. Certainly not six. And he had definitely not intended to head back in the direction of London, from which he had come just the afternoon before. But embarrassment and disaster can do strange things to both a man's intentions and his destination. Bath, and his reason for going there, would have to wait for another day.

He did not look embarrassed, of course, or the victim of disaster—at least, he hoped he did not. He was well aware that to appear either would only lower him in the esteem of the innkeeper and his servants to a point at which he would be treated with open contempt rather than with the icy, suspicious courtesy he had been favored with in the last hour.

He would not have made his nasty, embarrassing discovery until a far more civilized hour if it had not been for the barmaid demanding her pay before she went about her day's work. He had not known her like before. Barmaids in his experience did not awaken one rudely before the crack of dawn in order to demand payment for the night's sport. They trusted one to pay, and handsomely too, when one was settling the rest of one's reckoning after breakfast.

And it would be as well not to think of breakfast, Lord Kincade thought, shutting his mind resolutely to the image of bacon and kidneys and eggs that had flashed into it unbidden and unwelcome. Breakfast—and luncheon—would have to wait until he arrived back home in London.

His purse had been stolen. That was the conclusion he had been forced to after a search of his room—languidly made for the benefit of the maid who stood, hands on hips, waiting for payment, but frantically felt. He had searched her too, heavy-lidded eyes holding her indignant ones as his hands knowingly searched all possible hiding places. But as she had been not backward to point out, why would she have asked for payment if she had known his purse was missing and if she had been carrying it on her person? Was he daft?

And a young woman, he had discovered to his mortification,

who could be all bright eyes and enticing dimples and swaying hips and thrusting bodice during an evening of waiting on his needs, and all naked and giggling and experienced abandon during a night of energetic bed sport, could become a shrill and foulmouthed shrew when it seemed apparent that she would not be paid immediately for all her hours of hard work and might not be paid at all.

He had taken the offensive with the innkeeper, going downstairs immediately to demand in the languid, keen-eyed way that usually had all servants bowing and scurrying to perform his every wish what sort of a house this was in which a man's purse was not safe from thieves and pickpockets.

But the innkeeper had refused to be cowed, declaring that the like had never happened in his house before, that his servants were to be trusted, but that he would, if the gentleman insisted, line them all up in front of him that very moment, every last one of them, the arriving stage passengers notwithstanding, and strip them all naked to find if the purse the gentleman "claimed" to have brought with him were on any of their persons.

Lord Kincade had looked his host keenly in the eye and declined the offer. The purse was probably safe at the bottom of the nearest deep well by that time, and there was no way of identifying the money apart from it. Better to bow to the inevitable and at least retain some of his dignity.

"My bill," he had demanded, stretching out a hand as authoritatively as it was possible for one in his position to do, and regretting more than he could say his valet, preparing at the very hour no doubt to leave his town house with his trunks and rumble along behind him on the journey to Bath. "I shall have your money and more besides sent you by tomorrow. And yours too, Bessie," he had added to his recent bedfellow, who stood defiantly in the doorway behind mine host, hands still on hips.

Who were the other guests at the inn? he had asked the innkeeper before returning upstairs for his valise and repairing to the stableyard, where he fully expected to have to see to the harnessing of his own horses. But there was no satisfactory answer to his question, no potential thief there. It had been a slack night, he had been told. Only the gentleman with whom he had played cards the night before and his fancy lady and their servants. And only the two *ladies*—with an emphasis and a sneer on the last word—who had arrived without any servant save their lone coachman and who had kept to their rooms since their arrival.

And Lord Kincade had suddenly realized that his humiliation was not yet quite complete. He had lost a tidy sum to Mr. Martin the evening before and had agreed to that jovial gentleman's suggestion that, as the hour was late and the company congenial and honorable, the debt could be settled in the morning. Now he would be forced to awaken that gentleman, who was doubtless asleep in the arms of the female who accompanied him, and beg the indulgence of an extra day or two in which to settle his debt.

Mr. Martin had proved thoroughly decent about the whole business, even offering to lend the destitute viscount the money with which to continue his journey. And at Lord Kincade's embarrassed refusal, he had smilingly reminded him that at the very least he needed the price of the turnpikes between where they were and London. The viscount had reluctantly accepted that exact sum, not a penny more.

And so here he was, he thought, tapping his whip against his boot and beginning to feel annoyance at the slowness of the ostler, yet considering it prudent to maintain his indolent stance, since he did not have a spare penny with which to tip the man as he left.

He turned as the inn door opened behind him, and stepped aside to allow the two burly individuals who emerged to pass.

Viscount Kincade, however, had not lived for twenty-eight years—most of the last seven of those in London—for nothing. Indeed, it did not take a good deal of intelligence or experience to recognize thugs and bullies and to know when they were about their business.

The two new arrivals were about their business now, and clearly he was their object. His expression scarcely changed and his heavy eyelids scarcely lifted as he measured the situation during the second or perhaps two of grace that he was given. One of his would-be assailants was a great deal taller than he, the other shorter; both were considerably broader; both were unencumbered with long coat or cloak; both wore boots far heavier than his; both had bare knuckles while his were gloved. They were far too close for his whip to be of any advantage to him. He let it fall to the cobbles.

Lord Kincade deflected with his forearm the fist of one as it attempted to smash into his face, and at the same moment he turned and lashed out with his foot into the stomach of the second, who had lunged forward at him. He was given a moment's respite in which to turn away from the building into the open yard and prepare himself for the next double attack. They had chosen their time wrong. He was not feeling in a particularly good mood. In fact, he was feeling decidedly mean.

"All right," he said between his teeth, "who is for it first?"

But as they both came at him simultaneously, ignoring the hint that it might be more sporting to take him on one at a time, the feeling of exhilaration that was about to be born in Lord Kincade at the challenge, even though the odds were decidedly against him, died a stillborn death. A third, unseen force launched itself at his back, and he knew even as he bent to wrestle himself free that three against one in the present circumstances were just too many. A fist under his ribs robbed him of breath and all but caused his knees to buckle.

And then somehow, after a wordless, panting scuffle that could not have lasted longer than a minute, he found himself being held fast by two of his attackers while the third, the taller of the two thugs who had stepped through the door, stood before him.

"I 'ope yer took a good gawk at yerself in the glass this mornin', guv," he said, grinning to reveal a mouth in which there were the yellowed stumps of teeth on one side and none at all on the other. "Yer mug won't be so pretty next time yer looks."

At least they appeared to be without guns or knives, Lord Kincade thought with grim philosophy as a fist crunched into his jaw and felt as if it had mashed his brains. He was going to be allowed to live, then. Though apparently not in any degree of comfort for a while yet. What sort of thugs robbed a man first and then gave him a thorough drubbing? This sort, apparently. Rock-hard knuckles connected with one of his eyes as he wrestled uselessly with the two men who held him.

He did not hear the first words spoken by a different voice. His pain and his efforts to avoid more had taken precedence over all else. It took a moment for him to realize that his arms were free and that his three attackers were themselves warding off blows.

Thinking about it on the road back to London later, Lord Kincade was hard put to avoid breaking down entirely in helpless laughter. He might have done so, since for long stretches of the road he was alone except for his horses. But it would have pained his split lip and tender jaw and swollen eyes too much to smile, and his ribs would have protested loudly against laughter.

The new arrival was a woman—whether young or past her youth it was impossible to say at first. She was yelling shrilly something about cowards and bullies and rogues and scoundrels. And she was flailing about her with a gentleman's large black umbrella and poking with the point of it into the ribs of the only attacker who seemed inclined to stand up against the assault.

She was not a large female either in height or in build, a fact that made the outcome quite unbelievable and impossibly hilarious in retrospect. All three bullies, any one of whom could have picked her up with one hand and ground all her bones to powder, took to their heels, clattering out of the cobbled yard and into the street beyond without a backward glance.

Lord Kincade had only one eye with which to see. But it was quite enough. Quite enough! The female standing before him, bosom heaving, cheeks flaming, eyes flashing, was clad from neck to wrists to bare toes in a white flannel nightgown. Her light-brown hair hung in two thick braids to her waist. Her face glistened as if it had been freshly oiled. Her only adornment was the large black umbrella.

And she was young.

The viscount fumbled in his pocket as he felt the blood drip from his nose onto his coat.

"There, there," she said kindly and somewhat breathlessly,

as if she were talking to a witless toddler, "you will be all right now. They will not harm you anymore."

Miss Daisy Morrison was standing at the window of her room in the Golden Eagle Inn, gazing down absently at the stableyard below. It would have been more pleasant to overlook the front of the inn, she thought. And to have had a larger room and a less lumpy bed. The private parlor next door that she and her sister, Rose, had shared the evening before was not large enough to swing a cat in, as Papa would have said. Not that they had a cat with them, and not that she would have approved of anyone's swinging it even if they had. But any way one put it, the parlor was a small and shabby room.

It was as Mama and Rose had predicted, she supposed. And the Reverend Hammon. And Mrs. Ambrose, the doctor's wife. They had all warned her that it was not at all the thing for two young ladies to take to the road alone. Not that they were quite alone, of course. Gerry their coachman was with them, and the sight of his bulk and his shaggy black hair and jutting black eyebrows and the generally sooty look that clung to him even now, three years after he had last been down a coal mine, was enough to deter even the most dauntless highwayman, she had argued. Anyway, she was not afraid of highwaymen. Just let any one of them come close enough to their carriage to try to rob her and Rose. He would be given such a length of her tongue that he would soon go slinking away, his tail between his legs, his pistol hanging limply at his side.

Yes but, Mama had argued anxiously, highwaymen would not know her as everyone did for miles around Primrose Park. They would not realize, perhaps, that retreat was the best battle tactic when Daisy went on the offensive.

And besides, Mrs. Ambrose had tried to explain to her, there was more to traveling on the road to London than avoiding highwaymen. There were the proprieties to be observed. Gently bred young ladies just did not go jauntering around the countryside without their maids and their grooms and their companions or older female relations.

"But I am five-and-twenty," Daisy had pointed out quite

reasonably. "I *am* an older female relation. My presence will make Rose quite respectable."

Mrs. Ambrose had looked to Daisy's mama somewhat help-lessly, and Daisy's mama had looked back and shrugged. How did one explain to such a determined young lady that five-and-twenty was no very advanced age for all it was rather past the fashionable age for marriage?

And it would be silly, Daisy had continued to explain to both ladies, to load themselves down with servants only to have to send them all home again when they reached her Aunt Picker-ing's in town. One could not expect her uncle to take on a whole new battalion of servants and feed them too. Enough that she must call upon him to extend his hospitality to two nieces for the Season.

"If you would just wait, Daisy dear, for my brother-in-law to reply to your letter, you would probably find that he will send a carriage and servants too. And then you would not have to travel in that shockingly ancient traveling coach of your grandpapa's," her mother had suggested timidly.

"Your mama is right, dear," Mrs. Ambrose had said, nodding. "You were invited last year, it is true. But perhaps it will not be convenient to your aunt and uncle to have you this year. It is very unwise for two young ladies to travel all the way to town when they are not at all certain of their welcome."

All of which warnings and advice Daisy had swept aside with her usual forceful energy. Rose was nineteen already, indes-cribably pretty, boundlessly rich, and without any better matrimonial prospects than a match with Mr. Forbes or Mr. Campbell, gentlemen farmers both, blameless solid citizens both, and both entirely unworthy of her sister's hand. Rose must go to London. Rose must meet a lord worthy of her and make a dazzling match. She must live happily ever after.

Papa had been dead for two years. Mama would not venture farther than two miles from the door of the house where she had been brought as a bride almost thirty years before and remained ever since. There was only Daisy, five-and-twenty years old, who had singlehandedly organized their lives and run their home and modest estate and guarded her father's enormous wealth gathered during twenty years of quite ungentlemanly business dealings in coal. Only Daisy to see to it that her beloved Rose's life did not dwindle into a dull and ordinary one as a gentleman farmer's wife.

So they were on their way to London, Rose to make her come-out, Daisy to chaperon her, the faithful Gerry to convey them there in the enormous creaking, shabby coach that two fashionable louts who should have known more about good manners had hooted over in contemptuous mirth the day before when they had stopped for luncheon. Papa, for all his fabulous wealth, had scorned to spend any of his hard-earned riches on anything as inessential as a coach. Or on anything else for that matter, Daisy thought without rancor. Poor dear Papa had been a nip-farthing. A miser. No matter. There was all the more to provide Rose's enormous dowry.

Today, thank goodness, Daisy thought, they would finally arrive at their destination. It was true that she had not waited for her Uncle Pickering's reply to her request for hospitality. Once an idea was conceived in her head, she was far too impatient to wait around for a few weeks while someone else made up his mind to pick up a pen and dip it in an inkwell. But there would be no problem. Both her aunt and her uncle had begged her and Rose to come to town the year before after they had left off their mourning. At that time Daisy had declined, finding herself too busy settling her father's affairs and running his estate. She had not had the leisure at that time to realize that Rose's needs were greater and certainly more urgent than any other.

Daisy sighed as she gazed sightlessly down at the stablehands mucking out the stalls. She smoothed lemon oil over her face as she had been doing every morning she remembered to do so, which was not very often, since she was seventeen and Mrs. Hancock, the then rector's wife, had recommended it for freckles. She still had not quite lost her faith in the remedy, even though she had never succeeded in dimming the freckles that dusted her nose especially during the summer. If she could only remember to use the oil daily, her complexion would be flawless.

Servants at inns really did have a way of making their

contempt felt without a single word or gesture that one could grab hold of and take public exception to. This room, for example, and the parlor next door. They were surely not the best accommodations the inn had to offer. She had not been beyond the two rooms since their arrival late the afternoon before, but there had not been the noise and bustle she would have expected from a busy inn. There must be several empty rooms. And she did not believe that all the rooms were as small or as shabby.

Daisy glanced back to the high, lumpy bed, in which her younger sister still slept soundly. Rose had slept all night. How could she have done so on that mattress? And she would probably sleep for another few hours. It was still dreadfully early. It really was not worth getting dressed yet, Daisy thought glumly, continuing to smooth the oil over her face.

At least she was not the only person on God's earth to be up and about. A stagecoach had just departed, having taken up a full complement of subdued, sleepy-looking passengers. And of course there were plenty of servants busy in the stables. And a gentleman standing below her window, apparently waiting for his curricle to be brought forward.

Daisy could not see the gentleman very clearly. He was covered entirely by a greatcoat that looked heavy enough to bow him down to the ground. Except that he was not bowed down. He bore himself well, she noted with some approval. His beaver hat hid both his hair and his face from her view. But he looked very fashionable. And his curricle was certainly a smart conveyance, for all it was impractical with its seat that would accommodate no more than two persons. And his team was smart enough to make her itch to throw on some clothes so that she could descend to the yard to take a closer look. Alas, she must not do so. She was a lady on the road to London.

He might be seventy years old. He might be pockmarked and have ears that stuck out like cup handles and be the owner of a bulbous and broken nose. He might be any number of undesirable things. But from where she observed him she could dream. He was a handsome and fashionable lord. An *eligible* handsome and fashionable lord.

The inn suddenly caught fire and he turned, saw that there were ladies above him, and came charging to the rescue, taking the stairs three at a time. And he carried out in his arms a fainting but unharmed Rose. And they took one look at each other and Daisy knew that she did not even have to go on to London in order to find her sister an eligible husband. They could turn around and go back home and arrange the wedding there.

Instead of which, in reality, dreams aside, he was about to take himself away in that fast and sporting curricle, and a few hours later she and Rose would resume their lumbering journey after him or perhaps in the opposite direction. She had never been given much to dreams. They had nothing whatsoever in common with reality.

And then Daisy became aware of several strange happenings. The door below her opened and two other men stepped out. The ostler, who had been dawdling over the curricle, drew it and the horses back from the open yard. And one of the stable-hands, the one who had been almost out of sight right inside one of the stalls, put down his fork and stepped out into the yard. Perhaps not such strange happenings in themselves. But all four men—Rose's dream rescuer, the two who had come through the door, and the erstwhile stablehand—immediately put themselves into fighting posture. Daisy recognized it well. As who would not?

But who was about to fight against whom? She frowned. It was three against one. That was as plain as the nose on her face. And the three were no gentlemen, either in looks or in behavior. Three against one!

Daisy turned sharply from the window as Rose's gentleman sent the first two reeling backward and turned to defend himself against them. He clearly had not seen the third scoundrel creeping up behind him. She strode to the door of the bed-chamber without a thought to her appearance, turned back only long enough to grasp hold of the large umbrella of her father's that had sheltered her from many a storm when Mama's and

Rose's more elegant confections had been utterly useless, and that had beaten off many an animal from its less fortunate prey.

"Innkeeper," she called as she ran down the stairs. "Innkeeper!"

That individual emerged from the kitchen as she reached the bottom stair, the cook and Bessie close behind him. All stopped to gawk at her as if they were characters in a well-rehearsed farce.

"There is a gentleman at the back being thrashed by three bullies," Daisy announced, pausing only long enough to see if the innkeeper would take charge of the situation. In her experience, if Daisy did not take charge, no one did.

This occasion was to be no exception.

The innkeeper shrugged. "What do you expect me to do about it?" he asked, not bothering to address Daisy with any term of respect.

Daisy did not pause to answer the question, which was doubtless rhetorical anyway. She strode on to the door leading to the stableyard and went through it without checking her stride or pausing for breath or for a consideration of strategy. All three bullies were now attacking the gentleman. And soon Daisy was attacking the bullies, voice, free fist, and black umbrella all leading the charge.

And one of the bullies actually dared to turn his face to her and grin in a half-toothless way. Daisy in a rage poked at his middle with the point of the umbrella, not even caring if she caught him in a more strategic place.

"Be off with you, you bully and scoundrel!" she heard herself shriek before she realized she was alone on the battlefield, victor of the hour, the enemy having taken to its heels.

The gentleman was still there too, of course, dazed, battered, hatless, and bleeding. Impossible to say if he were the young, handsome man of her dreams. His face looked rather like a slab of raw meat. But his hair looked youthfully blond and far too thick anyway to be the thatch of an old man. His one working eye was regarding her with what she took to be undying gratitude. The poor gentleman. If she had not come to his rescue when she had, he surely would be stretched on the cobbles by now, senseless and decidedly more bloody than he already was.

Daisy lowered her weapon and regarded him with deep maternal compassion. "There, there," she said, "you will be all right now. They will not harm you anymore."

2

The back door of the Golden Eagle Inn spilled out its inn-keeper, its cook, one barmaid, and two chambermaids into the stableyard, the stables two stablehands and two grooms. Viscount Kincade found a handkerchief at last and mopped at the blood on his face. Daisy Morrison lowered the black umbrella, until its point rested on the cobbles before her feet, and continued to look with concern at the victim of the bullies whom she had just put to rout.

"You need cold water for your cuts and bruises," she said briskly, "and some raw steak for your eye. I am afraid it is going to be very swollen and very black. Innkeeper, some steak for the gentleman's eye if you please. And a bowl of cold water for his face, girl," she added to Bessie.

Lord Kincade, taking the handkerchief from his nose and finding it bright with fresh blood, was surprised to see both individuals turn as if they were about to obey the strange apparition who stood in their midst, apparently unaware or unconcerned that she was clad only in a nightgown, shimmering oil, and an umbrella.

"You may stay where you are," he said, wincing at the pain the effort of his words cost his cut and swollen mouth. "I believe my curricle is ready." He glanced coolly at the groom who held his horses' heads, and risked excruciating agony by lifting one ironical eyebrow. "And I now understand the, ah, slight delay in its preparation. I shall be on my way." He turned back to the innkeeper. "My reckoning will still be paid, since I imagine that you have not been fully satisfied by the alternative method of payment that you decided upon. And you too, Bessie. You gave admirable service, my girl, and earned your pay. Admirable! Ma'am?" He bowed to the apparition. "My compliments."

"You are never leaving in that condition," she said, picking up the umbrella, tucking it under her arm, and taking a few steps closer to him. "Why, your poor face is all blood and bruises. And there is blood on the capes of your coat. You must positively come back inside. I have a private parlor. I shall bathe your face myself."

Lord Kincade bowed again. "My thanks, ma'am," he said. "Fortunately the wounds are all superficial, and I would prefer to put as much distance between this place of hospitality and myself as I am able." He turned purposefully to his curricle.

"But you must wish to discover the identity of your cowardly assailants," she said. "Innkeeper, you must assist this gentleman. The good name of your house depends upon your doing so."

That individual shrugged expressively. "I can't help it if the gentry bring their quarrels to my house with them," he said. "Why should my good name suffer?"

Lord Kincade vaulted into the high seat of his curricle, disguising from the spectators the severe pain in the ribs and stomach that the effort cost him, dabbed once more at the blood on his face before putting his handkerchief resolutely away in his pocket, and turned to bow one more time at the female, whose appearance was beginning to make the stablehands snigger and Bessie smirk with contempt.

But before he could utter one final word of thanks, another female came hurtling from the inn. She was decently covered by a long dark-blue cloak and half-boots, though her blond curls looked suspiciously riotous. She was holding out a gray cloak before her and looking considerably agitated.

"Daisy!" she called. "Oh, Daisy, put your cloak on, do. Whatever can you have been thinking?" She was blushing with mortification.

Despite his pain and his anger, Lord Kincade looked closely

and appreciatively at the new arrival. She was somewhat taller than the female she called Daisy and undoubtedly younger too. And whole universes more pretty. In fact, she was quite undeniably lovely, disheveled hair and all. His almost certain knowledge that she had tumbled out of bed only minutes before set his eyes to straying down her body.

"Oh, goodness gracious me," the other female said, holding her arms out to her sides, the umbrella clutched in one hand, and looking down at herself. "What a sight I must be. Thank you, Rose. How thoughtful of you."

Lord Kincade touched his hat to both as he flicked the ribbons and set his horses in motion. Perhaps Bessie's energetic exertions in his bed had put him into such a deep sleep that he thought he was awake. Perhaps his purse was still inside his valise. Perhaps his ribs ached only from Bessie's head resting on them. Perhaps there was no oily faced female. And no black umbrella. And no flushed and tumbled and beautiful lady hiding her charms behind a blue cloak. And perhaps he had not just lived through surely the most embarrassing and uncomfortable hour of his life.

He set his horses' heads for London and home, looking about him for a stream or some source of water with which he might clean himself up sufficiently not to put a scare into the first tollgate keeper he encountered.

"Come inside, Daisy, do," Rose Morrison urged, taking her sister by the arm and trying to coax her in the direction of the inn door. "You must be dreadfully cold."

Daisy ignored the pressure on her arm. She turned to face the innkeeper. "How very peculiar," she said. "The gentleman clearly needed to have his face attended to. I hope he did not have broken ribs in addition to all those cuts and bruises. It was really a very cowardly attack. Three against one. And two of them were holding his arms while the other was punching him."

The innkeeper shrugged as he turned back to the door. "I have work to do," he said. "I cannot be bothering my head over every mill the gentry choose to indulge in."

"Ah, but three of them were not gentlemen," Daisy said,

"but common thugs. Two of them came from inside this very inn, my man, and the third from one of your stables. And kindly have the courtesy not to turn your back on me while I am talking to you."

The innkeeper stopped in his tracks and turned to face her.

Bessie put her hands on her hips and looked as if she were beginning to enjoy the scene.

"I do beg your pardon, my lady," the innkeeper said, making Daisy an exaggerated bow. "But I have guests inside who will be wanting their breakfasts soon. Now, if you will excuse me."

"I most certainly will not," Daisy said.

Rose tugged at her arm. "Do come, Daisy," she begged.

"At the very least your stablehands should be questioned," Daisy said. "They must have realized that a stranger was working among them. If he *was* a stranger, that is. And I would like to know your part in what has occurred in the inn in which I am paying for services and hospitality. The gentleman's words seemed to suggest that he suspected you of having a hand in what happened to him."

The innkeeper took two strides toward the upright little figure of Daisy Morrison, who stood her ground on bare feet, though she now looked almost respectable wrapped inside her gray cloak.

"How do I know that you will not go rattling off in that old coach of yours without paying your bill either?" he asked menacingly. "A man has to make a living. Do you think that having thugs give a customer a thorough drubbing in my yard here would satisfy me for the loss of a night's reckoning? I work for money here. Punches don't pay the servants' wages nor provide the food for the next night's guests."

"Are you telling me that the gentleman was unable to pay his reckoning?" Daisy asked as Rose dropped her hand to her side, realizing the hopelessness of her mission. "But I recall his saying that you would receive payment. A gentleman's word is to be trusted, surely?"

The innkeeper sneered. "That is the last I will ever see of that particular gent or his money," he said. "Had his purse stolen indeed! Does he think I was born yesterday?"

"And you feel no shame," Daisy said, regarding the man with severity, "doubting the word of a man you probably have never seen before or heard any ill of, and knowing that he only narrowly escaped a severe beating on your very premises?"

"I've never seen him before," the innkeeper agreed, "and have no wish to do so again. I was warned that he would try to slip out without paying his reckoning. He did the same last night to the gentlemen he was playing cards with. Lost, he did, and made excuses not to pay up until this morning. Well, that gentleman can kiss his winnings good-bye too. His servants told me all about our fine gentleman. All I can say is, it's a great pity you came along when you did and frightened those fellows away with your appearance."

"My feet are cold," Daisy announced, looking down at them and appearing surprised to notice that they were unshod. "Oh, dear, I did not stop to put shoes on. How careless of me, Rose. And I am very thankful for the cloak. It is a decidedly chilly morning. Now, my man"—she turned back to the innkeeper, her manner brisk—"we will go inside immediately, and I will pay both my reckoning and that of the gentleman who has just left."

"Daisy!" Rose admonished at her side. And then in a low voice, "Don't get involved in other people's problems. Oh, please do not. Not here. And not in London. You know that you always get into so much trouble when you do."

"Nonsense, Rose," her sister said, leading the way indoors and leaving the innkeeper and the indoor servants to trail in behind her. "I think that poor gentleman has been sadly maligned. I would not give these very unmannerly and inhospitable people the satisfaction of being able to complain that his bill has gone unpaid. As for me, I believe that he will return or at least send a servant back with the money."

"Sh," Rose hissed.

"I really do not care if I am heard," Daisy said. "I am not pleased with the service here."

When they all arrived in the taproom, the cook having been shed somewhere along the way, it was noticeable that the innkeeper's manner had become considerably more obsequious.

The lady might be peculiar to the point of eccentricity, but if she was willing and able to pay both her own reckoning and that of the gentleman who had just left, then she clearly was not a nobody, as he had assumed since her arrival the previous afternoon with only the one servant.

"Now," Daisy said, "the two bills, my man, if you please. And you will kindly send to wake up my coachman to prepare my carriage and horses for an immediate departure. No, we will not stay for breakfast. I cannot think what Gerry is about to sleep until this hour anyway."

The innkeeper bowed and retreated behind the bar to fetch the bills.

Daisy turned her attention to the barmaid. "The gentleman said that he owed you money too?" she said.

Bessie smirked and curtsied. "That he does, ma'am," she said. "A hard night's labor I put in for that gent. He would hardly let a body get a wink of sleep. And now a full day's work ahead of me and the dear knows what to expect tonight again."

Daisy fixed her with a severe eye. "You will tell me how much you earned with your hard labors," she said. "I will pay you. And if I were you, my girl, I would not boast so loudly about your exploits. You are part of a gentleman's bill just like the emptying of his shaving water and the blacking of his boots. Not very flattering when you look at it that way, is it?"

Bessie tossed her head and glared defiantly back. But she did not turn and flounce out of the room, though she looked as if she wished to do. If this lady was fool enough to pay her for what she had done between the sheets with a gentleman who was a stranger to the lady, then far be it from Bessie to stand on her dignity. She even wiped the smirk from her face, though it was hard enough to do. The lady must have fallen hard for the gentleman even though she had seen him only after his good looks had been spoiled. Poor lady. With her looks—Bessie allowed her eyes to rest on the shiny face and the rather untidy braids that were now inside the cloak—she was probably desperate for any man, gent or otherwise.

Rose appeared to have given up on her sister. She blushed

scarlet at Bessie's words and sat down at one of the tables. From the quiet air of resignation with which she sat there, it appeared that perhaps she was accustomed to such scenes.

"Now," Daisy said, having taken the two bills firmly in her hand and acknowledged with a nod the inflated sum Bessie had named, "I shall go to my room and be down in half an hour's time both ready to leave and to pay the two of you. But before I do leave, I will wish to see the gentleman whose gaming debts have gone unpaid. Kindly ask him to wait upon me here, my good man."

"Daisy!" her sister moaned halfheartedly from behind her.

But Daisy, once she was launched on a course of action, was not to be deterred, as Rose knew well from long experience. Why she should have expected her sister to change merely because they were on their way to London, she did not know. They both spent the following half-hour washing and dressing, doing their hair, packing away the belongings that had been taken out the night before.

Daisy glanced through the window when they were almost ready, and nodded with satisfaction. "The coach is ready," she said, "and Gerry is down there waiting to go. I am surprised he slept through all the commotion. I will be very glad to see the back of this place, will not you, Rose? How you could have slept on that mattress, I do not know."

"It was remarkably brave of you to go to that gentleman's rescue," Rose said. "I would not have had the courage to go anywhere near the yard. I could have fainted with fright when your leaving the room woke me up and I glanced out to see what was going on. You might have been killed, Daisy."

"Nonsense," her sister said, putting in the last hairpin to hold the heavily coiled braids to the back of her head. "Bullies are always cowards, Rose. If there had been only one man attacking the gentleman, I would not have been near as safe. But then, if there had been only one, I daresay the gentleman would not have needed my assistance."

"Do you not think it was unwise to rush downstairs at an inn without any thought at all?" Rose suggested tentatively. "You were wearing only your nightgown, dear. It was very fortunate that so few people saw you. There might have been any number of guests wandering around."

"No," Daisy said with all the logic of hindsight. "If there had been lots of other people around, those bullies would not have made their attack, you may depend upon it. Are you ready? Let us go, then. I hope you do not mind waiting for your breakfast, Rose, but I really think I would choke if I had to eat any of that man's food after the very discourteous treatment he has given both us and the gentleman. We should be on our way soon. It will not take long to talk to the other gentleman and settle that debt."

"Daisy!" Rose sat down on the lumpy bed and gazed imploringly at her sister with large blue eyes. "A strange gentleman's gaming debts are really none of your concern. You must leave well alone, you know. You do not know what the sum is, and though I know we are very wealthy and can afford even a large sum, it is not the thing at all, dear. We do not even know if the gentleman is worth your care. He is a gambler, and worse. That barmaid, Daisy!" She blushed and looked away from her sister's eyes.

"It is not for us to judge," Daisy said, stooping to pick up their large valise. "But it is certainly not the thing for that other gentleman's servants to spread unsavory stories in the servants' quarters, Rose. The innkeeper would have dealt with such gossip with the proper severity if he were any kind of man. No, I intend to pay those gaming debts, and then let them all say what they will."

She marched from the room and down the stairs without looking back to see if her sister followed. Rose sighed and got to her feet. Dear Daisy! She was always on some crusade in support of strangers, human and animal alike, and half the time the recipient was either unworthy or ungrateful or both. Daisy and her lame ducks! Rose had been sorry to see the gentleman the victim of such an unequal fight, and she had been horrified to see his face. But really, his problems were none of their concern. Certainly his unpaid debts were not their business. Rose even had a feeling that if he were a proper gentleman, he would not be grateful to Daisy for her intervention.

But how could one explain any of that to Daisy? After nineteen years of living with her, Rose still tried quite frequently. But she might as well talk to a brick wall. At least the wall would stay quiet while she talked and still until she had finished.

Rose followed her sister downstairs and stood a few paces from the table where Daisy sat with a smiling plump gentleman who gave Rose the shudders. She could not explain why. He probably could not help having soft fat fingers with dark hairs on the backs of each. And if he chose to wear a ring on each of those fingers, well, that was entirely his business. And one could not quarrel with a smile and a quiet, polite manner. But Rose found her lips curling in distaste and had to deliberately school her expression to blandness.

She was very relieved that the meeting was brief and to the point. She wished as fervently as Daisy that she need never set foot inside the Golden Eagle ever again. She had never been so glad to see the old carriage waiting in the stableyard and Gerry striding across the cobbles to take the valise from Daisy's hands and scold her for not sending him up for it.

Gerry, it seemed, had been sent clear to the other end of the village on an errand to the blacksmith's as a favor to the head groom of the inn, and so had missed the fight. But he grumbled his scoldings to Daisy for her foolish and dangerous intervention in the scuffle just as if he were her fond papa. He coughed and wheezed as he climbed into his high seat and took the ribbons in his hand. He would probably be dead by now, he thought as he thumped his chest, if it were not for Miss Morrison. Men who spent their lives down the mines from childhood on usually died young of coal on the chest. He must not complain of some congestion, frequent as it was. At least he was still alive and over forty years old. And he had the fresh air to breathe. He drew in a deep breath of it now, coughed again, and guided the carriage out onto the street.

Inside the taproom of the Golden Eagle Inn, the gentleman who had just recovered his gambling debts far sooner than he had expected, was smiling in a very self-satisfied way at the redheaded female who had just joined him at the table where Daisy had left him.

"This is far better than I hoped in my wildest dreams," he said with a soft laugh. "A little embarrassment and a little pain to keep him from Bath is what I had planned. And that would have been bad enough for the likes of Kincade. But this! He will never recover from the humiliation. I could kiss the lady, Kit, if I did not have a far more desirable armful right here with me. This triumph needs to be celebrated, my dear. And it is still very early. Come back upstairs with me for a while." He shook with quiet laughter again as he got to his feet and held out a hand for the redheaded female's.

She shrugged and put her hand in his. "It is as good a way as any of working up an appetite for breakfast, I suppose," she said.

Viscount Kincade was having breakfast in his London town house the following morning, talking with his brother, when the butler asked if he might admit his lordship's head groom to deliver a message.

"I am relieved to know he has returned so promptly and the whole sordid episode is at an end," Lord Kincade confided before the man came into the breakfast room. "You cannot imagine the embarrassment, Arthur."

The Reverend Arthur Fairhaven smiled his sweet smile. "There would be plenty to say that the treatment you were given at that particular inn absolved you from all obligation to pay your reckoning, Giles," he said. "It pleases me to know that you have done what is right rather than seek revenge."

"Don't try to make an angel out of me," his brother said before turning his head and raising his eyebrows inquiringly to the groom, who had entered the room and stood at the foot of the table. "If I could find those three louts, I would take them on one at a time and not let them go until they were mince-meat."

"And you would do it in a fair fight, I note," Fairhaven said.

"Yes, Chandler?" The viscount turned his attention to his groom. "The bills have been paid, the accounts settled?"

"Yes, my lord." The groom shifted his feet uncomfortably.

"Good," his lordship said briskly. "Now I will have to find out Mr. Martin today, and then all that will remain to be done is for the bruises to heal."

His morning face indicated that that would be no swift business. He sported a swollen upper lip, a shiny sore-looking cheek, and an eye as black as bootblacking might make it for a masquerade. The raw purple-and-yellow decorations around its outer edges, and the bloodshot appearance of the eye that peeped from swollen lids proved that this was no masquerade, though.

"Ah, my lord," the groom said, instead of turning and taking his leave as his master expected, "the reckonings had already been paid when I got there."

The viscount frowned. "My purse was found?" he asked.

The groom coughed. "A lady paid, it seems," he said. "A Miss Daisy Morrison."

Lord Kincade closed both good and bad eye briefly. "Miss Daisy Morrison," he said. "My savior, the glistening apparition. And did you get her direction, Chandler?"

"No, my lord," the groom replied. "The innkeeper did not know it, and she had not deemed it necessary to leave it. But she was traveling in the direction of London, he said."

"Oh, famous!" the viscount said. "It should be easy enough to find her, then, if we have narrowed the search to London." He eyed his brother briefly and turned back to the servant. "You settled that other matter, Chandler?"

The groom's cough was more pained than the last. "The lady had paid that too," he said.

"What!" Lord Kincade half-rose from his chair before sinking back and closing his eyes very tightly again. "The interfering baggage! My instincts told me from the start that she was no lady." He opened his eyes again. "Next, you will be telling me, Chandler, that she paid my gaming debts as well."

"Yes, my lord," the groom said crisply, not even taking the time to cough first.

Lord Kincade was lost for words. He clamped his mouth shut after staring at his head groom for an appalled moment. "Thank you, Chandler. That will be all," he said, and watched his servant scurry thankfully from the room. "The baggage! The effrontery! The sheer nerve of the woman! Arthur, what kind of female would rush to the rescue of a stranger being worked over by three thugs, armed with nothing but an umbrella and clad in nothing but a nightgown, pay that man's inn bill, settle his gaming debts, and pay off his wh—"

"His whore?" the Reverend Arthur completed. He smiled gently. "A courageous and a very generous lady, by my guess, Giles. A one-of-a-kind lady."

His brother glared at him from his one and a half eyes. "A madwoman," he said. "A one-of-a-kind lunatic, Arthur."

3

Daisy and Rose Morrison found their reception at Pulteney's Hotel in London scarcely any warmer than that at the Golden Eagle, though the proprietors of the hotel were a great deal more well-bred in their coldness. It seemed that anyone who wished to be treated with the proper respect must travel with a veritable army of retainers, Daisy said with a sigh as the door of their suite finally closed behind them.

Rose had not wanted to stay at the hotel. They really had no choice but to return home immediately, she had pointed out to Rose. They could be well on the road before nightfall, though they must be sure that dusk and the Golden Eagle Inn did not meet with them simultaneously.

But as usual, she thought, looking about the palatial dimensions of the parlor that adjoined their bedchamber at the hotel, she might as well have saved her breath. Their uncle and aunt Pickering were not at home. They were in Paris, their butler had explained when they had arrived in the middle of the afternoon. They were presumably taking advantage of the opportunity to travel beyond England's shores again for the first time in many years, now that the political situation made it safe to do so.

Rose had felt panic grip her for a moment. But she was not Daisy's sister for nothing. Daisy would surely ask if they might stay at the house for one night before beginning their return to the country the next morning. No real harm had been done beyond the fact that they had wasted several tiring and frequently embarrassing days on the road.

But Daisy had turned from their uncle's door, climbed back into the carriage, and appeared nonplussed for only a moment or two. She had then given Gerry the order to proceed to Pulteney's, the only hotel in London whose name she knew.

"We will stay there tonight?" Rose had asked. "Indeed, it will be pleasant to be able to relax for a few hours, Daisy. But would it not be wiser to start back immediately so that we might have some miles behind us before tomorrow morning?"

Daisy had given her an uncomprehending look. "We are not going back," she had said when she had caught the drift of Rose's meaning. "Gracious, Rose, we have traveled all these days and made all our preparations for London, and we have come here so that you might meet some eligible gentlemen and make a brilliant match. I will admit that the absence of our Aunt Pickering from town is a setback, but only a minor one. We have plenty of money, after all, and you are adequately chaperoned. We will stay."

"At Pulteney's?" Rose had asked, aghast. "For the whole Season, Daisy?"

Daisy had frowned. "I hope not," she had said. "We have one small problem, as I see it, Rose. We need an entrée into society. It is true that Papa was a baron and that as his daughters we should have no difficulty being received by even the highest society, for all that Papa was frowned upon because he enhanced his fortune in coal. But Papa never came near London and never deemed it necessary to cultivate the friendship of his peers. So we do face a little difficulty. But no matter. We will manage."

"Manage!" Rose had cried, appalled. "We do not know a soul in London, Daisy. There is no one to give us an introduction or an invitation to even the lowliest drawing room. The situation is impossible. We will have to go home and wait until Aunt Pickering comes back. Perhaps next year."

"Next year you will be twenty years old," Daisy had pointed out as the carriage drew to a halt before the hotel. "No, it has to be this year, Rose. You have waited long enough for a husband. We will contrive a way, never fear."

And the trouble was, Rose thought, wandering from the sitting room into the equally spacious bedchamber, Daisy probably would too, in a manner that would bring the maximum of embarrassment to both of them. Not that Daisy would notice, of course. She never did.

For the next three days they lived in splendid isolation at Pulteney's, eating in the public dining room so that Daisy might eye the other patrons and see if she might strike up an acquaintance with someone there. She did on the second day, but the lady with whom they talked for the whole of an hour turned out to be the owner and head teacher of a girls' academy in Brighton, who was in town in order to meet and accompany a duke's daughter back to her school. A very interesting lady, Daisy gave as her judgment after they had parted. And she was quite sincere. She seemed to feel no chagrin at a wasted dinner hour.

They found Bond Street and spent two mornings enjoying looking at all the fashionable shops and people on the streets. Daisy took Rose into the shop of a modiste that looked as if it might be the most fashionable and arranged for a whole new wardrobe for her, despite Rose's protestations that they probably would not after all be spending the Season in London. Daisy even ordered some new gowns and walking dresses for herself.

And, clad in a new walking dress each, they ventured into Hyde Park on the third day to see if it was true that the whole of the fashionable world promenaded or drove there in the late afternoon. It was true, it seemed.

"But we might as well be a hundred miles away," Rose said, capping an argument in favor of returning home the next day that she had been carrying on for the previous ten minutes. "We still know no one, Daisy, and we cannot just walk up to a stranger, introduce ourselves, and ask if she has any spare invitations she can drop our way."

Rose wished she had not said that particular speech as she heard the words coming from her mouth. She really would not put it past her sister to do just that. However, she was relieved to note, Daisy seemed not to be paying her a great deal of attention. She had stopped walking and was looking pointedly in the direction of a group of three horsemen who were exchanging greetings with a pair of ladies in a barouche.

"There he is!" Daisy announced suddenly. "I have been hoping we would see him, Rose. I must confess it has been at the back of my mind all these days. I was only afraid that his injuries might keep him at home for some time. His eye really does look nasty still, does it not?"

Rose followed the direction of her sister's gaze and saw the gentleman of the stableyard at the Golden Eagle Inn. Not that she would have recognized him except for his bruised eye. He was without the greatcoat now, and a very elegant figure of a gentleman was revealed to her gaze. And a handsome one, despite the purple eye. She felt acute embarrassment.

"Let us walk on, Daisy," she said, plucking at her sister's sleeve. "It is improper to draw the attention of a gentleman we do not know. Do come on."

Rose was to be saved from the embarrassment of seeing her sister wave her closed parasol in the air for all the *ton* to see as well as the gentleman whose attention it was designed to attract only because that gentleman looked up and spotted them even as Daisy prepared to go into action. He recognized them immediately, that was clear. And he came toward them with no more delay than a hasty explanation to his companions called for. Whether he was glad to see them or not was less clear to Rose. The look on his face could be eagerness or anger or scorn. It was hard to judge when one of the gentleman's eyes was brightly bloodshot and its surrounds an angry purple. Rose shrank somewhat behind her shorter sister.

"Miss Morrison," the gentleman said as his horse came up to them. He removed his hat to reveal a glorious head of thick blond hair. His one good eye looked unsmilingly down at Daisy. It was a clear gray, of the shade that might be described as blue by someone of a poetic turn of mind. "Good day to you, ma'am."

To Rose, who was used to encountering the victims of Daisy's kindness, it was immediately clear that what the gentleman really wished was that a thunderbolt would come down from the blue sky and strike her prostrate on the spot.

"Good afternoon, sir," Daisy called up to him, all smiles. "I am so glad to see you on your feet again, so to speak. Your eye is really quite nasty, but I trust that you have otherwise recovered. If you had come inside the inn, as I advised you to do, and applied a beefsteak, I would wager the bruise would not be half as purple. However, I can understand your wanting to get away from that horrid place as quickly as you could. Rose and I refused to stop for breakfast, too.''

The gentleman inclined his head, but showed no inclination to pursue this promising line of conversation. "I have been hoping to encounter you somewhere in London,'' he said. "You neglected to leave your direction with the innkeeper, ma'am.''

"Ah,'' Daisy said, smiling more brightly. "So you did go back to settle your account. I knew you would. No, sir, I did not think it necessary to leave my direction. You would have thought I was expecting you to seek me out with your thanks and repayment of the money I spent on your behalf. And both are quite unnecessary. I was only too pleased to help out a fellow traveler in distress.''

The gentleman bowed his head again. It looked to Rose as if he were making a heroic attempt to hold on to his temper. She bit her lip.

"May I present myself, ma'am?'' he said curtly. "Giles Fairhaven, Viscount Kincade, at your service. Perhaps you would give me your direction now, ma'am, so that I might call upon you and speak in more privacy?''

"We are at the Pulteney,'' Daisy said, "and would welcome your call, my lord, though you must not think it necessary to come with your thanks or your money. But we would be most grateful for your help, would we not, Rose?''

The viscount looked at Rose for the first time. And she noticed before she blushed with mortification and proceeded to engage herself with an examination of the grass at her feet that his expression softened somewhat.

"May I do myself the honor of calling upon you tomorrow morning?'' she heard him ask.

Daisy curtsied. "It will be our pleasure, my lord,'' she said. "You know, you were fortunate not to have permanent damage done to that eye. It is quite dreadfully red, is it not? But you are able to see?''

He nodded curtly and turned to rejoin his two companions, who were waiting for him at a discreet distance. "Good day,

Miss Morrison,'' he said without answering her question. He
nodded in the direction of Rose. ''Ma'am?''

Daisy took her sister's arm and squeezed it as they walked
on. ''I knew that something wonderful would happen for us if
we merely had patience,'' she said. ''You will have your introduction to society yet, dear, and your brilliant match. The
viscount will see to it that we are introduced to the right people.
He cannot fail to do so, you know, as he owes us something.
He really owes us nothing, of course, as I did not help him with
the idea of being repaid. But being a gentleman he will feel the
obligation, you see. We would be doing him a kindness by
allowing him some way of showing his gratitude.''

''Daisy,'' Rose wailed, pulling her arm free and turning to
confront her sister, although there were no fewer than six
pedestrians about to pass them on the path they walked along,
''you cannot be thinking of asking such a thing of Lord Kincade. Oh, indeed you cannot. He is a stranger, Daisy, and a
gentleman and a nobleman at that. Oh, it would not be at all
the thing. He will think us quite vulgar, you know, and he will
have good reason for doing so.''

''Nonsense,'' Daisy said, smiling happily and strolling on.
''I will not ask him to escort us anywhere, of course. That would
be most improper. I shall merely ask him to introduce us to
a suitable lady. He must have all sorts of female relatives and
friends here. I think he might be a quite extraordinarily handsome man without the eye, do not you, Rose? And the two
gentlemen with him were well-looking too. And he looked at
you appreciatively too when I mentioned you. Oh, Rose, this
has been a good afternoon's work. I scarce know how I shall
contain my excitement until tomorrow morning.''

Rose opened her mouth to speak, and shut it again. What was
the use? She would leave it to the viscount to depress Daisy's
hopes. She had seen in his face and heard in his voice that his
purpose in wishing to talk privately with her sister had nothing
to do with any desire to repay a debt of gratitude, though it
probably had a great deal to do with a desire to repay a monetary
debt. Lord Kincade did not feel kindly disposed at all to Daisy.
Not at all!

Of course, Daisy had seen none of that. Daisy was living

where she always lived: at one remove from reality. Daisy saw what she wanted to see and heard what she wanted to hear. And dear Daisy! She lived in a world which she could make perfect for those she loved and in which her own comfort and happiness mattered not at all.

Let her dream, Rose thought with a rush of warm affection. Let her enjoy this afternoon in Hyde Park, strolling shoulder to shoulder with the *beau monde*. Rose had a feeling that they would not enjoy many more such afternoons.

There were two possible ways to react to public humiliation, Lord Kincade had decided in the past two days or so. One could face it head-on, accept it as unavoidable, and determinedly and patiently live through it in the certain knowledge that very soon some other poor victim of gossip or scandal or ridicule would surely step forward and take his place. Or one could hide one's head, lie low, keep out of the public gaze, confident in the hope that if one did not die of boredom in the meanwhile, one could eventually step out again into a world that just might have forgotten.

He chose the first course.

How word had got out and spread in such a raging hurry he would never know. But then, having lived in London for all of seven years, he supposed he should not be particularly surprised. None of the servants at that infernal inn, surely, would have had the opportunity to tattle, unless someone who did enjoy spreading gossip had stayed at their inn the night after his sojourn there. Mr. Martin had been an amiable and an indulgent man. It seemed unlikely that he would have posted back to London in all haste to spread the word. That left the two females, presumably sisters. The Misses Morrison.

However it was, and whoever had made public the details of his humiliation, he did find himself two days after his return to London the butt of everyone's jokes, the man who single-handedly supplied the *beau monde* with the laughter needed to keep them healthy.

His appearance was bad enough. He had already braced himself to hear the usual comments on his face and had armed himself with the usual and universal reply: ''Ah, but you should

see what the other fellow looks like." He was only thankful
that he was not married so that the range of jokes was necessarily
cut in half.

But even before he sallied forth to one of his clubs in order
to face the music, he discovered that his appearance would not
be the half of it. Not nearly half! His closest friend, Lord
Doncaster, wandered in on him during the second morning after
his experience on the road to Bath and eased himself into a chair
in his dressing room while the viscount examined in the mirror
some bruises that had come to light after his recent shave.

"If they had only been obliging enough to do the like to your
other eye, Giles," Lord Doncaster said, "you could go to a
masquerade with only a domino to hide you and no mask at
all. Think of the sensation you would cause at unmasking time,
though."

Lord Kincade frowned into the mirror before turning
resolutely away. By no stretch of the imagination would he be
able to persuade himself that he did not look too bad, after all.
"You don't seem surprised, Peter," he said. "And thanks for
the sympathy. You could almost hook your grin over your ears,
you know."

His friend laughed outright. "Are you planning to come to
White's?" he asked. "You do know what is facing you there,
do you not?"

The viscount looked his suspicious inquiry.

"It is the barmaid detail that is the real coup de grace," Lord
Doncaster said. "Tell me, Giles, my boy, was she at least worth
the price? I could probably lure away a duke's mistress for that
sum. Did you at least make use of her for the whole night?
Didn't fall asleep after the first mount or two, did you?"

Perhaps it was not apparent beyond the disguise that was his
face just how aghast Lord Kincade was. "Good Lord," he said,
"how do you know about that? I haven't told Arthur that one.
And I haven't told anyone else about anything. And how much
was she paid, anyway?"

His friend roared with laughter. "You can't expect to keep
such a delicious story under wraps, you know," he said. "And
at that, I am not sure that the barmaid detail is quite the most
delicious. A small female in a white nightshirt and wielding a

gentleman's umbrella, Giles. A strange little angel of mercy, to say the least. Was it really a nightshirt or has that detail been twisted in the telling, alas? Could you see her ankles, m'boy? Her knees? Or were you too preoccupied with more personal matters to take note of such unimportant details?''

Lord Kincade, turning his back on his friend in order to don his watch and his fobs, was somewhat more interested in the little angel's neck at that moment. He wished he had his hands around it.

''She has been deriving a great deal of enjoyment out of the telling of the story, I see,'' he said. ''Clearly it is also common knowledge that she paid my bill, my gaming debts to a man I had never met before, and the barmaid who was obliging enough to warm my bed for much of the night. And so I perceive I am the laughingstock, Peter. And there are so many delightful details to the story that I am like to remain so for quite some time to come unless someone is obliging enough to murder his grandmother in the middle of Kensington Gardens within the next day or so.''

''I'm afraid so,'' his friend said, a trifle more sympathetically than he had been behaving thus far during their conversation. ''You could make yourself scarce, you know. That is why I came here, in fact, instead of meeting you at White's. You were on your way to Bath. Why not resume your journey and let the laughter die down a little?''

The suggestion was tempting, especially as he still felt the need to go there. But who would believe that he had not merely run from embarrassment? No, he must go about his life as if nothing had happened, as if he did not have a shining black eye that would catch the attention of the beholder from half a mile away, as if he had not been made an utter fool of by a small baggage of a female who had a loose tongue among other undesirable attributes.

And he must stay merely in the hope that he would come across her somewhere in London. If she had any pretensions to gentility, there was at least the chance that he might. And then he would deal with her, making sure that he did not carry out his plan to strangle her in too public a setting. He would find out what her motive could be for holding up a total stranger

to the ridicule of the whole of the fashionable world and a sig-
nificant portion of the unfashionable world too—he did not doubt
that his experiences were provoking as much laughter belowstairs as they were above.

And so, when Lord Kincade spotted Daisy Morrison in Hyde
Park while he was riding there in company with Arthur and
Lord Doncaster, he was not totally surprised. He had been on
the lookout for her despite the fact that his search had taken
him right out into the public eye, where he tired almost to the
point of violence of smiling good-naturedly at all the teasing
remarks that no one else seemed to consider unkind, and parried
with repartee that he had practiced during a whole evening and
night alone.

He made hasty excuses to the Misses Harlow, with whom
they were talking, directed his brother and his friend to wait
for him, and walked his horse through the press of riders over
to the footpath where the woman was waiting for him, daring
to smile.

He was surprised to find that she did not look any more like
a fiend than any of the other ladies strolling around her. Indeed,
she looked rather fetching in a russet walking dress and straw
bonnet, wisps of fair hair framing her face, wide and candid
gray eyes smiling up into his. A little slip of a thing, who looked
as if she might blow away in a strong wind. The cream-colored,
frilled parasol that she carried looked decidedly more feminine
than the umbrella he had last seen her wielding and poking at
the midriff of a poor unfortunate thug.

He was, in fact, amazed to realize that he had recognized her
at all. Her face did not glisten on this occasion, but beamed
rosily up at him. She had freckles on her nose.

He treated her as courteously as he must in such a setting.
And she readily agreed to allow him to call upon her the
following morning. Perhaps she did not realize that that slender
neck that stretched her face up to him was at dire risk. Perhaps
she had no conscience at all. Certainly she did not appear to
be stricken by it while she talked with him.

Tomorrow he would deal with her. Lord Kincade found that
he was relishing the thought as he turned his horse back in the
direction of his waiting companions. He almost hoped that she

would greet him with the same smile as she had worn today. He would enjoy wiping it from her face and grinding it underfoot. He would enjoy letting loose on her a few home truths before he finally came to the much-awaited finale of his visit and would at last be able to clasp his hands about her neck and squeeze to his heart's content.

"Pretty," Lord Doncaster commented. "Especially the blond in green who was hiding. Whatever did you say to make her blush so, Giles? And no introduction, my friend? You must keep them both to yourself?"

"You are angry," the Reverend Arthur said quietly, looking closely at his brother's face. "Let us ride on. Don't explode here, Giles. Keep it inside for a while yet."

Lord Doncaster turned his head sharply in the direction of the disappearing ladies and looked back at his friend with heightened interest. "Who were they?" he asked.

"Miss Daisy Morrison," Lord Kincade said shortly, smiling and touching his hat to an elderly lady who passed at that moment in a landau, a female companion at her side. "Ah, ma'am," he said, raising his voice in reply to a remark that the former had made and injecting just the right tone of light humor into his voice, "but you should see what the other fellow looks like." He lowered his voice again. "And her sister, Miss Rose Morrison, I believe."

His friend whistled. "She don't look tall or strong enough even to lift a gentleman's umbrella," he said, "let alone vanquish an army of three with it. Who is she, Giles? Must be wealthy at least if she can afford to pay your debts, including a king's ransom to a sporting wench."

Lord Kincade looked uneasily at his brother and glared pointedly at his friend. "I don't know who she is," he said. "But I intend to find out. I wonder if there are more sisters at home. Lily? Violet? Pansy? Jonquil? Buttercup? Or did the father run out of energy before he could make such an ass of himself?"

"I think it rather a charming idea to call one's daughters by the names of flowers," his brother said with gentle reproach. "And I would not talk disrespectfully about the ladies if I were you, Giles, before you even know them. What Miss Morrison has done, though it has brought you considerable embarrassment, was kindly meant, I believe. The lady looked at you just now with an open, guiltless countenance.''

"There speaks Saint Arthur," Lord Kincade said with the first genuine grin he had managed in four days. "And I am not speaking with sarcasm, either. You would find goodness in a hanged criminal, my dear brother.''

"I would hope so too," the other said seriously. "Our Lord did. Giles, are you going to pay the ladies a visit? Will you allow me to accompany you?''

"You would ruin my carefully laid schemes," the viscount protested. "I had every intention of strangling the wench, you know, but I suppose I cannot if you come too.''

"My thought exactly," his brother said, his smile giving quite unexpected and extraordinary beauty to his long, angular face.

4

Daisy dressed with care the following morning, putting on the blue muslin dress that she had already received from the London modiste. It was perhaps a little light for a chilly April day and perhaps a little frivolous for morning wear, but she liked it. It fell loosely from beneath her bosom and had a neckline low enough to free her neck, and sleeves that puffed in a youthful way from her shoulders.

Not that she had any wish to appear unduly youthful. It would be improper to receive a gentleman in a private parlor of a hotel if she were really just a young single lady. She saw herself as a steady aging spinster. But even aging spinsters can have their little vanities, she thought as she coiled her heavy braids high on the back of her head and glanced to see that Rose looked far prettier and far more youthful than she.

Rose had the good fortune to be perfect in every way, her sister thought with satisfaction. She was of medium height, slender but curved in all the right places; she had wavy blond hair that looked delightful in any style at all; her complexion was all peaches and cream. And to crown it all, she had the sweetest nature that Daisy had ever encountered. She was not exactly timid or shy; she was all soft and glowing femininity.

It was certainly a blessing that she had Daisy for a sister, that young lady always thought. Without Daisy to look after her, Rose would have been doomed to bloom unnoticed. Papa had never been much concerned about the fate of his girls. He was the most indulgent of papas, except when it came to spending any money, but he seemed to have considered that his duty to his offspring had ended when he had begotten them.

And Mama was of no earthly use to Rose except as a well of endless affection. Mama dithered and dreamed her way through life. She had married for love a man of small property and modest fortune, and had continued to love him and live in her quiet way even after he had amassed fabulous wealth. It was probably as well that Mama had not grown dreams and ambitions to match the riches. It was unlikely that she would have persuaded Papa to spend one penny of it on anything that he would have considered frivolous. And Papa had considered almost everything but the essentials of survival to be frivolous.

So, Daisy thought, consulting the pocket watch that had been her father's and feeling slight palpitations of the heart that her mind denied, and noting that it was well into the morning and surely almost time for the viscount to put in an appearance, it was fortunate indeed that Rose had her. Rose was sweet and placid enough to marry the first gentleman to ask her, and clearly a few of the gentleman farmers who were their neighbors were winding up their courage to do just that.

But Rose deserved far better. She must have a Season. She must have all the eligible dukes and marquesses and earls with which London was said to abound see her and come to appreciate both her beauty and the lovely character behind it.

Daisy's thoughts were interrupted suddenly by a light knock on the door of the sitting room. She squared her shoulders and dressed her face in its best sociable smile.

"He is here," she said brightly to Rose, an unnecessary announcement, apparently, as Rose had turned a shade paler and looked with anxious reproach at her sister.

"Daisy," she said, "we ought not to be doing this, you know. We really ought not."

"Nonsense!" her sister said briskly, and crossed the room to open the door.

Viscount Kincade took a deep breath as the door opened, and wished for the dozenth time that morning that his brother was not with him and standing now quietly at his shoulder. He would feel rather inhibited in his wrath with the gentle Arthur observing all. And of course, his brother had realized as much and had asked to accompany him for that very reason. Sometimes, for all his sweet gentleness, Arthur could be quite sly.

Yet again Lord Kincade found himself surprised at the appearance of Miss Daisy Morrison. She was very small—she reached barely to his shoulder. And her figure was girlishly slim. He thought somewhat irrelevantly that he could probably span her waist with his two hands if he tried, though that waist was hidden beneath the soft folds of her blue dress. Her fair hair was drawn back from her face and piled high at the back of her head. He had a flashing memory of those braids reaching to her waist. And her face was bright and eager, extremely pretty, in fact, if one ignored the dusting of freckles on her straight little nose.

It would be hard to imagine that such a bright, neat little package could contain such fiendishness if he did not have painful and lasting proof that it was so.

Lord Kincade hardened his heart and refused to respond in kind to the eager smile of greeting. He bowed stiffly and unsmilingly. "Miss Morrison?" he said.

"Oh, good morning, my lord," she said, opening the door wider and standing to one side to let him in. "I knew you would not fail us. How glad I am to see you."

Lord Kincade stepped inside the room and turned to indicate his brother. "May I present the Reverend Arthur Fairhaven, my brother?" he said. He inclined his head to the beautiful and uncomfortable-looking sister, who was hovering in the background.

Arthur took the hand that Daisy extended to him and bowed over it, smiling.

"I am very pleased to meet you, sir," Daisy said. "A vicar. How splendid!"

"A curate merely," Arthur corrected. "And not even quite that yet. I am waiting for my first posting in the autumn. And I am pleased to meet you too, ma'am, and to thank you for the help you have given my brother. It seems that you showed extraordinary courage."

Daisy looked up at the very tall, thin young man who still held her hand, and across at the viscount. "If you have come here to thank me," she said briskly, "then I will ask you both to leave immediately, for you will put me to the blush, and I hate to feel uncomfortable." She smiled dazzlingly. "I did only what any decent person would have done. Will you have a seat, my lord? Reverend? Shall I ring for tea?"

Lord Kincade, fascinated by the audacity of the creature, decided to take charge of the situation before it got out of hand and descended into a mere social tea-drinking occasion.

"I owe you money, ma'am," he said coldly. "If you will name the sum, I shall repay you without further ado."

"Oh, please do not mention it," Daisy said. "A trifle merely. I was glad to be of some service to you, my lord, for I must confess to a dislike of that innkeeper, whose manner was quite insolent for one who has taken upon himself to look to the comfort of travelers. I only wish he could be brought to justice for having had bullies set upon you merely because you had the misfortune to lose your purse at his inn."

"The sum, ma'am, if you please," Lord Kincade insisted, glancing at his brother and feeling quite heroic for holding on to his temper so well.

"I beg you to think no more of it," Daisy said. "And that girl, you know. I swear she was actually proud of herself and showed no shame whatsoever. It was as well to pay her immediately, you know, for I would not put it past her to gossip about you to the very next traveler who walked through the door. And it would never do for you to be gossiped about, would it?" She smiled warmly into the viscount's eyes.

Lord Kincade could feel himself flushing as the sister muttered an agonized "Daisy!" behind him. He took his purse from a pocket and drew a wad of bank notes from it.

"I know what my gaming debts were," he said, forcing the words past his teeth. "I will have to guess what you paid the innkeeper and the barmaid on my behalf. Here, ma'am." He held out the money and glared down at her from his one and three quarter eyes.

"Oh," she said ruefully, her head to one side, taking the bank notes from his hand, "you are going to insist. And of course, how foolish of me to forget that a gentleman has his pride. Forgive me, my lord. I did not mean to humiliate you."

She counted out a number of bank notes into one hand and held out the remainder of the pile to him. "There," she said. "Now we are even and your pride is restored."

The clever little baggage, Lord Kincade thought in a fury as he put his money away in his purse and thrust the latter back into his pocket. He had counted on her to argue more. By giving in so sweetly, she had cut the ground from under his feet and had allowed him no vent for his anger. There was nothing more he could do but to bow to her as icily as he could and take his leave.

"I did not consider you in my debt even before this," Daisy said, looking back up at him again and indicating the money in her hand before stuffing it into a pocket of her dress. "But now I feel more shy about the favor I would ask of you, my lord. Will you not sit down, please? You are both so tall that you put me at quite a disadvantage."

A favor? The woman must be mad. A candidate for Bedlam, no less.

"Thank you, ma'am." Arthur, his brother saw to his dismay, was smiling and accepting the invitation. "May I beg the honor of being presented to the other young lady?"

"Oh!" Daisy said. "How very rag-mannered of me. My sister, Rose Morrison, sir and my lord. I have brought her to town for the Season, you see, but we have encountered a quite unexpected and troublesome problem."

Lord Kincade found himself sitting on a chair and regarding the lovely and clearly mortified Rose.

"Yes?" Arthur prompted encouragingly.

"We have no one to sponsor us," Daisy said. "My aunt would have been glad to do so, but unfortunately she has chosen this very spring to visit Paris. And we do not know anyone else in London, my father—Lord Brigham, that is—having rusticated all his life."

Lord Kincade could thoroughly sympathize with the aunt who had taken herself off to France rather than be saddled with Miss Morrison for the Season. "Your aunt did not warn you that she would not be here?" he asked.

"We wrote to my uncle—Sir Charles Pickering, that is," Daisy said. "But I would not wait for his reply, for I know

how busy life in town must be during the Season and I feared
that by the time he thought to write back to me, the Season would
be well-nigh over. But we felt confident of our welcome as both
our uncle and aunt urged us last year to come.''

"You came to London without any firm invitation and without
chaperons?" Lord Kincade asked, wondering even as he formed
the words why he should be surprised at anything the little
baggage should choose to do. "Where are your parents, if I
may make so bold as to ask?"

"Papa is dead," she said, "and Mama does not have the will
or the courage to venture from home. And we are not without
chaperons, you know. At least, I do not need a chaperon, being
a spinster past my youth. And Rose has an older female to care
for her and make her respectable."

"You refer to yourself," Lord Kincade said. He did not need
to frame the words as a question. Why did he suddenly feel
like shouting with laughter? A spinster past her youth! She
looked not a day over twenty, though he supposed that if she
could make such a claim in all seriousness, she was probably
somewhat older. Where must be the mother's sense to allow
such a situation to have developed? But then, gazing at the
determined little face before him and remembering what the
woman was capable of, he felt a sudden and profound sympathy
for the mother.

"You find yourself in distressing circumstances," Arthur was
saying gently. "How may we be of service to you, ma'am? May
we arrange for your journey home? Do you have your own
carriage?"

"Oh, we are not going home," Daisy said briskly, "not after
we have gone to all the trouble of getting here. No." She turned
wide gray eyes on the viscount and smiled sweetly. "I want
you to help us, my lord. Would you recommend a suitable lady
to sponsor us? Just to secure us an introduction to society, you
see. Once we are launched, everything will be all right, for I
will be able to chaperon Rose wherever she goes. You must
have a mother or sisters or someone."

Lord Kincade stared at the smiling face and felt that he must
have walked into some bizarre dream. Indeed, it must be an
uncommonly long dream. He seemed to have been trapped

inside it for several days. Was it possible that the little slip of a female who had made him into the clown of London was now demanding that his mother—the Countess of Atherby, no less—give her an introduction to society? Even apart from the sheer gall of the woman, could she seriously expect him to do such a dreadful disservice to society? Society might never be the same again.

She was awaiting his reply. Lord Kincade drew breath. "I regret to say that my mother is in Bath with my father at present," he said, "and my older sister is incr— in a delicate state of health. My younger sister is not yet twenty."

"Oh!" Miss Morrison's face lit up eagerly. She seemed not to have recognized the set-down for what it was. "Rose is nineteen. Perhaps they can be friends. Is your sister making her come-out, my lord?"

"No," the viscount said, ignoring what had preceded the question. Miss Rose Morrison, he could see from the corner of his eye, was twisting her hands together in her lap. At least her older sister appeared to be one of a kind. Her audacity did not represent a family trait.

"There is Hetty," he was suddenly aghast to hear his brother say. And Arthur was looking at him in mild inquiry. He turned back to Daisy. "Our cousin, ma'am. Lady Hetty Parkinson. She is always lamenting the fact that she has no daughters of her own to bring out. Only three sons."

Daisy was on her feet, her hands clasped to her bosom, her face glowing. "Oh yes," she said. "It would be perfect. Oh, I knew I did not misjudge you when we were at the inn, my lord, for all the innkeeper swore he would never see either you or your money again. I knew you were a perfect gentleman. Thank you, thank you, my lord."

Did she think he was a ventriloquist? The words had come from Arthur's mouth, yet she was looking at him with such gratitude shining from her eyes that Lord Kincade closed his for a moment.

He rose to his feet. "I will call on my cousin this afternoon," he heard himself say, "and try to procure an introduction for you and your sister, Miss Morrison. May I have the honor of calling upon you tomorrow morning again?"

She was holding out both hands to him. "Our rector at home is fond of saying that a good deed always brings its reward even if one does not do it for that reason," she said. "And it is true. But the reward is far in excess of the small service I was able to do for you, my lord. If only Rose can be successfully launched into society, I shall be eternally grateful. Perhaps one day I will be able to do something else for you."

Had he really stretched out his own hands to take hers? Lord Kincade wondered, looking down in some surprise to find that indeed he was holding both her hands. Cool, slim hands that one could scarce imagine holding and wielding as powerful a weapon as a gentleman's umbrella. He had surely never seen such a mask of innocence as the pretty face that beamed up into his. He bowed over her hands, stopping himself only just in time from obeying instinct and lifting one of them to his lips.

"I hope the occasion will never arise," he said fervently. "We must take our leave, ma'am. Until tomorrow, then."

Arthur was bowing to Rose and smiling at her.

Lord Kincade's eyes strayed to Daisy's smooth slim throat with some regret. He had been so looking forward to having his hands there. Or even if everyday reality had kept his hands at his sides, then he had truly looked forward to ripping up at the woman, telling her exactly what he thought of her interfering, tattling ways. And yet here he was still clasping her hands—he dropped them in some haste—and allowing himself to be the object of her smile of warm admiration and gratitude.

The viscount preceded his brother from the room. Perhaps soon he would wake up, he thought with some desperation. Had he really just promised to secure an introduction to Hetty for those two females? He could not quite persuade himself to think of them as ladies. Good Lord, their situation was quite scandalous. Two unchaperoned young females, one of them masquerading as an elderly spinster behind a slim girlish figure and open, pretty face, were living at the Pulteney, seemingly without a servant between the two of them, trying—and apparently succeeding—to wheedle their way into the *beau monde*. For all anyone knew, they might be a couple of milkmaids or worse. Lord *who* had been their father? He had never heard of the man. Sir Charles Pickering was their uncle? And he was conveniently in France.

He must be mad. How had it come about anyway? He looked suspiciously at his brother as they came out onto the steps outside the hotel.

"Well done, Arthur," he said. "You have got us into quite a coil, my dear brother. I was hoping never to be forced to set eyes on Miss Daisy Morrison after this morning's business. Yet you suggested that Hetty might be delighted to shepherd them around London. I hope Hetty has your head for this."

His brother smiled his sweet, attractive smile. "They are a delight, Giles," he said, "and quite unaware of the true awkwardness of their situation. We owe it to them to help them. The older sister has extraordinary courage and is quite selfless in her designs. It will do you credit to assist her. Remember that she risked her own safety, perhaps her very life, to help you. And I believe Hetty will be overjoyed."

"Arthur," his brother said, coming to a full stop and staring at him, "I dread to picture your home when you begin your life's work. The beggars and frauds and cheats will be lined up for half a mile waiting to be handed your last pair of shoes and crust of bread."

The Reverend Arthur Fairhaven smiled sweetly. "If there is one among them who is truly in need," he said, "then I will not have given in vain, Giles."

The viscount shook his head, looked disgusted, and decided to laugh instead. "Has the whole world gone mad around me?" he asked. "Or is it a characteristic of a madman to think he is the only sane person in existence? Maybe I am the one who should be carted off to Bedlam."

Viscount Kincade had another visit to make that afternoon before accompanying his brother to their cousin's, and this was a visit he should have made three or four days before and had been avoiding. Was it just the knowledge that he was not in his younger sister's favor? he wondered as he dismounted from his horse before his brother-in-law's door and handed the reins to a waiting groom. Or was it the even more certain knowledge that she would enjoy seeing his battered face and crowing over the stories about him that she was bound to have heard?

He sighed inwardly as the butler took his hat and cane and preceded him to his elder sister's sitting room. But any hope he might have had that she would be alone was dashed as soon as the butler stood aside for him to enter the room. It was occupied by both sisters.

"Giles," Lady Julia Holmes said, rising to her feet with some difficulty to reveal a very pregnant figure, "you have come at last. Do let me have a look at your face. Have your good looks been quite spoiled, my dear?" She came unnecessarily close and grimaced at the still-purple remains of his black eye. "It will heal? There will be no permanent scar?"

"Absolutely not," he said, taking her hands and kissing her cheek with some difficulty, leaning across her bulk in order to do so. "Heavens, Julia, is it to be triplets? You seem to double in size every time I see you."

"Well," she said, "when you consider the size of Ambrose, it is hardly to be expected that his heir would be a pigmy. And our side of the family is not noted for midgets. Look at you. And Arthur."

"Hello, Judith," Lord Kincade said, turning and smiling somewhat uncertainly at his younger sister, who sat straight in her chair and eyed him stonily. "No hugs and kisses, dear?"

"Don't you 'dear' me," she said, lifting her chin a good inch. "And don't you come over here looking for sympathy either. If both your eyes were as black as coal and all your teeth knocked out and all your ribs poking out through your back, you would not draw one tear from me, Giles."

"Well," he said, seating himself next to his older sister and nodding his acceptance of a cup of tea, "I thought you might aim for some originality, Jude. You were saying much the same things the last time I saw you, except that then, I believe, you were babbling on about knives and pistols and, er, boiling oil, was it?"

"I hate you," she said, "and I am glad you did not reach Bath, and if you have come here to wheedle your way back into my good graces again, you have wasted your time. I hope you choke on your tea," she added spitefully as he lifted his cup to his lips.

"Enough, Judith," her older sister said, laughing despite herself. "All Giles did, when all is said and done, was stop you from going to the public masquerade, and you know that I would have stopped you had I not believed your story about going to the theater with the Billingses, and that Papa surely would have done so if he were here."

"I hate having an older sister and brothers," Judith said, tossing her dark hair and glaring with deep-brown eyes. She was the only member of the family to have inherited her mother's dark coloring. The other three all favored their father. "You all think that because I am not yet twenty, I am just a child and must be given no freedom at all and no power to think for myself."

"Since it is apparent that you would use that freedom to tie yourself to a wastrel and a scoundrel," the viscount said, sounding bored, "and your power to think to place your fortune in the hands of a man who would dissipate it in a fortnight, then clearly you must be treated like a child, Jude."

"Lord Powers is not a wastrel and a scoundrel and he is not interested in my fortune," Judith cried, leaping to her feet. "And if that is what you were planning to tell Papa, Giles, you are a liar and a rogue and you deserved more than that black eye."

"As you said before," he said dryly. "I planned to advise Mama and Papa to come home before you elope and put yourself beyond the pale of respectable society for the rest of your life, little spitfire. Julia is at something of a disadvantage these days and cannot be expected to chase after you. And one cannot expect Ambrose to do so. Whenever Hetty escorts you somewhere, you succeed in giving her the slip with great ease as soon as she becomes involved in gossip, as she so easily does. Arthur is so sweet-natured that you would probably be able to persuade him to drive your coach to Gretna. And I, frankly, have better things to do than to act as your jailer."

Judith exploded into unexpected laughter suddenly. "Like bedding down with barmaids," she said before blushing.

"Judith!" Her sister's cup clattered back into its saucer. "Mind your manners, do. Oh, it is quite right that Mama should be here. I am finding it impossible to manage you."

Lord Kincade was pale and tight-lipped. "I suppose you enjoy that little tidbit of scandalous gossip even more than this eye, don't you, Jude?" he said. "It was a cheap shot, my dear. Very cheap. Now, news has obviously got into this house during the last six days, but have you been out at all during that time?"

She glared at him before sitting down. "You know I have not," she said. "You sentenced me to house arrest for one whole week or until either you or Papa returned from Bath, do you not recall?"

"Then fetch your bonnet," he said. "I will take you for a walk now before paying a call on Hetty with Arthur. You will need some fresh air."

"Well, hooray," Judith said with exaggerated sarcasm. "I am to have an outing. With my brother. I can scarce contain my excitement."

"Now, Jude!" her brother commanded, pointing to the door. "Before I change my mind."

He looked at his older sister after Judith had flounced out of the room. "Has she been a dreadful handful?" he asked. "I hate to think of your having to put up with her tantrums when I am sure you are in need of rest and tranquillity."

"She has had a trying case of the sullens," Julia admitted, "but has not tried to escape. I think your threat of an, er, walloping if she did had some effect, Giles. And she knows very well that Papa would carry out the threat even if you would not."

Lord Kincade frowned. "Powers has not tried to see her?" he asked.

She hesitated. "I have a feeling that some notes have passed," she said. "But I am afraid that I have played craven and pretended ignorance."

"Can she not see that the connection is wholly ineligible?" the viscount asked, exasperated. "It is true that his father is the Marquess of Chalcott, but that is the only fact that could possibly recommend him. And no one seems ever to have seen the marquess anyway. The Lord knows what he is like. But

Powers, Julia! He has every vice one could name, and has been intent on winning a wealthy bride by fair means or foul for the past two years or more. Can Judith not see that?''

"He is very handsome, Giles," his sister said, "and can be very charming. And Judith is very young and very impressionable. We will just have to see that she grows safely out of it."

Lord Kincade sighed. "I suppose I should go to Bath after all," he said, "or at least send a long and explicit letter. I don't enjoy being older brother to a spitfire, Julia."

"Is it true that a lady saved you from a thorough beating?" she asked, looking closely at his bruised eye again. "Poor Giles. What a dreadful experience. Who could possibly have wanted to do such a thing? And it happened after your purse was stolen, it is said, not before. Who was the lady?"

Lord Kincade was thankful for the return of his younger sister to the room at that moment, though the look she gave him would have felled him on the spot if it had been loaded with bullets. Enough to have one troublesome female at a time to occupy his thoughts. He did not even want to think about Miss Daisy Morrison for the next hour or two. Indeed, he would be very happy if he never had to do so.

"Well, my dear," he said, "would you care to take your jailer's arm and pick up your ball and chain? You may have to squint your eyes when we step outside. The daylight may dazzle you after such a lengthy incarceration."

"I hate you, Giles Fairhaven," his sister said, thrusting her arm vengefully through his.

5

"You look just perfect, Rose!" Daisy, her hands clasped to her bosom, was gazing in delight at her sister, who was dressed in a pale-lemon muslin dress with bonnet to match and looking the picture of youthful loveliness. "Lady Hetty Parkinson cannot fail to be taken with you. Oh, this is all turning out like a fairy tale. Soon you will be going to balls and concerts and theater parties, and the gentlemen will be flocking around you. And your only problem will be deciding which one's suit to encourage and accept."

"Daisy," Rose said, turning speaking eyes on her elder sister, "we have not yet met Lady Hetty. We know nothing of her except that she is Lord Kincade's cousin."

"And that she has three sons," Daisy reminded her. "I wonder what their ages are, Rose. His lordship did not say."

"I cannot like this," Rose said as she pulled on her gloves nevertheless, seeming to realize that her protests would be ignored, as they always were when Daisy had set her mind on something. "The viscount did not half like the suggestion that he present us to his cousin. And indeed it is a great imposition."

"There you are wrong," her sister said, putting on her own straw bonnet carefully over her piled braids. "He is an extremely civil man and a man of pride. You could tell that he felt beholden to us, Rose, by the ridiculous fuss he made over the money. He must be grateful to have something to do for us in return. And indeed, he is a very handsome man. Did

59

you notice? Despite his black eye, I think his good looks are evident. Perhaps he will become enamored of you. I would not be at all surprised.''

Rose's shriek of dismay was drowned out by the sound of knocking on their sitting-room door. Daisy strode across the room to open it, excitement putting a spring in her step.

Yes, he was indeed handsome, she thought as she beamed up at Viscount Kincade and noted his tall, broad-shouldered figure, his thick and shining blond hair, and his regular features, marred temporarily by the bruised eye. And it would not be at all surprising if he developed an attachment to Rose, who easily matched him in coloring and beauty. She would certainly not stand in the way of such a match.

Lord Kincade had sent a servant that morning with the message that he would wait on the ladies during the afternoon in order to convey them to his cousin's home. Daisy had been waiting in excited anticipation ever since.

"Good afternoon, my lord," she said all in a rush. "We are ready, as you see. We certainly did not wish to keep you waiting when you are doing us such a particular favor. And such a beautiful day it is too. Is the Reverend Fairhaven not with you this afternoon?''

Lord Kincade bowed. "My brother is accompanying my younger sister to Madame Tussaud's," he said. "Judith has not had many outings during the last week."

"How lovely it must be to have brothers to accompany one everywhere," Daisy said. "There are just the two of us in our family. Here is Rose all ready to go, as you see. I am taking the place of a brother, in a way, by seeing to it that she has this chance to go into society. Is it not fortunate that I am six years her senior and can act as her chaperon? I am talking too much, am I not? You must forgive me; I always do that when I am excited and somewhat nervous. You cannot imagine how important this visit is to me, my lord.''

Lord Kincade bowed to Rose and offered his arm. Daisy smiled to herself at the handsome picture they made together and whisked herself out of the room ahead of them when he offered her his other arm.

"Oh, that is quite unnecessary," she said. "I have been told that I stride along so briskly that a man finds it difficult to suit his pace to mine.''

Lord Kincade was left with one arm hanging on midair. He glanced at Rose and raised his eyebrows.

"Daisy is very independent," Rose said hesitantly. "She always has been. But then she has always been responsible for the organization of our lives for as far back as I remember.''

"Perhaps Daisy would do as well to learn that country manners are not necessarily town manners," he said quietly, though the low volume was hardly necessary. Daisy was already halfway down the stairs and out of earshot.

"I doubt if Daisy will ever realize that," Rose said, staring at her sister's disappearing back with a mixture of fondness and exasperation.

Lord Kincade handed Rose into an open barouche and took his seat opposite her and Daisy, his back to the horses. He looked assessingly at both. The younger sister was quite exquisitely beautiful and would undoubtedly take well if Hetty was willing to take them on. And she probably would. She had been quite delighted by the idea when Arthur had suggested it to her the afternoon before—Arthur had persuaded his older brother to allow him to make the explanation. It would be a treat to have two young ladies to shepherd around, she had declared, instead of having nothing to think about except the latest scrapes of "those horrid boys.''

The older sister did not have the serene beauty of the other, but she was decidedly pretty nonetheless and had already drawn one appreciative glance from a doorman at the Pulteney, taken off his guard when she had smiled dazzlingly and thanked him for handing her into the barouche, instead of ignoring him as she was supposed to do. She must have windmills in her head if she thought that anyone was going to mistake her for an aging spinster chaperon. She was six years older than her sister, she had said. Could she really be five-and-twenty?

Daisy exclaimed with enthusiasm over everything they saw on their journey—just like a child, Lord Kincade thought. Perhaps all her indiscretions on the road to London were due to an unfortunate gaucherie rather than to a deliberate fiendishness. He began to relax in the fresh spring sunshine.

"Oh, stop!" Daisy cried suddenly, surging to her feet so that the viscount in a reflex action caught at her waist to prevent her from being thrown over the side. "Stop this coach! Immediately!"

The viscount's startled coachman obeyed instinctively and with such haste that the horses almost reared up, and certainly caused some commotion on a busy Bond Street. And Daisy was gone from the viscount's hands, gone from the barouche, though whether she had gone through the door or over it was not at all clear to a dazed Lord Kincade.

"How could you be so cruel!" he heard with some horror even before he could react and vault out of the carriage after her. "You deserve to be horsewhipped yourself, sir, and see how you would like it."

Daisy Morrison was standing in the middle of the street on quite the most fashionable stretch of Bond Street, brandishing a pink parasol in the air with one hand and shaking the fist of the other at the surprised driver of a sporting curricle—Mr. Cecil Durrell, prominent Member of Parliament, Lord Kincade noted. And looking fiercely angry.

But before the unfortunate Mr. Durrell could decide whether to draw his horses to a halt or not, and before the spectators could decide whether to stop to watch the show or be more well-bred and stroll onward as if nothing were happening, and before Lord Kincade could reach Daisy in order to throttle her and stuff her out of sight onto the floor of his barouche, she dived off into the thick of a crowd of pedestrians on one of the pavements and emerged seconds later clutching a bundle of gray hair, which turned out to be a dog of predominantly Pekingese origin.

"Did you see that?" Daisy announced indignantly to a small gathering of shoppers and strollers and a viscount who wished profoundly that he were anywhere on earth at that moment except where he actually was. Mr. Durrell had decided that the commotion had nothing to do with him and was making his escape at leisurely pace along the street. "That man"—she stabbed a finger in the direction of the departing politician—"that man actually struck at this poor creature with his whip."

An unidentified young man sniggered. "The dog was under

his horses' feet and might have caused them to bolt," he was unwise enough to say.

"What?" said Daisy. "You are defending the bully, sir? There can be no excuse—none!—for striking at poor dumb animals who look to us for protection, not wanton cruelty. All he had to do was to get down from his seat and remove the little dog gently onto the pavement. But oh, no! It is so much easier to lash out with one's whip. Someone should take a whip to him."

"Hear, hear," a couple of gorgeous dandies said, applauding and grinning at this unlooked-for sideshow.

Lord Kincade took a firm hold of Daisy's arm and sincerely hoped he would leave bruises for a fortnight. "Set the dog down now, Miss Morrison," he said quietly but in the firm tones that he always expected—justifiably—to bring instant obedience, "and come back to the carriage."

"And know that the same thing will probably happen as soon as my back is turned?" she said, directing wide, surprised eyes and glowing cheeks at him. "No, indeed, my lord, I could not be guilty of such negligence and live with my conscience afterward. I will take the dog with me. Your coachman will tend to it while we are visiting your cousin, I am sure."

She turned toward the barouche, and the viscount relaxed his grasp of her arm and smiled rather foolishly at the few people who were still looking curiously their way. Miss Rose Morrison, he noted in one swift glance, was sitting quietly in the barouche, clearly trying to pretend that she was not there.

"Daisy!" she said reproachfully as her sister came up to her, the dog still clasped in her arms. But it was a token protest, Lord Kincade could see, almost a reflex action. Miss Rose Morrison, he saw in an unwelcome flash of insight, was perfectly well-accustomed to such scenes.

"Poor little dog," Daisy said, looking down at the animal for the first time. "You are sadly in need of a haircut, I can see. It is difficult to know which end is which." She looked up at Lord Kincade and smiled warmly. "Thank you so much for stopping, my lord. Can you believe that the world holds such brutes?"

Lord Kincade, in the process of handing her back into his carriage and drawing breath in order to make a final protest against the added presence of the dog, froze suddenly to a heartrending shriek from behind.

"Thief!" the voice screeched. "Stop, thief! They have my Marmaduke. Stop them, someone! Help!"

Lord Kincade closed his eyes briefly and waited now—surely now—for his dream to end.

During the ensuing fracas, which drew a far larger audience than the first, Lady Jemima Hawken and Miss Daisy Morrison went at each other's throats with a series of accusations, threats, and counterthreats. Daisy was a thief and a butcher and a brazen hussy, among numerous other things. Lady Jemima, to summarize, was not worthy of the sacred trust of having an animal to care for if she could be so intent on buying baubles for herself that she would let the poor creature wander out onto the street to be struck at and killed.

Lord Kincade took the animal firmly from Daisy's arms and placed it in the other lady's with a bow and a winning smile and an abject apology for the fright they had caused her.

"Oh, it is you, Kincade," she said, looking with suspicious hostility back to Daisy. "Well, I suppose it has all been a misunderstanding, then. And Marmie seems to be unharmed. But you must understand how I felt when I saw him about to disappear into a carriage with an unknown lady."

Lord Kincade made soothing noises until the dowager turned back to the pavement and her maid, and a disappointed crowd had begun to disperse.

He sat in stony silence when his barouche finally started on its way again, picturing to himself in graphic detail what he might expect when word of this afternoon's circus and the identity of his female passenger became public. Perhaps he should emigrate to Brazil while he still retained some vestiges of his sanity.

He stared at Daisy as she sat very upright, her bosom still heaving, her cheeks still flushed, her eyes still bright, and thought it decidedly unfair that the prize exhibition she had just put on for the destruction of his good name had only made her a great deal prettier than she had been before. The little fiend! His stare became a glare.

She smiled at him after noting the direction of his gaze. "I do not wonder that you are out of temper, my lord," she said. "Can you quite believe that anyone could be that careless? Even to take a poor dog to such a crowded place as Bond Street seems a type of cruelty, but to allow it to run loose is beyond belief. And that man in the curricle! In one way I am glad he did not stop, for surely you would have got into fisticuffs with him, and we would all have made spectacles of ourselves. Though I do, of course, applaud your intent."

"Yes," Lord Kincade said after a moment's incredulous silence. "I think it as well under the present rather public circumstances to curb the violent urge that is almost beyond my control." He stared very directly and very coldly into her eyes.

She smiled fondly at him. "What sort of a person would name a poor little dog Marmaduke?" she said.

The visit to Lady Hetty Parkinson was even more of a success than Lord Kincade had expected. More of a success for the ladies, that was. For himself, he could have wished that Hetty and Miss Morrison would have taken each other in such instant dislike that the visit would be concluded almost before it had begun and Daisy Morrison forced to retreat to the country, where she belonged. Though there were probably hundreds of poor souls there, he thought with some sympathy, who would be willing to put up a stiff argument to prove that she belonged in town.

Lady Hetty clapped her hands as soon as she set eyes on the two young ladies, even while Lord Kincade was trying to present them formally.

"Oh," she said, "you are the Misses Morrison. And pretty beyond my fondest hope. Giles, dear, neither you nor Arthur thought to mention that they are pretty. And I see that I am to have double delight. I thought it was to be only one young lady and her chaperon. But I see it is to be two."

"I am the chaperon," Daisy said, walking forward, hand

extended to shake Lady Hetty's, instead of curtsying prettily as she was supposed to do. "People are forever mistaking me for a green girl. It is because I am so small, I suppose—a minor irritation passed on to me through my mother's line, I am afraid. But I am five-and-twenty, you know. No girl, at all, but merely an older relative to accompany Rose."

Lady Hetty shook Daisy's hand, acknowledged Rose's curtsy with a nod, and motioned them to sit down. "You must tell me all about yourselves," she said. "Everything, right from the beginning. If I am to take you under my wing, which I am already strongly inclined to do, then I must feel that I know you almost as if you were my daughters."

"I will certainly tell you what you wish to know, ma'am," Daisy said, "but you must not think that we are here to impose upon you to any great extent. All we need is an introduction to society. Our father was a baron, you know—Lord Brigham— and Sir Charles Pickering is our uncle. And Rose is excessively lovely and sweet-natured. I am sure that once she has been seen a few times, we will have plenty of invitations, and then we will not have to inconvenience you any longer."

"Gracious, child," Lady Hetty said, "you will not be an inconvenience. This is the chance of a lifetime. I could produce nothing but sons, you know, during my breeding years—three of them. But though at the time of the births everyone was loud with congratulations at my good fortune in producing three possible heirs for their father, I have discovered that sons are no use at all once they grow up. They want to be off on their own all the time and have no interest at all in attending assemblies and balls—especially with their mother. Is that not right, Giles? And I can see that the next hour is not going to be a thrilling one for you. Why do you not go into the billiard room and find Albert? He was complaining less than an hour ago that, despite the existence of three men in the household, not one other was willing to play a game with him."

Lord Kincade got thankfully to his feet. "Perhaps that is because it is almost impossible to beat him, Hetty," he said. "The novelty of being thoroughly outclassed soon palls, I would imagine."

He bowed to all three ladies and made his escape. And being

soundly thrashed in a game of billiards, he reflected philosophically somewhat later, was infinitely preferable to sitting and waiting for the next embarrassing *faux pas* of Daisy Morrison.

He hoped that Hetty would talk to her and her sister for long enough. The trouble with Miss Morrison was that she looked like a perfectly normal and harmless female much of the time. If Hetty talked to her for only half an hour or so, she might make the dreadful mistake of thinking that the woman really was normal. Poor Hetty! He should never have agreed to allow Arthur to do the talking the afternoon before. He should have explained the whole dreadful truth himself.

He shuddered, drawing a grin from young Albert, who thought his reaction due to the thorough trouncing he was receiving at the table. He might have known that driving along Bond Street on their way from the Pulteney to Hetty's house on Hanover Square would be disastrous. Had he had any sense at all, he would have taken the quietest street he could find even if he had had to add five miles to his journey. And he should certainly have brought the closed carriage—with all the curtains drawn across the windows and both doors locked.

And now all the gossip and laughter, which had surely almost run their course, would be revived and redoubled in strength. There had been several people on Bond Street whom he knew, and the others would not take long to discover his identity, especially when he wore the distinctive badge of a mottled violet eye. And he would not even allow himself to hope that Daisy Morrison's identity would long remain a secret, or the interesting fact that she was the identical lady who had saved his hide with an umbrella and paid his whore for a night's service.

Lord Kincade shuddered again. How could such a very small package be capable of inflicting such harm? Rather like a cannonball or a bullet, he supposed. He remembered the feel of her as he had grasped her waist in the barouche. His hands really had almost met around her. She was soft and feminine and quite damnably pretty. And he was not using the word "damnably" in any profane sense, he thought wryly. If only the devil were feminine—perhaps he (she) was; no one had ever seemed to think of that—he would readily believe that her pseudonym was Daisy Morrison.

"Ach," he said in disgust. "You are just too good for me, Albert. Tell me, do you do anything else all day but practice in here to humiliate poor innocents?"

When Lord Kincade returned to the drawing room, he could see at a glance that any faint hope he might have had that the ladies had had a falling-out could safely die a natural death. All three were sipping tea and looking thoroughly pleased with themselves. He did not allow even a glimmer of optimism to deceive his mind at his cousin's opening words to him.

"Ah, Giles," she said. "Well-timed, my dear. I need your assistance. We have had a serious falling-out here."

Lord Kincade strolled across to the fireplace and leaned one elbow on the mantelpiece. He looked his inquiry.

"First of all, you must add your voice to mine, Giles, and assure Daisy that it is quite imperative that she and Rose move here from the Pulteney."

Must they? Lord Kincade wondered.

"It is quite improper for two young ladies making their come-out to be staying in a public hotel without the presence of their mother," Hetty said.

"But it is only one young lady, staying in the presence of her older sister," Daisy said patiently. It sounded as if she had made the same argument several times before.

"And that is the other point," the older lady said, looking at her younger cousin. "I wonder you have not explained yourself, Giles, how absurd it is for Daisy to see herself as a spinster past the age of marriage and social involvement. Of course she must make her come-out too. I can think of a dozen gentlemen who would be only too pleased at an introduction to her. I have no doubt at all that I can find husbands for both young ladies before the Season is out."

Heaven help the unsuspecting dozen, Lord Kincade thought fervently. He drew breath to speak.

"I have no intention whatsoever of marrying," Daisy said spiritedly, "even if I were young enough to be thinking of such a thing. I gave up the notion years ago. I am afraid I am rather a managing person, you see. At least I have always managed our household for as far back as I remember, even when Papa was still alive. Papa was so busy amassing his fortune that he had no conception at all of what was going on around him. So I took charge.''

"Quite admirable," Lady Hetty said. "You will be all the better prepared to run a gentleman's household, my dear.''

"The trouble is, though," Daisy said, frowning, "that I would also run him. And I do not think I would be able to bear being married to a man who would allow himself to be dominated by me. So I decided long ago that marriage is not for me.''

"But Daisy has had many offers," Rose said.

She rarely spoke, Lord Kincade thought, looking at her in some surprise. Yet when she did, there seemed to be some suggestion of sense in her words and manner.

"But she has always been far more concerned about the well-being of others—even that of strangers—than about her own," Rose went on. "I do think it would be a splendid idea for you to enjoy yourself too, Daisy, if we really must be a part of this Season. And it seems we must. I do thank you most sincerely, ma'am, for being willing to take in two complete strangers. I still cannot help feeling that we are imposing dreadfully, but I can also see that you are really pleased by the idea.''

"Ah, bravo!" Lady Hetty said, clapping her hands and looking back to Daisy.

"Well," that young lady said, "it seems we will accept your hospitality, then, ma'am. And it seems that I will have to step out into society too, though I shall be very nervous about doing so. Sometimes, you see, I forget myself and speak out when I should not, or do something that I should not. And it would be embarrassing for both myself and my companions, would it not, if I should make myself conspicuous?''

Lord Kincade stared at her, fascinated.

"I am sure you exaggerate," Lady Hetty said. "So, Giles, it is all arranged. I do thank you, my dear, for helping me persuade Daisy. I was having little success before you came back in and added your persuasions to mine.''

Lord Kincade bowed. "Always pleased to be of assistance to you, Hetty," he said, ignoring the growingly familiar urge to break down into hysterical laughter.

She smiled at him. "I will have the young ladies and their belongings moved here tomorrow morning," she said. "And there is no point in delaying, as the Season is already well under way. There is the Riplinger ball tomorrow evening, Giles. I had accepted my invitation, though without a great deal of enthusiasm, for what is there to do at such entertainments for a woman with three grown sons except to sit with the chaperons and gossip or play cards in the card room and lose money? But I know Gussie Riplinger well. I shall pay her a late call this afternoon and see to it that Daisy and Rose have invitations too."

Lord Kincade bowed, noting out of the corner of his eye the bright smile that lit up the face of his little fiend.

"Julia has told me that you have an invitation too, Giles," Lady Hetty said, "and that she is hoping to persuade you to honor it so that you can accompany Judith there. Arthur is going, apparently, but everyone knows that Arthur has two left feet when he dances, for all that he is popular with the ladies because of his sweet smile. You will go, will you not, and dance with Daisy and Rose? There will be nothing like your attention to them to bring them into fashion, though I am sure that their own beauty and the news of their late papa's fortune will do that regardless."

Lord Kincade was furiously searching around in his mind for excuses—any excuse!

"Daisy for the leading set, I think," Hetty said, frowning in concentration. "She is the older, after all, and it would be appropriate for you to dance with her first. You can have the second dance with Rose, provided it is not a waltz. The third, if it is."

"It would be my pleasure," Lord Kincade said, inclining his head first to Miss Morrison, who was still smiling, and then to her sister, who at least had the decency to look somewhat embarrassed.

"How happy I am," Daisy said. "Your first ball tomorrow, Rose, and you have one set reserved already. Oh, everyone there will admire you, I know they will. Just you wait and see. Thank you, ma'am. Oh, thank you." She rose to her feet and extended her hand to Lady Hetty. Then she turned glowing eyes on Lord Kincade. "And thank you, my lord. The very best thing I ever did, I think, was to rise early at the inn that morning—the bed was so lumpy—and happen to look out into the stableyard to see that you needed my assistance. I am positively glad that the innkeeper put us back there because we did not have any servant but Gerry with us and he held us in contempt as a result.''

For one dreadful moment, as she made a little rush at him, Lord Kincade was afraid that she was going to cast herself into his arms. But it was only her slim little hand that she extended. She stopped her forward motion a full foot away from him and beamed up at him.

And the most mortifying thing that had happened in the whole dreadful afternoon happened then. He smiled back at her—a strange reflex that he recalled afterward with utter incredibility—and he raised her hand to his lips and kissed it!

6

Daisy was almost beside herself with excitement as she stopped before the pier glass in the dressing room that was attached to her room at Lady Hetty's. She twirled around twice and smiled at herself in thorough satisfaction. She was wearing one of her new ball gowns, a pale-green silk with netted tunic, new slippers to match, and the pearls that Papa had surprised her with on her twenty-first birthday. Her hair was dressed in its high braids, though Penny, the maid who had been assigned to the sisters, had done fascinating things with curled tendrils at her neck and temples.

She picked up the ivory fan that she had run back for, having realized at the last possible moment that she had forgotten it and having declined Lady Hetty's suggestion that a footman be sent to fetch it. She unfurled it before her nose and batted her eyelids over the top of it at her reflection. Then she laughed gaily, turned, and ran from the room again.

Daisy had not been admiring her own appearance. Indeed, it was probable that she had scarce seen her reflection. And she was not excited at the knowledge that she was on her way to her first ball and that she would probably attract at least a few dancing partners. She was not exuberant over the fortunate realization of all her hopes when it had seemed on their arrival in town that they would have to leave it again for home.

No, Daisy was happy because she had seen Rose, and Rose was looking more lovely than even Daisy had thought possible.

She wore a white silk underdress overlaid with delicate lace. There were no fewer than three ruffles at the hem, and the neckline was low, though not indecently so. And the inestimable Penny had done marvels with her hair, which Lady Hetty had persuaded her to have cut, taking her out immediately after luncheon and only two hours after their arrival in the house in order to have the task accomplished and ready for that evening. Now Rose's hair was in soft blond curls around her face and along her neck.

Rose would be the sensation of the evening, Daisy was convinced. She could not fail to attract every eligible gentleman there even before their identity became fully known and the size of their fortune. The latter knowledge would bring a mixed reaction, of course. It was true that they were enormously wealthy. But it was true too that Papa had amassed that fortune in coal, and the *ton* would turn up their well-bred noses at that, she had heard.

As for herself, Daisy would dance the opening set with Lord Kincade as she had promised, and then she would find a quiet corner where she could sit undisturbed and observe Rose's triumph. Rose had, of course, already met a few eligible gentlemen. There were Lady Hetty's three sons, all of whom lived at home, and all of whom were older than Rose and younger than herself. But they seemed to be very much boys still, especially Albert, the oldest, who appeared to spend his days playing billiards.

And there was Viscount Kincade himself. Daisy had not failed to notice right from the start, and despite the fact that she had never seen his face unblemished, that he was an exceedingly handsome and distinguished gentleman. She liked his tallness and approved the wide set of his shoulders and the muscularity of his frame. And she had always admired blond-haired gentlemen.

But it was not merely his looks that had drawn Daisy's interested attention. He was a viscount, the son and heir of an earl, and a gentleman in every sense of the word. He had been remarkably kind to her and Rose, though she acknowledged that he had been somewhat in their debt. And he must be an affectionate family man. His cousin had been only too pleased to oblige him; he obviously had a friendly relationship with his brother; and he must be fond of his sisters, if he was willing to accompany one of them to the ball in order to please the other.

There was only one blemish on Lord Kincade's character, as far as Daisy knew: that was his penchant for spending nights on the road in the arms of dreadfully vulgar creatures like that Bessie at the Golden Eagle. But gentlemen were like that, she had heard. There were such things as wild oats that they felt compelled to sow before they were ready to settle into steady citizens. It was nothing to worry about.

He was, then, Daisy had concluded the night before while lying awake beside her sleeping sister at the Pulteney, ideal for Rose. Perfect. She would do everything in her power to promote the match. But she would not be blind to other possibilities. Before the Season was at an end, there would probably be a score of men clamoring for Rose's hand. Between them, she and her sister would have to choose the most eligible, and one whom Rose favored.

Though there would surely be no problem in Rose's favoring the viscount. He was, Daisy thought with sisterly smugness, quite gorgeous. She could feel his strong hands at her waist even now. Indeed, she had almost wished there in the barouche that the necessity of rushing to the rescue of the poor little dog had not been quite so urgent. She would not have minded at all lingering for a few more seconds. And she could feel now his strong hand holding hers and his warm lips kissing it. She had felt quite a thrill all the way to her elbow. And he had the loveliest smile. She had seen it only the once, just before he kissed her hand, but it had been directed wholly at her. She had felt almost weak at the knees for a moment.

Yes, even though they must keep an open mind for a few weeks at least, it seemed almost a foregone conclusion that Rose must succumb to the charm of Lord Kincade. How could she help it!

"Here I am," Daisy called as she ran lightly, and in quite unladylike haste, down the stairs. "And here it is." She waved the fan in the air. "It was on the washstand, as I thought. Would it not have been dreadful if I had forgotten it? I would have nothing to wave energetically before my face if someone makes me angry.'' She laughed gaily.

She watched in some satisfaction as the Honorable Humphrey Parkinson offered his arm to Rose, and followed behind with Lady Hetty to the awaiting carriage.

At least he knew that his younger sister could still smile, Lord Kincade thought ruefully as he handed her out of his carriage and led her up the carpet-lined steps and into the hall of the Riplinger mansion. She had smiled quite dazzlingly at Arthur when the two of them had called at Julia's to collect her. It had been a deliberately warm smile, of course, so that he would feel the more punished by being accorded only a stiff nod.

But Judith was unable to hide her excitement for all her attempts to imitate a dowager duchess. He supposed that it was natural that she should be excited at being taken to a ball again after a week during which her only outings had been in the last two days, and both times with one of her brothers for escort. But he had a gloomy premonition that there was more to her suppressed delight than just that fact. He suspected that Lord Powers was to be at the ball too. As was most natural, of course. That particular nobleman was almost invariably to be found wherever the gathering of young, gullible, and rich females was likely to be the thickest.

He would have to see how the situation developed. He had told Judith two afternoons before when they were out walking that he would not after all either go to Bath or write to their father. He would give her another chance to show that she could behave with the decorum and good sense that one might expect of a young lady of nineteen who was in her second Season. He had no way of knowing if Judith appreciated that second chance or not. She had not replied in any way to his announcement.

Well, Lord Kincade thought, removing his hat and cloak and glancing up the stairs to note that there was quite a cluster of people at the top, presumably waiting to pass the receiving line, if Judith chose to have a fit of the sullens whenever he was in the vicinity, that was her problem. He had far more pressing worries of his own. Not the least of which was the knowledge that Miss Daisy Morrison was to be in attendance at this very ball and that he was engaged to dance the opening set with her.

He wondered, trying not to get his hopes too high, if it would be possible to dance with her for the whole of half an hour and get away from her again without any disaster overtaking him. Not that it mattered, of course. By now, it seemed, everyone who mattered knew about the fiasco of the previous afternoon, and somehow—how did these matters ever become public?—everyone also knew that the lady who had so disgraced him was the same lady who had stood in her nightgown and her bare feet in the stableyard of a certain inn less than a week before defending his person from harm with her umbrella.

What could possibly happen to embarrass him further? Matters were at such a low ebb that surely they could only improve. But then the fates that had so sensibly decreed such a pattern of existence had surely never known Daisy Morrison. He would believe his fortunes to be on the upward rise when he knew the woman to be safely back in the country again, managing her family as she claimed to have been doing all her life. And even then he would never again feel quite secure in the dignity of his name.

Any nasty hope Lord Kincade might have harbored that his cousin would have been unable after all to wrest invitations for the Morrison sisters from Lady Riplinger were dashed as soon he and his brother and sister had reached the end of the receiving line and arrived in the doorway of the ballroom. She was there already.

How he knew so instantly was not clear. They were not close to the doorway, and there was no greater press of people around them than around many other groups of ladies. Humphrey had come, and Colonel Appleby was there, and young Hancock. That was all. But he saw her immediately anyway. She drew his eyes rather as an insect bite draws one's scratching fingers. And in fact, he thought, the simile was very apt. The best way to handle an insect bite was not to handle it at all, but to ignore it, forget it was there. He liked the analogy as it applied to Daisy Morrison.

"There are the Misses Morrison with Hetty," Arthur said, indicating the ladies with a beaming smile in their direction. "Let us go and pay our respects, Giles. You will like them,

Jude.'' He smiled down at his sister and patted her hand as it rested on his arm. She had pointedly ignored her elder brother's, extended to her when they had reached the end of the line.

Well, Lord Kincade thought with a mental shrug, he had to dance the first set with Miss Morrison anyway. It was always as well to give the insect bite a good scratch before starting to ignore it. He followed his brother and sister across the room, nodding to several acquaintances as he went and seeing more significance in their smiles than mere social politeness.

Daisy Morrison was, of course, looking decidedly lovely and as far removed from the appearance of a chaperon as the equator from the north pole. He pitied from his heart the poor colonel, who was conversing with her and smiling at her and probably reserving a set of dances with her. He did not realize that he was far safer in battle waiting as the thundering hooves of a cavalry charge advanced on him. At least one recognized both the enemy and the danger in such a situation.

In fact, Lord Kincade thought as she looked up and noticed their approach, it would not be stretching the truth too far to say that she outshone her sister. Miss Rose Morrison, while quite exquisite in white silk and lace and with a new and becoming style of hair, was no more outstanding than a dozen other young ladies making their come-out. Miss Daisy Morrison, with her animated face and dazzling smile, was definitely one of a kind. Very definitely!

She and Arthur greeted each other as if they were long-lost friends, Rose and Arthur with a little more decorum. Arthur drew Judith forward as Daisy turned her smile on Lord Kincade.

"I am very pleased to meet you," she said to his sister. "Your brothers have been very kind to us, you see. And I am pleased for Rose's sake. You and she are of an age, though this is only Rose's first Season. I am sure the two of you will get along famously."

She beamed at Judith, happy now that she had a new victim whose life she could organize, the viscount thought nastily. He turned his attention to Hetty, who was always an entertaining companion as she never failed to have all the latest *on-dits* at her tongue's end. Of course, he supposed he was the very latest and hottest *on-dit*, but it was soothing to hear within the next five minutes that there were a few other unfortunates in town who had involved themselves in scandals almost one-tenth as embarrassing as his.

He snapped to attention when he realized suddenly that Judith and Rose Morrison were in conversation with Lord Powers. He must remember that he was not here tonight either to enjoy himself or to indulge in gossip, however soothing to his battered self-esteem. He strolled over to them, smoothing the lace of his cuffs over the backs of his hands as he went.

"Ah, good evening, Powers," he said, his voice at its most bored. "Quite the squeeze again, is it not?" He avoided his sister's glowering eyes.

The baron bowed. "Kincade," he said. "At each occasion of this kind one becomes convinced that one must have seen every lovely lady in the land. And yet each time one is amazed to find that there are other lovely blooms of whose existence one was unaware." He inclined his head in Rose's direction.

"Yes, indeed," the viscount said. He smiled at Rose. "Did I hear Arthur soliciting your hand for the first set?" he asked, though he knew the answer perfectly well, having been standing beside her when Arthur had asked.

"Yes," she said. "I am quite overwhelmed, my lord. My card is full already. Lord Powers was obliging enough to sign his name in the one remaining space just a few moments ago."

Lord Kincade looked at the baron through lazy, heavy-lidded eyes. "You were fortunate to come along when you did, Powers," he said. "And you, my dear?" He turned to Judith. "You have partners?"

"Of course," she said. "I am afraid there is not one set free for you, Giles." She looked defiantly at him. "Lord Powers has reserved two sets with me—a waltz before supper and a country dance after."

"Enjoy yourself, then," Lord Kincade said, noting that the musicians were tuning their instruments and their hosts standing in the doorway looking as if they were to begin the dancing at any moment.

"A nasty eye you have there," Lord Powers said.

"Yes," Lord Kincade agreed. "It posed quite a problem tonight. I had to choose a coat that would not clash with violet."

Rose laughed. "It is looking far better than it did the first time I saw it," she said.

"And doubtless far better than it would look if you had not had a champion to save you from a worse drubbing," the baron said.

"Oh, quite," Lord Kincade agreed. "But then my dilemma over colors might have been eliminated altogether, Powers. I probably would not have been in attendance at this ball or any other for some weeks to come."

Lord Powers tutted. "It is too bad that these days one has to look to one's safety not only on the open road but even in public and seemingly respectable inns," he said.

"If you will excuse me." Lord Kincade bowed. "I believe it is time to claim my first partner."

"Enjoy yourself," the baron said with a friendly smile. "We must hope that none of Gussie Riplinger's many poodles wanders into the ballroom during the next half-hour, must we not, Kincade?"

The viscount laughed at the pleasantry about as heartily as Rose did.

For all that she had had little wish to come to London for the Season, and for all that she had no desire even now to attract a wealthy and noble suitor and make a dazzling match, and for all that she had been embarrassed out of all countenance by Daisy's manner of acquiring them a sponsor, Rose was vastly enjoying the ball.

She was fortunate, she believed, to dance the opening set with the Reverend Arthur Fairhaven. She was feeling particularly nervous and self-conscious before the dancing began. But it was impossible to remain so with that particular gentleman, whose good nature and kindly smile would surely put a person at her ease if she were about to have a noose placed around her neck. Indeed, she thought with something of a jolt, that was the job of a clergyman, was it not?

There was the added consolation of knowing that the Reverend Fairhaven was not one of the more handsome gentlemen in the room. Oh, he had a pleasing countenance indeed, and his fair wavy hair looked baby-soft. And he was very tall—he topped his brother by at least three inches. But he was also a little too thin and there was a suggestion of a stoop about his shoulders, as if he were conscious of his great height and wished to be more on a level with ordinary mortals.

But the most endearing quality about him under the circumstances, Rose found, was that he could not dance. More than once during the country dance he began to skip off in a direction quite out of keeping with the pattern of the set, and the first time he had to twirl her down the set he tried to turn anticlockwise when even a novice dancer should know that one always turned clockwise. Before the set was even half over, Rose was smiling and relaxed, her fears that her dancing skills were not up to such a distinguished gathering put entirely to rest.

"You can see why I decided on a career in the Church, can you not?" he said with a good-natured grin as he guided her back to Lady Hetty's side after the music had stopped. "Nobody would employ me as a dancing master, alas."

And Rose found that Lady Judith Fairhaven was quite prepared to accept her as a friend and drew her into a group of young ladies between sets. The talk, she discovered, was all centered on the gentlemen present and who was more handsome than who, and who danced better and dressed more fashionably than who, and who was reputed to be in search of a bride and who intent on mere dalliance.

"Colonel Appleby has fixed his interest on me," Judith confided, "though he has not said anything openly yet. I just know. He is very handsome, I think, and very distinguished. But he is past thirty. Do you think that rather old?"

"If you would be comfortable with him," Rose said, "then I do not think the age gap too great."

Judith leaned closer to her. "My particular beau is Lord Powers," she said. "He is very handsome and very charming, and his father is a marquess. And he loves me and is quite determined to marry me."

"You are betrothed, then?" Rose asked.

Judith's face became stormy. "By no means," she said. "Dear Giles has taken it into his head that Lord Powers is a fortune-hunter merely because he has gambled away his fortune and merely because he tried to elope with Miss Hamilton last year—she is a great heiress, you know. But he has explained to me that he agreed to that only because she was very importunate and he was too chivalrous to deny her. He was vastly relieved when her papa discovered their plans and put a stop to them.''

"He would have married her just to avoid hurting her feelings?" Rose asked.

Judith ignored the question. "We are very much in love," she said dramatically, her eyes wide on her new friend. "But Giles is being cruel and quite gothic and has forbidden me to be alone with him. But I must, Miss Morrison—may I call you Rose? I mean to steal away to the library with him after supper when we are supposed to be dancing. Will you help me? Tell Giles that I have torn my hem and gone to the ladies' withdrawing room?"

"That would be lying," Rose said. "And it is not proper to be alone with a gentleman, is it?"

"But we are being kept asunder by force!" Judith said tragically. "Giles had me locked up for a whole week before this ball."

"Oh, dear," Rose said, her eyes straying to that gentleman, with whom she had danced and enjoyed the second set. For all his handsome good looks and manly bearing, she had found him ready to make conversation and set her at her ease. And he had been very good to her and Daisy, though she realized full well that her sister had unwittingly pushed him into doing far more for them than he had intended to do. He had also shown great restraint in not ripping up at Daisy on Bond Street when she had quite unknowingly exposed them to dreadful humiliation. Lord Kincade a ruthless jailer? She had her doubts.

"You will do it for me?" Judith asked. "You will, I know. You are a dear, Rose. I will do as much for you one day."

"I really think you ought not," Rose said.

But she was led away at that moment by her next partner. She looked critically at Lord Powers, who was in a set adjacent to her own, looking very handsome and smiling attentively at his partner. Had she promised, or had she not? Certainly Judith seemed to think she had. And was that not the same as actually making the promise?

The very next set was the one that Lord Powers had reserved with Rose. She had had several partners already and was feeling quite able to cope with having such a darkly handsome one.

Lord Powers smiled a very white-toothed smile as they waited for the music to begin. "You are Lord Brigham's daughter," he said. "I have just discovered that fact."

"Did you know him?" Rose asked.

"I did not have that pleasure," he said, "but I certainly knew of him. As who did not? But I did not know that he had such a very beautiful daughter."

Rose smiled a little uncertainly.

"Indeed," he said, "I have found since I entered the room and first set eyes on you that I have the utmost difficulty directing my eyes at anyone else. I believe you have quite slain me, Miss Morrison."

The music began at that moment. It was the only set of the evening so far that Rose did not enjoy. Indeed, by the end of it, she felt so uneasy at his lordship's extravagant gallantries that she decided to seek out Daisy and confide her problem.

"Lord Powers pretends to be quite smitten with me," she said.

"Pretends?" Daisy, whose face was glowing with her enjoyment of the evening, laughed. "I am not at all surprised, Rose. You look beautiful enough to slay all the gentlemen here tonight. I have seen the way several others have looked at you too."

"But he is supposed to be in love with Lady Judith," Rose said. "He wants to marry her. And he tried to elope with an heiress last year. Lord Kincade calls him a fortune-hunter."

Daisy's eyes sharpened. "Lord Kincade says so?" she said. "I have the greatest respect for Lord Kincade. Well, you must be careful, that is all, Rose. But I know I can trust to your good sense, dear. I know I will not have to be chasing off to Gretna Green on your heels. I wonder if he knows who we are."

"Yes, he does," Rose said.

"Ah." Daisy nodded. "Steer clear of him, then, Rose. There are plenty of other eligible gentlemen here. Did you enjoy your dance with Lord Kincade? I saw that he was talking with you through the whole of the set."

Rose was not listening. "Lady Judith is planning a private

meeting with him in the library later this evening," she said. "And I believe she thinks I have promised to lie for her so that her absence will not be remarked upon."

Daisy tapped her sister's arm with her fan. "Then you must disabuse her mind," she said, "and then relax and enjoy yourself. I shall keep an eye on Lady Judith. It is the least I can do for Lord Kincade, who has been so remarkably good to us."

"Will you?" Rose asked dubiously.

"Don't I always look out for other people in trouble?" Daisy asked cheerfully.

Rose looked even more dubious. "Yes," she said.

7

Daisy danced three of the first five sets, and would indeed have danced all five if Lady Hetty had caught her sooner refusing partners on the ground that she was there merely as an observer and chaperon for her sister. She absolutely must not do so, Lady Hetty said, when she was looking so perfectly splendid in her netted gown and when she looked not a day above twenty. And when Lady Hetty herself was so obviously filling the role of chaperon to both young ladies.

Daisy vastly enjoyed dancing the opening set with Lord Kincade. He looked so very magnificent in his ice-blue coat and silver waistcoat and knee breeches, with a quantity of white lace at neck and cuffs, that she positively gloated over the fact that he was to dance with Rose next. And how splendid they would look together. Then, of course, he was an accomplished dancer, and Daisy found to her surprise that she remembered the steps of the dance. She had never given a great deal of attention to her dancing lessons.

Perhaps best of all was the fact that he did not make a great deal of conversation, with the result that Daisy could count steps and memorize the pattern of the dance and soon feel quite confident that she could continue without conscious thought. Lord Kincade merely looked at her steadily and unsmilingly. He too was anxious to get on to the next set and a younger and more attractive partner, she thought entirely without rancor. She wished it too. She would not be dancing the following set and would be able to watch the two of them together.

She smiled. "You must think it very forward of me, my lord," she said, "to be dancing when I am five-and-twenty years old and here really in the capacity of chaperon."

"Not at all," he said. "I am eight-and-twenty, ma'am, and can still execute the steps without shouting from the pain of the rheumatics."

Daisy laughed. "You know that is not what I meant," she said. "I am in the best of health, I assure you. But as far as propriety is concerned, you may be glad to know that I have refused partners for the next two sets. Indeed, I would have sat demure and content among the chaperons for the rest of the evening had not Lady Hetty stepped in and scolded me for not dancing."

"I doubt that the dowagers and pillars of propriety will be unduly shocked to see you kick up your heels, Miss Morrison," Lord Kincade said, looking down at her with his one violet eye and the other good one. "I assure you that you carry your advanced age very well."

"If you say so," she said doubtfully. "I hope you are not merely being kind. I trust you to be honest with me."

Daisy could not interpret the expression that flashed across the viscount's face and was gone. But she was not too bothered by the mystery. She smiled again. "Do you not think Rose looks quite beautiful?" she asked. "I think she outshines any other young lady present, though I will admit that I am partial. And I happen to know, of course, that there is a very sweet person behind the beauty."

"She looks very lovely indeed," Lord Kincade agreed, and Daisy beamed up at him warmly before missing a step and having to concentrate again on counting.

For the next couple of sets she observed both her sister and the viscount with satisfaction. She was pleased to see that Rose had made friends with Lady Judith and a group of other young ladies. She was ecstatic to note that Lord Kincade talked to her during most of the second set and even smiled several times. The viscount seemed to be a man not given much to smiling.

And she was gratified to note that his other partners were not one-tenth as lovely as Rose and that Lord Kincade did not appear to be unduly enamored of any of them. Her one fear—for Rose's sake—had been that perhaps he already had a lady to whom he was paying serious court.

Her own partners she found quite satisfactory. It was true that the Reverend Fairhaven was not nearly as good a dancer as his brother—or nearly as handsome, for that matter—but she liked him vastly. He won her everlasting affection by complimenting her on Rose's appearance. He amused her by extending those compliments to herself.

"Come, sir," she said. "I know it is a clergyman's job to make people feel good about themselves, but clergymen are not expected to tell outright bouncers of lies, you know."

"Miss Morrison!" Arthur looked astonished and completely lost his way in the set. He recovered himself with an apology and a smile. "Indeed you do look very lovely, quite one of the loveliest ladies in the room. Ask Giles or any other gentleman. No, I suppose you cannot do that, can you? But I do assure you that I am not lying."

Lord Doncaster, who had asked Lady Hetty to present him and had introduced himself as a particular friend of Lord Kincade, was an amusing young man, who appeared to have a permanent twinkle in his eye. He commended Daisy on her courage in coming to the rescue of his friend with no deadlier weapon than an umbrella, and on her generosity in paying his debts when she had no assurance that she would be repaid.

"As for that," Daisy said, "I did not even wish to be repaid, though Lord Kincade, of course, being a gentleman of honor, insisted. I just did not like to see a gentleman who as far as I could see had done no one any harm, publicly humiliated. That innkeeper was a thoroughly unpleasant man and had given Rose and me a small bedchamber at the back of the inn merely because we had no servant with us except Gerry. And that barmaid I despised because I could see that she enjoys what she does. I could sympathize if I felt that poverty forced her to it, but I do not believe that is so."

Lord Doncaster was grinning widely, his shoulders shaking. Daisy frowned. "I should not say such things in a polite society, should I?'' she said. "I am afraid I am used to speaking whatever is on my mind, for if I did not, you see, nothing would ever be accomplished in my home.''

"Please treat me with the freedom you would accord a friend,'' he said. "I am not easily shocked, ma'am.''

"Thank you,'' Daisy said. "That is very civil of you. I was glad to pay that gaming debt too when I saw Mr. Martin. I did not like him above half.''

"He looked as if he might go for Giles' blood?'' Lord Doncaster asked.

"No.'' Daisy frowned again. "He looked as if he cared not at all for the money. He looked as if he was enjoying the whole situation. He smiled and smiled, but if one could have put a book up over his nose and seen only that part of his face above it, one would not have known at all that he was smiling. I daresay he was disappointed that I paid him, for then he had no more reason to despise the viscount, did he?''

"No, I suppose not,'' Lord Doncaster said faintly, his shoulders still shaking.

Daisy was enjoying the ball, but her brief talk with Rose had alerted her instantly to possible danger from the smiling, handsome Lord Powers. Earlier she had thought him a possible suitor for Rose, since he had begged an introduction to her through Judith and signed her card without delay. But, yes, she thought now, he could very well be a villain. His smile had the same sort of insincerity as that horrid Mr. Martin's had had.

She would watch after Rose, she decided, though she trusted to the good sense of her sister not to be charmed by a man whose motives she already suspected. But she must also keep an eye on Lady Judith, who was clearly young and foolish and intent on ignoring the warnings of her older and wiser brother. If she did try to slip away with Lord Powers despite Rose's refusal to help her, then Daisy would go after her and make sure that no harm came to her.

The moment came after supper, when Judith was dancing with Lord Powers for the second time. For a minute or two they were there, and then they were gone. Had Daisy not been particularly watching, despite the fact that she was dancing with Colonel

Appleby, she might not have noticed until it was too late. But she had been watching. Rose had told her that indeed she had declined to lie for her new friend but that Judith had merely tossed her head and said that she intended to spend some time alone with her beau anyway.

Daisy discovered without more ado that her hem was down and her slipper like to catch in it at any moment and send her sprawling. She clutched the side of her gown in what she hoped was a convincing manner, apologized profusely to the colonel, and hurried from the ballroom.

She had thought earlier of speaking to Lord Kincade or the Reverend Fairhaven about their sister's plans. But she had rejected the idea. Lady Judith's parents were in Bath, apparently, and Lord Kincade was in charge of his sister during their absence and during the confinement of the older sister. And it seemed that there had been some conflict already over Lord Powers. Poor Lady Judith would be in trouble if she were discovered in a private and forbidden tryst with her beau, or even perhaps if she were suspected of having planned such a meeting. And Lady Judith was just a young and foolish and impressionable girl—no older than Rose.

There was no need to get her into trouble. Daisy would handle the matter herself. And she would have a good talk with the girl tomorrow if she could, and doubtless persuade her to see sense. Lady Judith was very pretty and very young. She would have numerous chances to make an advantageous marriage. Colonel Appleby, for example, was clearly very interested in her.

So when Daisy slipped from the ballroom, she did not stop to enlist anyone's help. She made straight for the library downstairs, having had the forethought to ask a footman the way. And sure enough, a peep around the door into the room, which was lit only by two candles on the mantelpiece, revealed two figures wrapped in each other's arms. Daisy coughed and stepped inside. She shut the door firmly behind her.

"Goodness me, how pleasant it is to find a room that is relatively quiet for a few moments, is it not?" she said. "But I see that you two have had the same idea as I." She smiled.

Judith and Lord Powers jumped apart and turned to face her.

"Oh," Judith said. "You have followed me here. You have told Giles. I might as well be in a prison."

"The umbrella lady," Lord Powers said with a faint smile and a bow. "Good evening, ma'am."

"Well, yes," Daisy said with a smile, "I did follow you here, Lady Judith. But tell your brother? Why should I do such a thing? The room would be decidedly crowded if he were here too, would it not? And I perceive that you would like a little time to converse alone. That is quite understandable. The ballroom is indeed crowded. But you forgot, you see, that you need a chaperon to make your tête-à-tête respectable. I will be that chaperon."

"I do not need a chaperon," Judith said indignantly. "I am nineteen years old and in my second Season, and everyone treats me as if I were a child."

Lord Powers, behind her, looked at Daisy with a half-smile and raised one eyebrow.

"Of course you are not a child," Daisy said. "If you were, you would need a nurse. You are a young and lovely young lady, and need a chaperon. I shall go over to that corner of the library"—she walked purposefully to the part of the room farthest away from where the other two stood—"and examine the books. I think I can amuse myself here for the ten or fifteen minutes that must be left in this particular set of dances. And I shall hum a tune to myself to keep up my spirits. I shall neither observe nor hear your conversation, you see." She smiled brightly and turned her back on the pair.

Fierce whispering broke out behind her as Daisy suited action to words and hummed along with the music that could be heard faintly in the background. After a couple of minutes Judith spoke.

"We are going back to the ballroom now, Miss Morrison," she said. "Lord Powers brought me down here because I was feeling faint and short of breath from so much dancing."

Daisy turned and smiled. "I do not wonder at it," she said. "I have noticed that you have been much in demand with all the young gentlemen. Lord Powers is to be commended for his kindness and concern."

That young gentleman regarded her with the same half-smile he had worn earlier. "But you were quite right, Miss Morrison," he said. "I should have taken the time to realize how improper it was to bring Lady Judith here without the added presence of a chaperon. It seems, ma'am, that you have undertaken the task of being guardian angel to the Fairhaven family."

Daisy nodded briskly. "I shall precede you back to the ballroom, then," she said. "I expect you will be a minute or two after me."

"Miss Morrison?" Judith said as Daisy turned away. "You are not going to tell Giles? Promise?"

"Of course I promise," Daisy said. "Why would I wish to tell your brother that all the dancing has tired you? He might forbid you to attend any more balls. And that would be quite tragic for a young lady, would it not?"

She left the library, trusting full well that the two truants would follow on her heels after a brief kiss, which she thought it prudent to allow them. Her hand held the handle of the door, which she intended to leave ajar. However, when she ran literally into Viscount Kincade, coming in the opposite direction, she pulled the door shut and smiled.

"How very embarrassing," she said. "I came downstairs hoping for a few moments of quiet and walked in on a, er, tête-à-tête. I would advise you not to go in there, my lord."

"Judith and Powers?" he said. "I have every intention of going in, Miss Morrison, if you will stand aside."

"Oh, gracious no," she said. "You are mistaken. Are they together? And did they leave the ballroom? Perhaps they are in here, then. Let's look."

She caught him by the arm and almost dragged him through the door of the room next to the library. It was a small salon, she saw, also lit by a pair of candles on the mantelpiece. She crossed the room and spread her hands to the blaze that was not there. She must give Lady Judith time to return to the ballroom. She had promised not to get the girl into trouble.

"What are you up to, Miss Morrison?" Lord Kincade asked suspiciously from behind her.

Lord Kincade had not been enjoying the ball. It was never

his idea of pleasure to spend a whole evening dancing and making small talk against the background of vigorous dance music. Although he attended balls, he liked to spend at least part of the evening in the card room and part in some anteroom in conversation with sensible gentlemen.

But on this occasion he had to stay in the ballroom the whole time, pretending to enjoy himself while keeping his eye on Judith. He hated the role of jailer. And it was one he was unaccustomed to playing. His parents had been in London during the previous Season when Judith made her come-out and for the first weeks of this Season until his father's ill health had sent them both to Bath in search of the healing waters. His own relationship with his younger sister had always been good. She was high-spirited and headstrong, but he had never seen any particular vice in her. But he had never before been responsible for seeing that she did not do anything irrevocably foolish.

Judith had been attracted to a handsome face and to a practiced charm, and she refused to admit what she must know deep down. He was sure that that was the truth of the matter. If he could only prevent her from doing something quite foolish, like eloping with Powers or allowing him to draw her into such a compromising situation that she would be forced to marry him, then soon surely the truth would be as plain to her conscious mind as it must already be to the unconscious.

But patience was not his best virtue. And patience on such an evening would have been almost impossible to achieve anyway. There were two irritants that would be almost beyond the endurance of a saint.

First were the almost incessant jokes wherever he turned. By suppertime he felt that it was altogether possible that he would do dreadful violence to the next person who mentioned umbrellas or dogs in his hearing, wittingly or unwittingly. It would be marvelously satisfying to level one of the jokers and to watch blood well from the fallen victim's nose. Instead of which, he had to smile and counter as best he could with witty repartee.

Second was the presence of Daisy Morrison in the room. Her smallness, her daintiness, her bright smiles, her prettiness, all seemed to multiply the jokes against him. He still felt that strong compulsion to wring her neck.

Perhaps the only blessing of the evening was the fact that the first set had passed without any incident more serious than a single stumbling step she took while talking to him. He had thoroughly convinced himself that she would succeed in doing something during that dance to make him feel conspicuous and foolish. But it was not so. He was going to escape further embarrassment from her for one night anyway, he was thinking some time after supper as he stood and talked with Lord Doncaster and a few more acquaintances who seemed finally to have run dry on witticisms concerning his experiences of the past week.

But the evening was not to be without event, he thought ruefully as he noticed Judith and Powers waltz past half the doors leading out into the hall and through the other half. Drat the girl! He did not wish his friends to be aware of what was happening. He waited for all of a minute for there to be a lull in their particular line of conversation before excusing himself and strolling in leisurely fashion around the edge of the floor and out into the hallway.

By that time, of course, his sister and Powers had disappeared. He spent several minutes strolling from anteroom to anteroom and finally downstairs to the main salon, an office, and a smaller room of indeterminate function. As he approached another room, a little figure stepped out through the door, collided with him, and shut the door firmly behind her. Lord Kincade did not even have to look down to know who it was. It was, inevitably, Miss Morrison.

And how he found himself a mere few seconds later in another, empty room with her, the door shut behind them, he did not know. But there he was, standing inside the door while she had whisked herself over to the fire to warm herself. Except that there was no fire. One quickly learned to notice nothing strange about such a fact when Miss Morrison was involved. But her manner was agitated. Embarrassment only at having walked in on a couple in the middle of an embrace? He doubted that Daisy Morrison was capable of embarrassment.

"What are you up to, Miss Morrison?" he asked suspiciously.

She turned around and smiled dazzlingly as he walked closer to her. "Up to?" she said. "Nothing."

"I am in search of Judith," he said. "She has disappeared with Powers. That in itself would be enough cause for concern. But Powers is not a savory character, Miss Morrison. I mention that because I notice he has been paying some attention to your sister, who is, I believe, a wealthy young lady. Powers has a weakness for wealthy young ladies. Now, if you will excuse me."

"Oh," she said, catching at his arm, "I daresay that Lady Judith will be back in the ballroom by now. I am sure you have nothing at all to worry about. Is it not pleasant to be away from the noise and the motion for a minute?" She smiled a smile that was as false as any he had ever seen.

"That *was* Judith and Powers in the next room, was it not?" he said, frowning down at her.

The smile held for a moment and then faded a little. "But you must not be unduly cross with her," she said. "I do assure you that no harm was done, for I was there as chaperon. And, really, you know, she is such a very young lady. It is easy for you and me to be sensible and wise. We are much older and have had more experience with life. Lady Judith is at an age when she sees with the heart. She must be saved from such as Lord Powers, of course, but gently, my lord, and with patience. And I did promise that I would not get her into trouble."

Lord Kincade's eyes had narrowed. "You are telling me from the wisdom and experience of your age how I should treat my sister?" he said with ominous calm. "You are stepping within the bounds of my life again to solve my problems? You recommend gentleness and patience?"

Daisy smiled. "I don't mind," she said. "You must not feel that my evening has been spoiled, you know. I am only too glad to have been of some help. I am a woman, you see. Perhaps I can understand Lady Judith a little better than you."

Lord Kincade felt every force within him that made him a gentleman snap. If he could not—because he was a human being as well as a gentleman—lift his hands and encircle her neck with them, he could certainly blister her with his tongue. Enough is enough. More than enough is intolerable. He opened his mouth and drew breath.

It was several hours later before he had leisure in which to try to reconstruct the events of the next few minutes. At the time he seemed to act from pure instinct, though he realized afterward that his mind must also have worked at lightning—and utterly mad—speed.

The door opened behind him, and he heard simultaneously the voice of Lady Hutchinson, one of London's most notorious gossipmongers, in conversation with someone else. He realized a few seconds later that it was Mrs. Whittaker, a woman to whom the same description would apply. They would immediately see him and probably know him even from a back view. They would not see Miss Morrison because she was standing directly in front of him.

And they must not see Miss Morrison. Not alone with him in a room far removed from the ballroom. It would be bad enough for them to see him with any lady in such compromising circumstances. But definitely not Miss Morrison. He would never in all his days live down the gossip. Yet in a moment they would see her. He would be compelled to turn around, and they would see her. Or else she would open her mouth and they would hear her even before he turned or they advanced.

There was only one thing to do, and he had only perhaps a second after the opening of the door to make his decision. He wrapped his arms around Daisy Morrison, drew her slim body against his own, and brought his mouth down on hers—open so that her own mouth was safely imprisoned by his lips.

"Oh!" Lady Hutchinson said. "Sorry, I am sure."

"Who . . . ?" Mrs. Whittaker said in her rather shrill voice. "Oh, dear."

And yet, for all the embarrassment their words suggested, it seemed an age before the door finally closed. They had obviously been looking their fill.

And it was at that point—when the door closed—that the truly mortifying part began. Mortifying because he did not immediately jump back, as he expected to do, as if he had been shot from a cannon. In fact, he did not jump back even *almost* immediately.

He went on kissing Daisy Morrison, becoming aware of her slim, warm body fitting itself to his, her hands moving up to rest on his shoulders, the fragrant, seductive scent that clung to her hair, letting one hand run down her back to her waist and lower, tasting her mouth with his own, reaching with his tongue for a deeper taste of her.

And thus and otherwise making an utter idiot of himself, he realized several seconds or minutes or hours later when he began to come to himself and discovered that he was enjoying a thoroughly intimate and indecorous embrace with Daisy Morrison! He lifted his head and relaxed his hold on her.

She looked up at him with uncomprehending eyes for a few moments, her hands still resting on his shoulders, her body arched to his. ''Oh,'' she said at last, ''why did you do that?''

''To save your reputation, ma'am,'' he said, knowing the lie, knowing that it had been his own reputation that had concerned him far more. ''It would have been in shreds if that particular pair of tabbies had seen you alone here with me.''

''Oh,'' she said, ''how kind you are. You felt yourself in my debt again, although there was no reason to do so, and you have repaid it already. Thank you, my lord.''

''Please do not mention it, ma'am,'' he said. ''I shall return you to the ballroom.''

He spoke from instinct. He did not know what he said. He had just noticed the mirror over the mantelpiece. The two gossipmongers must have had a quite perfect—and lengthy—view of both Daisy Morrison and the openmouthed kiss he had given her for the protection of both their reputations.

8

" "So." Lord Kincade examined his Hessian boots, which were resting—with his feet inside them—on the desk in his library. He noted absently that there was one spot at the level of his inside left ankle that did not shine like a mirror. "What am I to do? Do I have to marry her?"

The words sounded like a death sentence indeed when they were finally verbalized. He twisted his feet the other way to see if there was any other spot on his boots that had suffered since his valet's loving care of them the night before.

Lord Doncaster and Arthur Fairhaven sat on either side of the fireplace, looking rather like judge and jury, Lord Kincade thought—or God and St. Peter, or the executioner and the chaplain. The three of them had mulled over his problem during a morning ride in the park and during the almost half an hour they had been shut up in the library since.

"I still think not necessarily so," Arthur said. "I like Miss Morrison, as I said before. She has a splendid courage and is very good-natured. But the truth is that for some reason you do not like her, Giles. And I cannot think that holy matrimony would be appropriate under those circumstances. You would both be unhappy."

"Here we go, talking in circles again," Lord Kincade said wearily, rubbing his eyes with a finger and thumb and wincing a little as he touched the bruised one. "But the fact remains that I have compromised her. And the story was certainly

97

exaggerated by the time those tabbies had finished with it. I practically had the woman naked and half-ravished. And how can I protest? The more I do so, the more the masses will believe what they want to believe. And it is too, too delicious to know that the woman I was so voraciously ravishing was the same who paid my whore a week ago. Sorry, Arthur.''

''I still think this decision you are bursting your brains over is an academic one, Giles,'' Lord Doncaster said. ''From my observations, I would say that Miss Morrison has considerable character. The chances are that she will refuse you, you know.''

''Yes,'' his friend said, ''but I can't make her an offer on that assumption, Peter. I have to make it—if I have to—with the firm conviction that I am taking on a life sentence.''

''I am not sure I would mind a life sentence with that particular female,'' Lord Doncaster said with a grin. ''She really is a delight, Giles. And remarkably pretty for a woman who should be past her first bloom. It is my guess that you will not know a moment's dullness with her as your wife.''

''That is what I am afraid of,'' Lord Kincade said gloomily.

''Perhaps I could marry her, Giles,'' Arthur said hesitantly. ''She would make a quite splendid helpmate to a clergyman, I am sure. She has great energy and much cheerfulness.''

''Good heavens!'' Lord Kincade scrambled to his feet. ''I would not wish such a fate on my worst enemy, Arthur. Absolutely not, though it is just like you to make the suggestion. No, if Miss Daisy Morrison is to be married—and I know deep down, avoid the truth as I may, that she must—then it must be by me. And may the Lord help both of us. I shall doubtless throttle her before the first week of our marriage is out and have the hangman do the like for me soon after.''

''Oh, come now, Giles,'' Lord Doncaster said, ''it is not as bad as that. The woman is kindhearted. She likes to help other people. It is a singular misfortune that her efforts during the past week have all worked to your disadvantage. She has not meant you harm. And kissing her last night, by your own admission, was entirely your cork-brained idea.''

''Thank you,'' his friend said, sinking back into his chair again. ''I really need to be reminded of my lack of intelligence this morning.''

"But you did it for a noble reason," Arthur said gently. "You wished to protect the lady's reputation, Giles, and for that you are to be honored. It was unfortunate about the mirror."

"So," Lord Kincade said again, "what am I to do? No, don't answer. I know the answer. And I am keeping you both. Peter, you were on your way to White's. The morning papers are waiting for you there. Arthur, you were on your way to visit . . . whom? The home for destitute mothers, was it, this morning?"

"The home for sick chimney boys," his brother corrected. "I visited the mothers yesterday, Giles, and had the happiness of seeing one of them depart for the country with her child, where her brother is to take her in and set her to weaving with his wife."

"And presumably you are the one who wrote to the brother and arranged it all," the viscount said.

Arthur smiled sweetly. "It was the least I could do," he said. "I know how to read and write, Giles. You would be surprised to find just how many people cannot do either."

"Well, Arthur," Lord Doncaster said, standing up and stretching, "Giles wants to be rid of us, I can see. He wants to contemplate the horror of his situation unencumbered by our words of comfort and encouragement. Are you riding my way?"

And Peter was right too, despite the facetiousness of his words, Lord Kincade thought as he closed the library door behind them and returned to his former position at the desk. Damnably right.

He could not quite believe that he was sitting there contemplating marriage with Miss Daisy Morrison. His bad dream was turning into a nightmare, and he could not shake himself free of it, try as he would. He had not even known the woman until a week before—eight days to be exact—and since then she had been the plague of his life. And yet he found himself now in the position of having to offer her marriage.

The world had gone mad!

As he had expected the night before as soon as he saw that mirror, the story of his encounter with Miss Morrison had preceded them upstairs and was already raging around the ball-room when they returned. And as he had expected, the story was quite inaccurate. Even then, it would have been bad enough. He had kissed her openmouthed, and had pulled her body against his own so that they had touched at all points, two things that he had never even dreamed of doing with a lady before. But in the story, Daisy had also been half-unclothed and his hands had been lost inside the half that was still covering her. Indeed, general belief seemed to be that the two fortunate dowagers had only just succeeded in reaching the safety of the hall outside the love nest before he lowered Daisy to the carpet to have his lustful way with her.

For himself, he had had to endure only more of the interminable teasing that was becoming a way of life to him. Indeed, he seemed to have risen in the esteem of some very young bucks, who gazed at him for the rest of the evening with admiration bordering on awe.

For Daisy Morrison, matters had been worse, of course. Ladies shunned her as pointedly as they could. Only one notorious rake and one of the very young gentlemen and Arthur had danced with her afterward. Peter had left, or he certainly would have done so too, he had protested that morning. Whether Miss Morrison was very upset with the turn of events, Lord Kincade did not know. He had stayed as far away from her as possible for the rest of the evening.

He must marry her. Her reputation would never recover unless he did. But how could he stomach doing so? Daisy Morrison was one of the few people he had ever thoroughly disliked. He could not stand her, the forward, interfering baggage. He would be driven insane in a week. He *had* been driven insane in a week.

Physically, of course, she was attractive. Despite his first impression of her as some strange apparition, probably from hell . . . What on earth had she had on her face that morning? And how long was her hair when unbraided, for goodness' sake? He had found in the week since that she was extremely pretty and had a slim, attractive body. And he had certainly lost his head over her for a few minutes the night before when he had found her unexpectedly warm and yielding, her mouth enticingly soft and inviting. Indeed—horrid admission—there had been a few moments during which he had had nothing else on his mind but laying her down and possessing her.

But that had been only at the most mindless moment of the embrace, when he had forgotten that she was Daisy Morrison. It was a mortal shame that such a fiendish, unfeminine character had to be housed inside such a very feminine and delectable body. But the body would be small consolation to him when he married her. Because with the body he had to take the person inside. God help him!

Lord Kincade crossed one booted foot over his knee and rubbed at the dull spot on the ankle. He would have to go to Julia's in the afternoon to see how she did. Ambrose was convinced that her time was very close, though the doctor said there were all of two weeks to go yet. And he must talk to Judith, try to get her to see sense without blowing up at her or sentencing her to another jail term. That had certainly not been a good idea of his. He had a great deal to learn about the handling of young people.

And then he pushed himself decisively to his feet. No, much as the visit to Julia's needed to be made, he must not use it as an excuse. The visit to Hetty's was even more urgent. It must be made after luncheon before he did anything else. The idea certainly did not do wonders for his appetite, Lord Kincade thought ruefully.

Daisy had not noticed anything different about the atmosphere in the Riplinger ballroom after her return there with Lord Kincade. It was true that she had only three dancing partners for the rest of the evening, and that two of those did not dance very well and the third tried to flirt with her in a manner she thought decidedly silly. She had told him so in the end quite bluntly and had added the chilling news that she was five-and-twenty. She had considered that the end of the matter.

There were perhaps several different reasons why she did not detect the cuts that many ladies were at such pains to deliver her. First, Daisy had not expected to be the focus of any favorable attention at the ball. She had not even hoped to be noticed. Even the three partners she had were three more than she had expected to have. She was quite delighted.

Second, she had been busy after her return observing Lady Judith and Lord Powers. They were not together when she entered the ballroom, and stayed apart for the rest of the evening. Lord Powers did not dance, but spent his time talking with other men and doing a great deal of laughing. Judith danced each set and did not look unduly sullen or upset. Daisy hoped she had handled the situation well. She still had much work to do to help that young lady. Scolding her or otherwise sending her into a fit of the sullens would accomplish nothing.

And her first concern must still be Rose. It had been gratifying to watch her sister dance each set, and to note that several of her partners were young and distinguished-looking. Surely at least one of them was also eligible and already languishing after Rose. It was a pity, she thought, that Rose appeared to tire early. The sparkle disappeared from her eyes and the smile from her lips not long after Daisy returned from downstairs. She was very young, Daisy thought fondly. She would get used to late nights and incessant dancing.

But despite all these concerns with which she had very deliberately filled her mind, one other had loomed very large there and probably would have made her unaware of the scandal brewing around her even without everything else.

Lord Kincade had just kissed her!

Daisy had been kissed several times before when she was younger, pecks on the cheek and on the lips, once a hand against the side of her breast that she had slapped away before soundly slapping also the face belonging to it. But all that had been years ago, when she was young and foolish, before she had grown up and settled into a comfortable spinsterhood.

She had not remembered that a kiss could be so disturbing, that it necessarily brought one into quite such close proximity to a gentleman. Not just a closeness of body—she had had no idea that a gentleman's thighs and chest and shoulders could be quite so solid and splendidly muscled—but a closeness of mouths. Lord Kincade's kiss had not been merely a meeting of lips. More, it had been a meeting and intermingling and invasion and tasting of mouths.

All very disturbing indeed! Her knees had felt decidedly weak and her heart had been palpitating quite uncomfortably at the end of it all. And there had been a foolish disappointment—was that all? No more? She had not felt nearly finished. But finished what? In order to finish, something had to have started. And nothing had started. It had not been an embrace. Lord Kincade had merely been shielding her from the view of the two ladies who had been about to enter the room.

So it was foolish—of course it was foolish—to find even an hour later that her knees still felt shaky and her breath still short. And foolish to dart glances at him five times in every minute, so tall and handsome and fashionable, and remember that such a thing had happened. She really should have left such silliness behind with her girlhood.

She had concentrated ultimately on thinking of him as Rose's possible future husband. It really would be a very splendid match for her. He was heir to an earldom, and was a very distinguished and titled gentleman even apart from that. But Rose would have at least as much to bring to the marriage as he. She was lovely and sweet-natured and, of course, very wealthy.

And so Daisy had been taken completely by surprise when she found in the carriage home that Lady Hetty was quiet and tight-lipped and Rose quiet and tragic.

"You both look extremely tired," she had said. "Perhaps we should have come home earlier."

Rose had burst into tears.

"Rose!" Daisy had said, aghast. "What is it, dear? Did you not enjoy yourself, after all? Was someone unkind to you?"

"N-no," Rose had wailed. "It's y-you, Daisy. Miss Kershaw and her sister were saying horrid things about you and Lord Kincade before they realized I was in their group. About you being d-downstairs alone with him."

"Oh, dear," Daisy had said, "those two did see me after all, did they?"

"It is true, then?" Rose had asked miserably.

"Poor Lord Kincade," Daisy had said. "He was very chivalrous. He tried to hide me from their view because we were alone in the room, you see. I had been down there chaperoning Lady Judith and Lord Powers, and then he came, but I could not let him see them, so I pulled him into an empty room so that they would have time to return upstairs. But those two ladies walked in on us, and Lord Kincade, who had his back to the door, pulled me close so that I would not be seen, and he kissed me so that they would not come in and find out who I was. That was all, Rose. Nothing to get at all excited or upset about, dear.''

"Oh, dear,'' Lady Hetty had said. "I am afraid you do not understand the ways of London society a great deal, my dear. The story had been a great deal embellished, I am afraid, by the time it had made the round of the ballroom. I am afraid your reputation has been severely tarnished.''

"Well, what utter nonsense!'' Daisy had said briskly. "How very foolish people are. As if Lord Kincade would have any interest at all in seriously kissing an aging spinster like myself. You must neither of you take on so. I shall certainly not let any silly gossip bother me at all. And I shall tell anyone who cares to mention the matter to me exactly what happened. Though, of course, I would not be able to mention Lady Judith or Lord Powers.''

And although Lady Hetty had continued serious and Rose had continued to sniff into her handkerchief, Daisy had refused to admit that the evening had given rise to any problem. She slept quite soundly after only an hour of persuading herself how silly it was to recall and relive every minute detail of an embrace that had not been an embrace at all, and that she would not have wanted to be an embrace anyway.

When Lord Kincade arrived at his cousin's house after luncheon, it was to find the three ladies gathered in a sitting room, Daisy with one foot on a stool.

He looked suspiciously at her when the other two rose, Hetty to receive his kiss on the cheek, Rose to curtsy to him. "You have hurt yourself, Miss Morrison?'' he asked.

"Yes.'' She looked down at her foot and shook her head. "I twisted it this morning, I am afraid, when running along Bond Street, and my ankle is swollen. But it is nothing to worry about. There are no bones broken, I think.''

Running along Bond Street? And without him there to participate in the joy of such a spectacle? "I am sorry about the injury," he said. "May I ask why you were running? Was there a shop on fire?"

"Oh, no," she said. "It is just that I saw one of your assailants from the Golden Eagle Inn and tried to catch him. Silly, was it not? I might have known he would be able to outrun me. I should have used more cunning to effect his capture. I am afraid I frequently act before I think."

Yes, Lord Kincade thought, he knew all about that. "One of those three thugs?" he said. "Are you sure?"

"I do not see how you could be, Daisy," Rose said. "You saw them only fleetingly in the stableyard, and this morning he was gone almost before you had seen him. I think it was just your imagination."

"No, indeed it was not," Daisy protested. "I had a very good look at him that morning because he was the one who looked as if he were going to attack me but changed his mind when I poked him in the midriff with my umbrella. It is a good thing he ran when he did, for I might have poked him somewhere else next. And I did have a good look at him this morning. He was grinning at a poor young girl who had upset her basket in the street, and I knew him from the fact that he has teeth only on one side of his mouth. At least that was what made me sure. I recognized him even apart from that."

"We were in the carriage on the way to the library," Lady Hetty explained to the viscount. "We were passing a boot-maker's when suddenly Daisy shrieked for the coachman to stop and was out of the door before we had even stopped. It is a miracle that she did not break an ankle then."

"It was very foolish of me," Daisy admitted. "Of course, our friend looked to see what was happening, and as soon as he saw me, he took to his heels. I chased after him, but I lost him very quickly."

"Tell me," Lord Kincade said, seating himself in a chair opposite hers. "What were you planning to do if you caught him?"

"I certainly would have found out who he was and who had set him on to attacking you," Daisy said.

"And how were you planning to extract such information from him?" he asked. "If memory serves me correctly, he must be at least four times as large as you, Miss Morrison.''

"Oh, I had no fear for myself," she said. "I was not his intended victim last week, after all, and I did have the forethought to grab my parasol as I jumped from the carriage.''

Lord Kincade stared at her. "Do you not realize what danger you were in, Miss Morrison?'' he said, unable to keep the exasperation entirely from his voice. "You must not do such a thing again. I must insist. I want your promise.''

She smiled. "You need have no worry for me," she said. "I am well able to look after myself. Ask Rose if that is not so.''

Lord Kincade got to his feet and stood in front of the stool on which Daisy's foot was propped. "You are in London now,'' he said, "not in the country. And this morning's business has cost you a sprained ankle, even though you did not touch the man you were after. He could break you in two without even putting any strain on his muscles. And clearly he is not the local thug, hired by the innkeeper, that I took him for. If you see him again, Miss Morrison, you must not try to apprehend him. And I must have your promise on that. Now!''

Daisy looked up into his steady gaze. "Well," she said, "if I see him and do not catch him, who will?''

"If you do not hold the world on your shoulders, who will stop it from collapsing?'' Lord Kincade said quietly.

"That is silly,'' she said.

"Your promise, Miss Morrison,'' he said.

"Oh, very well," she said grudgingly. "But I hope I never see that man again, for I know I will find it well nigh impossible to keep my promise if I do.''

"You will keep it," Lord Kincade said with conviction. "You will have me to reckon with if you do not.''

Daisy looked at him with interest.

"You are a blessing indeed, Giles," Lady Hetty said with relief. "I was never more frightened in my life than when I realized that Daisy was in pursuit of that great hulk of a man. And as the mother of three sons, I am used to frightening situations. It is a good thing that Lord Powers came along when he did, or Daisy might have fallen to the pavement before either Rose or I could reach her.''

"He was most civil,'' Daisy agreed, "and helped me to hop

back to the carriage. He was kind enough to offer to carry me, but I did not want to draw attention to myself. I hate to be conspicuous.''

"Quite so,'' Lord Kincade said, resuming his seat and eyeing her in some fascination.

"Shall I ring for tea, Giles?'' Lady Hetty asked. "Or would you prefer something stronger?''

"Neither, thank you,'' he said. "Might I beg a private word with Miss Morrison, Hetty? I would ask her to step into another room, but under the circumstances, perhaps I might ask you and Miss Rose Morrison to do that?''

Lady Hetty jumped to her feet, her eyes sharpening. "Certainly,'' she said. "Rose, dear, you wanted some advice on which bonnet to wear when you go driving in the park with Sir Phillip Corbett later this afternoon?''

"Yes,'' Rose said. "Will you help me?''

"I know what you want to say to me,'' Daisy said as soon as they were alone. "And it is quite unnecessary. Really she was in no danger at all, you know. I would never be so foolish as to put her deliberately into danger.''

Lord Kincade, who was on his feet, his hands clasped loosely behind him, frowned in incomprehension. "Who was not in danger?'' he asked.

"Rose,'' she said. "She was safe inside the carriage with Lady Hetty. I do not doubt the coachman would have moved off in a hurry if that bully had tried to go for her.''

"Good heavens,'' Lord Kincade said. "I do not doubt that Miss Rose Morrison was as safe as it is possible to be, ma'am. How could she have been your sister for all of nineteen years and not learned something about survival?''

Daisy looked a little uncertain.

"But I thought you would have known the purpose of my visit and my wanting to speak alone with you,'' Lord Kincade said. "I thought you would have been expecting it. I have come to ask you to marry me, of course.''

9

The Reverend Fairhaven and Judith arrived in Hanover Square soon after Lady Hetty and Rose had left Daisy and Lord Kincade alone together.

"Arthur came to see Julia," Judith explained. "But she is in a very cross mood today, the poor dear. She complains that she can neither sit nor stand nor lie, and no one has yet invented another way of positioning one's body. Even Ambrose begins to think that perhaps she is bearing twins. But when one considers how enormous Ambrose is, one can well believe that there is only one child, after all."

"You will be embarrassing Rose," Lady Hetty said briskly.

"Oh, not at all," Rose said, quite unperturbed. "We live in the country, you know, with a large farmyard very close to the house. One learns a great deal about life in such a setting."

Arthur smiled. "I did sit for five minutes rubbing poor Julia's back," he said. "I have heard from—from certain ladies I know that that often helps ease the aching muscles. But Judith wanted to go out walking, and Julia drove me away, saying that I would do her far more of a favor if I took Judith off her hands for an hour. Poor Julia. She would not say such a thing even in jest if she were herself."

"We have come to take you walking in the park, Rose," Judith said.

"Sir Phillip Corbett is to take me driving there later," Rose said. "Oh, what a shame. I would so like to have come with you."

"But there is lots of time," Judith said. "The fashionable hour for driving is not until about five o'clock. Do run along and fetch your bonnet."

"Yes, please do," Arthur said, smiling warmly at Rose. "I shall have an empty arm otherwise. I feel quite lopsided with a lady on only one side of me, you know."

Rose glanced inquiringly at Lady Hetty, noted her nod of approval, and ran up to her room for a shawl and bonnet.

It was a beautiful day for a walk, and she had been into Hyde Park only the one time with Daisy. Now, although the hour was rather too early for it to be crowded, she felt far more at home. She was on the arm of a very pleasant and very tall gentleman, and his sister, her new friend, was on his other side. And she found that she recognized, even if she could not name, several of the people whom they did meet.

She was beginning to feel more comfortable in London. Not that she had ever looked for any grand excitement from life or a wealthy and prominent husband—that was all Daisy's idea. She would have been quite content to settle eventually with one of the gentlemen who lived close to them at home, though she had developed no particular attachment to any one of them. She would be quite happy to go back home again at the end of the Season.

But she thought now that she would enjoy it while she was here. And her hopes for Daisy had been raised. It had always seemed sad to Rose that Daisy had never married and now showed no interest in doing so. And there was no point at all in trying to convince her that she looked, and indeed was, far too young and pretty to have settled herself into the role of spinster. Daisy was certain that she was so far past the age of matrimony that no one would even think of her in such terms.

Yet it seemed entirely possible that Lord Kincade was offering for her that very afternoon. Daisy had made very light of the events of the previous evening, of course, but then Daisy, for all her seeming practicality, almost never saw the world the way it really was. She had been very badly, even scandalously, compromised the evening before, and it seemed that the viscount had little choice but to do the honorable thing.

That was the only detail that disturbed Rose. She liked the viscount. She loved her sister. She thought they would make a splendid match. But it would have been far better if he had been coming to make his offer from choice. But no matter, Rose assured herself. He would grow to love Daisy. It might take time, because poor Daisy had embarrassed him several times, though she was blissfully unaware of the fact. But eventually he must realize that she had a heart of gold and deserved some happiness for herself.

And Lord Kincade might be just the man for Daisy, Rose thought. She had stared openmouthed at the way he had talked to Daisy earlier, threatening dire consequences if she dared break the promise he had forced her to make. Rose could not remember any person—male or female—who had talked to Daisy that way and received such a meek capitulation.

"Oh," Judith said in casual surprise, "here comes Lord Powers."

Arthur looked down at her with gentle reproach. "Jude!" he said.

She had the grace to blush and hang her head. "Well, you are with me, Arthur," she said, "so there will be nothing improper."

"And conveniently we will be two couples," Arthur said quietly. "That is a little like using people, dear."

"Oh," she said, looking up at him, tears forming in her eyes. "That is not fair, Arthur. You know that I love you dearly and like to be seen with you because everyone else loves you too. And you know that I like Rose and want to be friends with her."

She curtsied to Lord Powers, who was upon them by that time and expressing his pleased surprise at meeting them in the park at such an unfashionable hour.

"But may I join you?" he asked pleasantly. "I was just strolling along here, wondering what I would do to fill in an afternoon for which I have no plans."

Judith slipped an arm through his without looking at her brother again, and the two of them strolled on ahead of Arthur and Rose.

Arthur looked down and smiled at his companion. "This is very naughty of her," he said. "This meeting was clearly planned."

Rose smiled back. "But as long as you are here, sir," she said, "nothing dreadful can happen."

"And are you as cunning when you have a *tendre* for a certain gentleman?" he asked.

"I have never had a *tendre* for anyone," Rose said, "and don't expect to. But if I had, I do not know how I would act. I am not willing to judge someone whose shoes I am unable to put my feet into."

"You are a wise young lady," Arthur said.

"You are to take up a post as a curate in the autumn?" Rose asked.

"Yes," he said. "I find that time is moving with irksome slowness."

"It is a job that you wish to do, then?" she asked. "It is not that you have been forced into the Church because you are a younger son?"

"Goodness, no," he said. "Indeed, my father did his best to dissuade me, saying that everyone would consider him a pauper who could not support more than one son. But I cannot imagine any other life for myself. I am happy only when I can be serving others. I am entirely selfish, you see."

"You must find life in London very tedious," Rose said.

"Oh, not exactly," he said. "I am very attached to my family and am particularly glad to be here at the moment when Julia is going through such an uncomfortable time. I also like to visit all sorts of charities. Giving money to various institutions is quite unsatisfactory and not at all what our Lord means us to do in support of one another, I believe. I like to meet the people themselves and help when I can. It is better to help one person directly than to give money to twenty whom one never meets, I think. But I am delivering a sermon. You must stop me when I do that, Miss Morrison."

"Oh, no," she said, looking up at him with glowing eyes. "I think that is similar to what I feel when I tell Daisy that I like living in the country and have no craving for life in town. It has nothing to do with charity, of course, but in the country one can know everyone individually and communicate closely with them. Here there are such crowds. So many people last night, and almost none that I can now name, and none at all that I feel I know.''

Arthur patted her hand. ''If you ever tire of the artificiality of society,'' he said, ''you must let me know, and I will take you to see one of the schools for poor boys, or one of the orphanages or homes for the elderly. But of course you must enjoy the Season! You are young and you are pretty, and there is a time for enjoyment and a time for more serious activity. This is the season of enjoyment.''

But she was wrong, Rose thought. There was one person in London whom she felt she was getting to know. And the Reverend Arthur Fairhaven was such a very likable gentleman that she was glad indeed that she knew him.

''You will be wanting to get home,'' he said, ''if you are to come back here later for a drive. And Judith has been given long enough. The minx,'' he added tenderly.

''You have come to ask me to marry you,'' Daisy said blankly. ''Why?''

Lord Kincade frowned down at her. ''You can ask me that after last night?'' he said. ''After the way you were treated? It must have been an agony to you to be so snubbed.''

''I did not notice,'' she said, ''or even know of it until Lady Hetty and Rose told me in the carriage on the way home. It was all nonsense, in my opinion.''

''Perhaps the idea of people behaving so is nonsense, ma'am,'' he said, finding it difficult to believe that anyone could be so appallingly innocent or so impervious to feeling. ''But the effects are not so. You will suffer as a consequence of last evening. There will be certain members of society—ladies mainly, and unfortunately those with most influence—who will be unwilling to acknowledge you in public or to allow you to mingle freely with them in various *ton* events. You will suffer, ma'am, and that will not be nonsense.''

''It is all foolishness,'' Daisy insisted. ''People may say what they will about me. I do not care. And if they say anything *to* me, then I shall tell them what nonsense they speak.''

"Miss Morrison," he said, "will you consider what was observed last night? You and I were alone together, and in very close embrace."

Daisy flushed and prevented her eyes from slipping away from his only just in time, he saw. "That is nonsense too," she said. "You were not really kissing me."

"I was holding your body to mine and had your mouth covered with my own," he said bluntly. "In the vocabulary of most people, that constitutes a kiss, even something more than a kiss. And those ladies exaggerated what they saw."

"They saw nothing," she said. "I was hidden by you."

"There was a mirror," he said, "behind you. Unfortunately I saw it only afterward. Otherwise, most of this awkward situation might have been avoided. We would have been guilty only of being in a room alone together."

"How did they exaggerate?" Daisy asked suspiciously.

"You would not wish to know," Lord Kincade said.

"Oh, yes, I would," she said. "Tell me."

Lord Kincade looked at her with exasperation. "I would ask if you have smelling salts at the ready," he said dryly. "But somehow I imagine you have the fortitude to withstand the shock. It seems that I had my hands on your naked breasts, not to mention lower parts of your anatomy, Miss Morrison. Now do you see? You will have to marry me."

"No one will ever believe such a thing," Daisy said scornfully. "Why, I am five-and-twenty years old. Who would possibly believe that you would feel such desire for an aging spinster?"

"In short, almost everyone," Lord Kincade said. "Strangely enough, five-and-twenty years are not seen by everyone as qualifying one to enter one's dotage. And you do not look your age, Daisy Morrison. And what is more, you are remarkably pretty."

"Oh," she said, and laughed after a moment. "How silly."

"This conversation gets to be tedious," he said, realizing in some surprise that she entirely believed what she said. She was not merely indulging in false modesty. "Come, give me my answer. Will you marry me?"

"I certainly will not," Daisy said.

Lord Kincade leaned over her chair and regarded her neck with some longing as his hands twitched behind his back. "I shall borrow a leaf from your own book," he said, "and ask you why not? And please do not mention your age and confirmed spinsterhood again."

"I am not in search of a husband," she said. "I do not want a husband. I would rule him in a moment and then I would despise him for the rest of my life. Besides, I have Mama and Rose to look after and all the servants at home. Nobody knows how to go on when I am not there."

"You are the most conceited person I have ever known," Lord Kincade said, straightening up again, annoyance growing in him.

"Conceited? I?" she said. "When I do my best to look after other people's needs?"

"Do you think the sun will not rise in the morning if you do not wake up to watch it safely over the horizon?" he asked.

Daisy stared at him.

"Are your mother and her servants in a state of utter collapse now that you have taken yourself to London?" he asked.

"Of course not," she said. "I gave careful instructions before I left."

"All of which they are probably ignoring with great glee," he said. "You are not indispensable, Daisy. No one is. It is a blow to one's conceit when one realizes that, is it not? And I will tell you another thing: if you marry me, you will not rule me in a moment, you will not rule me in a hundred years—or a thousand. That is one thing I can safely promise you. And you may suffer more than once from a sore posterior if you learn that fact slowly. Now what do you have to say?"

Daisy closed her mouth, which had strayed open during the previous rather irate speech.

"Now," Lord Kincade said, realizing that he had rather enjoyed the exchange and careful not to lose the advantage by also losing his temper completely, "you had better say yes, and we can have this betrothal properly announced by tomorrow."

"If you ever tried to beat me," Daisy said, "I would beat you right back, you know. I am fully aware that I would not win because you are much larger than I and I know you are very strong. But I would inflict enough damage that you would know that this lady would not give in meekly to such a cowardly, dastardly creature as a wife-beater.''

Lord Kincade did not stop to analyze why he felt like laughing. ''I shall have the black umbrella destroyed on our wedding day,'' he said. ''Your answer, Daisy.''

''No,'' she said. ''I do not want a husband, and you do not want a wife. At least, you do not want me. And the only factor that would even make me consider marrying would be an attachment, a mutual attachment. But it will never happen. I am not made for love. Not for romantic love, that is.''

All that was reasonable in Lord Kincade's mind was shouting at him to leave well enough alone. He had made his offer and been rejected. He should make his escape without delay and stop running when he had reached the opposite side of the globe. All that was stubborn in his mind was determined that this time the little fiend would not get the best of him. ''What about your sister?'' he asked. ''Would you not consider marriage for her sake?''

Daisy frowned.

''If you are to be ostracized,'' he said, ''your sister's Season will come to an abrupt end. You may find, for all your indifference to your own feelings, that you will be forced to retreat to the country to save your sister's.''

''Oh, no,'' she said. ''That must not happen. I have my heart set on Rose's making the right connections here.''

''Yes, I know,'' he said, fixing her with a severe eye. ''Will you marry me, Daisy?''

''Is there no other way?'' she asked. She shifted impatiently on her chair. ''Drat this leg. I want to be on my feet pacing. I can think better so.''

''And you would probably tread on my toes every time you passed me,'' Lord Kincade said.

''Come,'' Daisy said briskly, ''admit that you do not wish to marry me any more than I wish to marry you.''

He looked down at her with raised eyebrows. ''Frankly,'' he said, ''I had not thought of marriage at all, Miss Morrison. I have been quite content as I am. But that is beside the point, is it not?''

Daisy was tapping one finger against her lips. "What if we were to pretend to be betrothed?" she said. "That would serve, would it not? Rose would have her Season and meet her eligible gentleman. And at the end of it you could go back to the way of life you enjoy, and I could go back home to look after my people again. Everyone would be happy."

"And you would be seen as a jilt at the end of it all," he said.

Daisy made a dismissive gesture. "What foolishness," she said. "Do you think I would care for that?"

"No," he said. "Not for a moment."

"Very well, then," she said. "Will you agree to my suggestion?"

Lord Kincade regarded her with a frown and rocked back on his heels. He did not have to marry her? Only endure her for another six weeks or so? For another eternity or so? "It would seem a satisfactory arrangement," he said, "though with you in the thick of it, Daisy Morrison, doubtless I will come to regret it."

She smiled and held out her right hand. "We must shake hands on the agreement," she said.

Lord Kincade took her small hand in his and looked down at it as if he expected it to explode. "I will expect you to behave as my betrothed," he said. "I will not expect you to defend my honor with black umbrellas, parasols, or any other weapons, including your fingernails. And I will not expect you to shoulder the burdens of the family of which I am the head in my father's absence. Do you understand what I am saying to you, Daisy?"

"You are afraid for my safety," she said with a warm smile. "You have no need to be, but it is kind of you to feel concern."

"No," he said, raising her hand to his lips and kissing it, and looking at her over it rather vengefully, "I did not think you would understand."

"May I ask you one thing?" she asked hurriedly. "Will being betrothed to me prevent you from showing an interest in Rose? You said last night that she was looking very lovely, and it seems possible that she is just the sort of young lady who might attract your interest."

"Good Lord!" Lord Kincade dropped her hand as if it were a hot potato. "I am suddenly very glad indeed that I am safely involved in this mock betrothal. I see I have had a narrow escape from a matchmaker. Did you really have me picked out for your sister?''

Daisy blushed a full crimson this time. ''I did think it might be a splendid match,'' she admitted.

He leaned over her chair again. ''You may set your mind at ease,'' he said. ''I am not nursing a hopeless and undying love for your sister, or for any other young lady. My tastes do not run to young girls no more than a few years beyond the schoolroom.''

''To more experienced women?'' she asked.

''Daisy,'' he said, leaning a little closer to her, ''ladies do not refer to such matters in polite conversation. But if it interests you, in private here and for this one time only I will tell you that Bessie was the exception rather than the rule in my life. And she is much regretted, by the way. And during the duration of our betrothal, mock or real, I will pay you the courtesy of staying away from other, experienced women. I would not dare do otherwise. I might beggar you with paying their bills.''

''I doubt it,'' she said. ''I am very rich.''

Lord Kincade straightened up and smiled fleetingly. ''A tour of Bedlam could not be more interesting than a conversation with you, Daisy,'' he said. ''Stay there. I am going in search of Hetty and your sister. It is time to bring a little sanity as well as propriety back into the room.''

Lady Hetty was delighted by the news. Although she had not for a moment considered turning off her charges as a consequence of the events of the evening before, she was quite familiar enough with London society to realize just how difficult her task would be for the next days and even weeks. Miss Daisy Morrison, behaving so scandalously on her very first public appearance among the *beau monde*, would not easily be forgiven.

But of course a betrothal and an impending marriage wiped out all sins. And Lady Hetty had quickly developed a fondness for both her protégées even in the little more than one day she had had them with her. Both were without affectation and not in any way missish. She was happy to know that Daisy was to marry her second favorite cousin. Arthur, of course, was everyone's favorite.

Lady Hetty's exclamations of rapture were scarcely at an end, and Daisy's smile was already feeling stretched and forced, when Rose returned home in company with Arthur and Judith. Lord Kincade repeated their announcement, and Daisy smiled harder.

She really felt the most dreadful impostor. The temptation to blurt out the truth was almost overwhelming. Daisy had never been comfortable with lies and deceit and secrets, even in a good cause. And really there could be no harm in their own families knowing the truth, could there? But she had not thought to discuss the matter with the viscount, and since the two of them were involved equally in the mock betrothal, she must not act without consulting him.

The restraint would kill her! For six weeks or so she was going to have to think of herself as half of a couple instead of a whole, independent person. She would never be able to do it. Despite Lord Kincade's brave words, she would be ruling him before the week was out. She would not be able to help herself. It was just her nature.

But on this occasion, Daisy clamped her teeth together and smiled. And felt thoroughly oppressed by the presence of her "betrothed" seated on the arm of her chair, his hand on her shoulder. He had the advantage of sitting on a level above hers as well as his superior height. He towered over her, and there was nothing she could do to equalize matters. She was trapped on her chair by the misfortune of a sprained ankle.

Daisy smiled on.

Rose bent over her and kissed her and shook Lord Kincade's hand, and looked altogether so happy and so glowingly lovely that Daisy lamented again the fact that her sister could no longer hope to be courted by the most handsome man in London. But there was no point in crying over spilt milk, she thought with practical good sense. They would just have to seek out the second most handsome. Sir Phillip Corbett was a distinct possibility, and Rose was to drive with him later in the afternoon.

The Reverend Fairhaven took one of her hands in both of

his and smiled kindly down at her. ''I am so very fond of my sisters, Miss Morrison,'' he said, ''that I can conceive of no greater delight than to add to their number. And I am pleased more than I can say that Giles has chosen you. I am an admirer of your courage and spirit.'' He raised her hand to his lips.

''Thank you, sir,'' she said, feeling the color rise in her cheeks at her own deception. ''I have always wished I had a brother, you know, and I can think of none I would rather have than you.''

Arthur turned his attention to his brother, and was soon pumping his hand in front of Daisy's face.

And then it was Judith's turn. And then tea was brought in, and everyone was merry, and everyone was speculating on where and when the wedding was to be and whether or not Arthur would help officiate at the wedding service and where the wedding trip was likely to take the newly married pair and what entertainments they should attend for the next few days in order to celebrate their betrothal and so on until Daisy felt like spreading her arms and yelling, ''Stop!''

She was usually the one in the forefront of such discussions. She was usually the one to make plans, for unless she did so, other people became so hesitant and muddleheaded that nothing was accomplished at all. But now, while a theater party was planned, and an evening at Vauxhall, and a dinner and evening party at Lady Hetty's, Daisy remained silent.

And smiled.

Lord Kincade bent closer to her in the end. ''Are you not feeling well, Daisy?'' he asked. ''I thought you capable of being so quiet only in death.''

''My ankle is throbbing,'' she said, giving in to quite uncharacteristic self-pity. And realizing as she said the words that they were quite true.

''Is it? Would you like to go to your room to rest for a while?'' he asked.

Daisy needed to recoup her spirits. ''Yes,'' she said. Very unwisely, as she was soon to find.

''Daisy needs to rest,'' Lord Kincade announced to the rest of the room. ''Will you send her maid and some laudanum to her room, Hetty? I will help her there.''

But instead of taking her arm and helping her hop along to the stairs and up to her room, and allowing her to salvage some of her self-esteem, he bent over her, scooped her up into his arms, and strode from the room with her.

And Daisy, who had never needed to lean on anyone, who had never been indisposed in any way, and who had never felt the need of any medicine, found herself being carried past the footmen, up the stairs, and into her room, and deposited gently on her bed. And when she would have risen to remove her slippers and release her braids from their knot at the back of her head, she was told in no uncertain terms to lie back down again until her maid arrived. And when Penny did enter the room and Daisy told her she might take the laudanum away, Lord Kincade turned back from the door, which he had been about to exit, and told her quite courteously that she would take it.

And she did.

And meekly lay in her bed and allowed sleep to overtake her, even though she was convinced that there must be a thousand and one important things to be done, including making sure that Rose was ready in time for her drive with Sir Phillip Corbett.

Give her one more day, she thought as she slid into oblivion. In one more day she would be ruling him, and then life would return almost to normal until it did so completely at the end of the Season.

Fancy a gentleman being strong enough to carry her all the way upstairs and still have breath left at the end of it to bully her!

10

Lord Kincade sat back in his chair after setting his quill pen down carefully beside the blotter. He regarded his head groom, who was standing quietly across the desk from him.

"Well, Chandler," he said, "what did you find out?"

"Not me exactly, your lordship," the groom said. "I would have been too easily recognized. I sent Baker. Baker is a good man and has had some dealings with, er, shady affairs."

"Baker is presumably the one that the Reverend Arthur saved from a life of crime and probably from a hanging, is he?" Lord Kincade asked dryly. "An admirable choice, Chandler. What did he discover?"

"The individual you described is not one of Lord Powers' servants," Chandler said.

"Hm," the viscount said. "So much for that guess."

"However, your lordship." Lord Kincade noticed not for the first time in their eight-year association the dramatic flair of his head groom. The man should be on the stage, not wasting his time in someone else's stables.

"Yes?" the viscount prompted, as he knew he was meant to do.

"The man is known to deliver messages to Lord Powers," the groom said. "Baker's drinking companion thought he might be a servant of the Marquess of Chalcott."

Lord Kincade's eyebrows rose and he stared at his groom for a moment. "The reclusive marquess," he said. "Powers' father. Interesting, Chandler. Very interesting. Baker was satisfied he was the same man?''

''He described him very carefully to his drinking companion,'' Chandler said, ''even down to the yellow teeth on one side of the mouth only, your lordship.''

Lord Kincade nodded slowly. ''Good,'' he said. ''Thank you, Chandler. And convey my compliments to Baker. Would he be willing to do something else for me that would take him from the stables, do you suppose?''

''If you ask me, your lordship,'' Chandler said confidentially, ''he is willing to do anything in preference to working in the stables. Not that he is a bad worker, mind,'' he added hastily. ''But his heart is on the streets, if you understand my meaning, your lordship.''

''I know that Lord Powers is an impecunious gentleman,'' the viscount said. ''He has expensive tastes. I should like to know more about the circumstances of the marquess. It might be difficult to find out. No one of my acquaintance has ever even seen the man. Do you think Baker can do it?''

''There is no knowing, your lordship,'' Chandler said. ''But if anyone can do it, Baker can, I daresay.''

''Good,'' Lord Kincade said, and nodded as an indication that the servant was dismissed.

So it had not been coincidence that Powers and the man who had tried to rearrange the features on his face were on the same street at almost the same time. And it seemed that there was possibly more to that attack on him than the desire for revenge of a rather uncouth innkeeper. Had Powers been that desperate to see that nothing came between him and his plans to marry a rich wife?

It was an intriguing question, Lord Kincade thought, resting his elbows on the arms of his chair and steepling his fingers beneath his chin. And certainly one worth pursuing.

In the meantime, he thought, pulling a copy of the *Morning Post* toward him across the desk and glancing again at the announcement, hoping yet again that this time it would not be there and he would realize that it had all been a dream, he had a betrothal to get on with. A mock betrothal, thank the Lord, but still one with all the obligations of a real engagement for as long as it lasted.

He must take Daisy into the park that afternoon if the weather held and if her ankle was not too sore. But if his guess was correct, she would die rather than admit to a weakness as she had the afternoon before. And doubtless her spirits would have rebounded and she would have a whole arsenal of schemes designed for his embarrassment. Not that she was a scheming female. Far from it. Miss Daisy Morrison, he suspected, acted almost wholly from instinct. It was just a pity that instinct always seemed to hit at the most public and awkward moments.

He must be thankful for small mercies at least. He had not been present with her on Bond Street the day before. Pretty soon some entrepreneur was going to start charging admission to Bond Street and make a fortune at it. People would flock from miles around to view the latest indiscretion of Miss Daisy Morrison, affianced bride of the Viscount Kincade!

Cringe as he might, though, when he imagined her behavior of the morning before, Lord Kincade nevertheless felt great relief that she had escaped with an injury as slight as a sprained ankle. He could cheerfully throttle the woman himself, and had derived decided satisfaction the afternoon before at the prospect—which he knew, alas, he would never put into practice—of walloping her posterior until she was doomed to walk the earth for the ensuing week and more. But he would not want to see her the victim of a hired thug. He had had a mercifully brief taste of the kind of pain that particular thug was capable of inflicting.

The trouble with Daisy was that she rarely seemed to think. The more he thought about the way she had come to his rescue at the Golden Eagle Inn, the more he turned cold at the thought of what might have happened to her. It was a good thing—a very good thing—that he was not doomed to marry her, after all. He would spend half his days rescuing her from danger and the other half hiding his head from the embarrassment of her latest escapade.

What a treat it had been yesterday to see her incapacitated and confined to one spot, he thought, realizing full well the

unkindness of his thought. He had been able almost to relax.
And how pleasant to be able to carry her to her bed and order
her to stay there, knowing that she did not have the ability or
strength to disobey. It had been almost unfair, almost cowardly
to gloat so much on his triumph.

But he might as well enjoy the memory of his moment of
power, Lord Kincade thought ruefully. Doubtless he would have
to load a ton of bricks on her head today if he wished to hold
her down. Life had not been so challenging for many a year.
Or so unsettling. Or so damnably mortifying.

"Oh, Arthur dear, you are an angel," Lady Julia said. "Just
a little lower, if you please. I am sure you could think of a dozen
things you would rather be doing than sitting here rubbing my
back."

"Not a single one," Arthur assured her. "Is that better? If
I am bringing you some comfort, dear, then there is nothing
I would prefer to be doing."

"You will make a wonderful husband, Arthur, if you can ever
find a wife worthy of you," Julia said. "Poor Ambrose! He
was excessively attentive at the beginning, you know, and even
until a few weeks ago. But I believe he has taken fright and
is consumed with feelings of guilt. He has even abandoned our
bed to give me more room, he says. It alarms him to hear me
moan and groan and huff and puff every time I wish to change
position, and to know himself at least partly responsible. I am
sorry, Arthur dear, am I embarrassing you?"

"Not at all," he said.

"I very much fear that the doctor is right," Julia said, "and
this little monster will not put in an appearance for two more
weeks. You see he is still high under my bosom, Arthur, so
that I am forced into perfect posture whether I wish it or not.
And how dreadfully self-centered we expectant mothers are.
Let us change the subject. Tell me something about your
charities."

"Young Lizzie and her baby have gone into the country to
live with her brother," Arthur said. "And Tommy has been

taken on by Mr. Menteith as a stable boy. He will do well, although he is so very undergrown. He has an eagerness to please. His years spent climbing chimneys have not brutalized him.''

"They are all going to miss you when you take up your post as curate,'' Julia said.

"No, no,'' Arthur said. "It is the Lord's work, Julia. The Lord will provide. I am quite unimportant.''

Julia turned and looked at him fondly, clearly unconvinced. "Rest your arms, Arthur,'' she said. "They must be tired. What about this betrothal of Giles'? Will it serve? Is Miss Morrison the right bride for him?''

Arthur hesitated. "Yes, I think she is,'' he said. "She is splendidly courageous, you know, and full of high spirits. And she has taken a great burden of responsibility on herself in the last few years, I believe. It is she who has brought her younger sister here for a Season, though she is very young herself and their mother is still alive.''

"Why did you hesitate, then?'' she asked.

"Giles has taken a dislike to her,'' Arthur said. "It is unfortunate that her courage and generosity in rescuing him from that situation on the road to Bath made Giles feel foolish. And then, of course, the other night when he tried to protect her, he plunged her into scandal instead. It is not an auspicious beginning for a betrothal. But I am sure it will turn out well.''

"I suppose I will not even meet her until monster here is born,'' Julia said with a sigh. "Ambrose said last night that we would not have any more children. And I feel so thankful, though I have always said that I would like four—two boys and two girls, like Mama. Will I change my mind, do you think, Arthur? Will I join the ranks of the women who are foolish enough to go through this more than once?''

But Arthur had no chance to reply. Voices were heard on the stairs, the door opened, and Judith, who had taken a maid with her in order to pay a morning call on her new friend, Rose Morrison, entered the room, followed by that young lady and Daisy leaning on her shoulder and hopping along beside her.

"Here I am, home again,'' Judith said, undoing the strings

of her bonnet and tossing it in the direction of a nearby chair. "And I have brought Rose with me. And Miss Morrison insisted on coming too in order to meet you, Julia, though she is not supposed to be up on her foot at all. Oh, hello, Arthur."

Arthur had risen and was bowing and smiling to the ladies. He kissed his younger sister on the cheek.

"Miss Morrison," he said. "You should have sent word that you were in the carriage. I would have come down and carried you upstairs."

"I know," she said. "But you cannot know how mortifying it is to have to rely on other people to carry me from place to place. We brought my coachman with us. He carried me upstairs; he would have brought me all the way in here, but I thought what a dreadfully lowering way that would be to meet my future sister-in-law. How do you do, Lady Julia?" She hopped toward that lady, who had also hoisted herself to her feet. "Do sit down again. Do you mind if I sit here beside you?"

"But how delightful of you to come," Julia said, taking both of Daisy's hands as the latter sank into a chair. "I did not think you would, and have been wondering if I might ask Giles to bring you. Most people prefer to pretend that pregnant ladies do not exist, you know, especially when they get to look the way I look right now."

"What nonsense," Daisy said. "You look in perfectly good health. You have a while to go yet, though, do you not? The baby is still high."

Julia looked a little disconcerted before laughing and lowering herself into her chair again. "I was just telling Arthur the same thing," she said.

"You know," Daisy said, "the very best thing for you would be exercise. Do you go out each day for a good long walk?"

"Heavens, no!" Julia said. "The *beau monde* would have a collective apoplexy. I am supposed not to exist until I can reappear as my more normal self after the baby is safely in the nursery."

Daisy shook her head. "The *beau monde* is a very silly institution," she said. "Each day I am more and more glad that I live in the country."

Julia smiled. "You will get used to it," she said. "Giles likes to live in town for much of the year. I am so pleased to meet you, Daisy. May I call you that? Giles told me that you are pretty. He did not also mention that you are slim and dainty. How envious I am!''

Arthur had carried over a pouf to support Daisy's sprained ankle. "Is it any better today?" he asked. "You must be well enough to dance at Vauxhall in the next week or so, you know."

"Vauxhall," Julia groaned. "Is Giles organizing a party there, Arthur? And I cannot go. How provoking!"

"The sprain is nothing," Daisy said briskly. "I daresay that I could walk on it now, but everyone around me squeals when I so much as suggest doing so. It is all nonsense. I have no intention of making myself an invalid, sir."

Judith and Rose meanwhile had settled into a corner of the room and were whispering together, their heads almost touching.

"Do you like him?" Judith asked. "I do not favor auburn hair on men myself, but I must concede that he is a handsome man, and Annabella Bailey—do you remember her, the one with the hair so blond that it is almost white?—comes near to swooning every time he enters a room. Rich too and heir to a splendid property in Northumberland."

"Yes, I like him," Rose said. "He is charming. He drove me around the park for all of an hour, but we were stopped and conversing with other people more than we were moving."

"That is what it is always like in the park at that hour," Judith said. "Were you offended earlier when we met Lord Powers? I was hurt when Arthur said that I was merely using him and you, and ashamed too because there was some truth in what he said. I do love Arthur, Rose, and I like you excessively too. But, you see, I must take every opportunity I have to meet Lord Powers, for Giles is so gothic about the whole matter."

"Do you love him?" Rose asked.

Judith thought for a moment. "Well, I do not love him exactly," she said. "But he is extremely handsome, and he loves me so desperately, and he thinks up the most romantic schemes, Rose. How can I resist him? It is so exciting to have some intrigue in one's life."

"But if one of his schemes was elopement," Rose said, "is

that not going just a little too far? Would you like to be married to him for the rest of your life?''

"But he loves me so much," Judith said. "I could not bear to let him down and see the hurt in his eyes and know that he would waste quite away and probably die because of my cruelty.''

Rose nodded.

"Are you going to marry Sir Phillip, do you think?" Judith said. "Are you going to do all in your power to attach his interest?''

"Gracious, no," Rose said. "I am in no hurry to make my choice.''

"But he is so rich and so splendid," Judith said, "apart from the auburn hair. What do you think of Colonel Appleby? He loves me too, I think, but he is very unromantic. He does not tell me constantly how beautiful I am and how he cannot sleep at night for thinking of me and how one unkind glance from my eyes would slay him. If he did, I think I might like him exceedingly.''

"He is a sensible gentleman," Rose said. "I admire his military bearing. It is so manly.''

"Yes, it is, is it not?" Judith said, pleased. "I am going to tell Lord Powers about going to Vauxhall. It is such a very romantic place, Rose. Just wait until you see it. The very best of places in which to get lost for a few minutes with a handsome gentleman of your choice." She giggled.

"We must be going," Daisy said, raising her voice. "It is almost luncheon time. Not at all the time to be paying calls, but I did want to meet you, Lady Julia, and I was close to screaming after having spent a whole morning indoors seated in the same chair. If the *beau monde* will not countenance your going out, I feel for you deeply. Can you not disguise yourself as a fat scullery maid and slip out through the kitchen door?''

Julia dissolved into peals of laughter. "That would put Ambrose on a roar," she said. "Can you imagine him, Arthur? You would be able to hear him clear across town. No, Daisy, I will just have to content myself with sitting here for another few weeks and looking forward to Arthur's daily visits to rub my back and Giles' to chide me on poor Ambrose's neglect.''

"I will call on you too, if I may," Daisy said. "I do a tolerable imitation of a milkmaid, you know, if you want company on that walk."

Julia laughed again. "I cannot remember when I had such a merry time, Daisy," she said. "You are going to be so good for Giles. He is a perfect dear, you know, and I love him. But he is very careful of his dignity. The worst fate he can contemplate is to be made to look foolish. You are going to tease him into a better humor, I can see. I am going to love having you as a sister."

"And so am I," Arthur said with a smile. "May I carry you out to the carriage, Miss Morrison? I may not look particularly strong because I am so tall, and I am told that I stoop and have shockingly poor posture. But I assure you that I will not drop you."

"Indeed not!" Daisy said, leaping to her feet and provoking a shriek from Rose. "Your arm is all I will avail myself of, sir. Though, on second thoughts, perhaps someone should summon Gerry. He loves nothing better than a chance to display his superior strength. He was a coal miner, you know, whom I saw coughing so hard when I visited the mine with Papa that I really thought he would not survive the bout. I persuaded Papa to give him alternative employment, but I do not believe he thinks driving a carriage a particularly manly occupation."

"And Gerry will grumble at you for a month if he finds out that you hopped down the stairs, Daisy," Rose said.

"Then I will summon this dragon of a coal miner by all means," Arthur said, crossing to the bell pull.

Although Daisy was feeling a little bored later in the afternoon to be sitting alone with her foot up, a book spread open on her knee, she was nevertheless feeling pleased with the way the day was developing, and with their stay in London generally. When she kept her mind off her own affairs, that was.

Rose had made a splendid entrance into society. She had attended her first ball only two evenings before, and already she had attracted the attention of a very eligible gentleman indeed. Sir Phillip Corbett, Daisy had discovered from Lady Hetty, was not only a handsome young man of fashionable

appearance and pleasing address, he was also a man of means
and heir after his father to an earldom and to a substantial
property in Northumberland.

And he must be captivated by Rose. He had taken her driving
the afternoon before and to a garden party given by his mother
that afternoon. It all seemed just too good to be true. Daisy had
expected to have to chaperon Rose at a number of entertainments before there was any chance of her fixing her choice.
But who knew what would develop from this? Perhaps the two
of them would fall in love and be married before the summer
was out. Stranger things had happened.

Lady Hetty had gone visiting. She had offered to stay at home
with Daisy, but that young lady had insisted that she needed
no nursemaid and would enjoy an afternoon alone with a book.
And indeed it was a treat to read, Daisy thought, glancing down
cheerfully at the first page of the book that had been open before
her for all of half an hour. Life at home was usually so busy.
There was always something to organize, someone to help.
Perhaps she would be back there sooner than she had expected.

And that thought brought Daisy's mind back where it did not
particularly want to go. Why on earth had she agreed to this
stupid betrothal? As much as anything it was embarrassing.
Daisy had no wish to make a spectacle of herself, but she was
afraid she had certainly done that. How everyone would laugh
to know that poor Lord Kincade had been forced into engaging
himself to an aging spinster like herself, and one who had come
to London only to bring out and chaperon a younger sister. She
felt thoroughly mortified.

Lord Kincade was so very handsome, so very fashionable.
It must seem ludicrous that she was his betrothed. She wished
desperately that she could whisper in a few ears the fact that
they were not really engaged. And there would surely be no
harm in doing so to Rose and to his brother and sisters. They
really should know the truth.

She had felt dreadful that morning in Lady Julia's sitting
room, surrounded by his family and her own, all of whom
thought her betrothal real. And the trouble was that she liked
them dreadfully. The Reverend Fairhaven was a thorough dear.
She would give an arm and a leg for such a brother. Visiting

his sister every day in order to rub her back, indeed! And telling her just yesterday that since he loved his sisters so dearly, he could think of no greater joy than to increase their number. She could positively shed tears over such kind words if she were the type to shed tears.

And she liked Lady Julia, who must be three or four years younger than herself. The lady had a sense of humor, something Daisy always appreciated. And Lady Judith too was someone she could grow to love as a sister. Indeed, she would enjoy taking that young lady under her wing. She suspected that as the youngest in a close and affectionate family, Judith had been spoiled and, as a consequence, was very young even for her nineteen years. She was very much less mature than Rose. But for all that, there was a charm and a love for life about the girl that Daisy thought could be developed with careful handling.

And she had had to pretend to all three that morning that she was preparing to become their sister, the bride of their beloved Giles. When really she was to be no such thing. And had no wish to be. She was too old now and set in her ways even to think of marriage. She would never be able to live with the restraints. Not to mention the absurdity of this particular betrothal.

Daisy's pleasant afternoon of reading—she was still on page one—was interrupted by the arrival of Lord Kincade, who let himself into the salon after a token knock at the door.

"All alone, Daisy?" he asked. "Did they abandon you, or did you drive them out?"

Daisy looked at him suspiciously. "My foot is quite recovered, you know," she said, "though I have promised to keep it from the floor for the rest of today. I do not need to be carried to my room again today, if that is why you have come. And I certainly do not need any more laudanum. Once in a lifetime is quite enough for that. I woke up late yesterday evening with a headache and a mouth feeling as if it were full of moss. If you have plans for subjecting me to another dose of that, you will have to hold me down and ram it down my throat."

"I am delighted you are so pleased to see me," Lord Kincade

said with a bow. "But you need not be so effusive in your greetings, you know. I came to take you for a drive."

"Did you?" she said, brightening. "I must say that I have not been enjoying *Robinson Crusoe* excessively. I had heard that it was an exciting book."

"It probably becomes more interesting on page two," he said, glancing down at the book in her lap. "At least I seem to remember that that was where my interest picked up."

"You need not take me if you do not wish to," Daisy said. "I know it must be irksome to you to be seen with me and to have to pretend to a fondness for me. I am sorry now that I agreed to this betrothal. It is all nonsense."

"I have brought my phaeton," he said. "I thought that if I perched you high enough off the ground, you would be far enough away from spectators that they would not notice your wrinkles and gray hairs."

"Oh!" Daisy burst into laughter. "How silly. You know perfectly well what I meant."

"My only misgiving," Lord Kincade said, "is that you will spot a little dog or a suspicious-looking character or an insect about to be trodden on, and bellow out at me to stop when we are in the middle of Rotten Row."

"How absurd," Daisy said, smiling up at him. "That would embarrass you, and I would not want to draw attention to you. Or to myself, for that matter."

"Do you think I might have that in writing?" Lord Kincade asked. "Now, Daisy, if I ring for your maid, will she know what bonnet and shoes to fetch? That dress is very pretty, by the way. I don't think you will need a shawl or pelisse."

The matter of her dress was settled with the minimum of fuss. The matter of conveying her outside to the phaeton was not. Daisy declared, her look thoroughly mulish, that she would go for this drive only if she could walk or hop outside herself. Lord Kincade announced, looking somewhat bored, that they would proceed only if she traveled from her chair to the phaeton in his arms.

It was a protracted argument in which Daisy did all the talking. At the end of ten minutes, during which Lord Kincade had sat down and polished his quizzing glass with minute care, he carried Daisy down the stairs and out through the front door, and lifted her into the high seat of the phaeton.

"Oh," she said, forgetting immediately that she had given in only under the severest of protests and was going to take the drive in silent dignity. "What a splendid conveyance. I feel as if I am a mile above the ground. And what lovely animals. Might I take the ribbons, do you think? I am an excellent whip, you know."

"I have no doubt that you are," Lord Kincade said coolly, climbing into the seat beside her and taking the ribbons into his own hands. "You probably bowl along the roads at home at thirty miles an hour when you are not in a hurry. This is London, Daisy, these are spirited animals, and the answer is no."

She folded her hands in her lap, resumed her silent dignity, and felt a thrill of exhilaration as the horses moved off.

"Oh, but it would be splendid to move along at thirty miles an hour in this conveyance, would it not?" she said, turning a beaming face to him.

"Ladies who are five-and-twenty and well past their prime must be contented with the sedate pace of three miles an hour," Lord Kincade said.

Daisy laughed.

11

Lord Kincade had cause to be not displeased with his life less than a week later. It was true that he was living in a manner that was not quite of his own choosing, but he had learned in his twenty-eight years that life tended to be like that. It was a naïve idea of the very young or of those whose minds never developed to full maturity that one could make of life whatever one wished.

In some ways the association with the Morrison ladies was not a bad thing. Hetty was as happy as a lark and no longer fretted over the very private lives of her three sons. She had two young ladies to fuss over, to conduct to a wide variety of entertainments, and to boast about to her friends. She was proud that Daisy was betrothed to her cousin, and that Rose was so pretty and sweet-natured that she was attracting her fair share of notice.

And both Julia and Judith had certainly benefited. Poor Julia was still waiting for her confinement to end, though she had confided to him in some triumph that morning that the baby had fallen to such an extent that it could no longer be said that it was wishful thinking on her part. And Daisy visited her every day, amusing Julia with her constant chatter. Indeed, Lord Kincade thought with some unease, his sister was going to be very disappointed when she discovered that the betrothal was not real. She loved Daisy quite as much as if they were blood relatives, she had declared that morning.

And Judith seemed a great deal happier and somewhat more

steady since she had befriended Rose Morrison. The two of them
had to meet every day and spent their time talking exclusively
to each other, and giggling a great deal. The sullenness seemed
to have gone from his sister and the obsession with Powers.
As far as he knew, Judith had seen Powers only once in the
past week. She had gone driving with him in Kensington
Gardens one afternoon. But since Rose and Arthur had been
with them, Lord Kincade had not worried unduly. There would
be more to worry about, perhaps, if it appeared that there was
no communication at all between the pair who had been planning
an elopement a mere couple of weeks before.

As for himself, Lord Kincade thought, matters could be a
great deal worse. He had expected them to be. He had been
betrothed to Daisy for almost a week and there had been no
major mishap or scandal of any sort. Perhaps it had been
unfortunate coincidence, he was beginning to think, that she
had involved him in such hopelessly embarrassing and compromising scenes all within a week. Perhaps for the remainder of
the Season, the remainder of their betrothal, life would proceed
with some tranquillity.

No, not tranquillity. The word could not be associated in any
way with Daisy Morrison. There was nothing tranquil about
a young lady who pestered one so throughout a drive in the park
that one felt compelled to silence her by taking her out onto
the Dover road the following afternoon, putting the ribbons in
her hands, uttering a fervent but silent prayer, and allowing her
to tool his phaeton along the road, while she exclaimed with
delight and used all the superlatives he was aware of and more
besides to describe his horses and his conveyance.

And there had been nothing tranquil about finding during the
three days following his engagement that every time he insisted
on carrying her from place to place, she first felt obliged to
deliver a ten-minute monologue of protest. One would have
thought that after the first time—or the second if she was a slow
learner—she would have realized that he could be ten times as
stubborn as she when it was necessary for him to have his own
way.

And there was certainly nothing tranquil about her conversation. It was all very well for her to describe to him in all its

sordid detail a visit to and down a coal mine that she had made with her father several years before, when she had not realized until her eyes became fully accustomed to the gloom that the poor dirty animals who lived underground and were harnessed to carts of coal far too heavy for their strength were actually children. And all very well to describe her grief and frustration to find at her father's death that he had sold all his interests in coal so that she could not make of his mines something more humane, if less prosperous. But Lord Kincade lived in some terror that she might introduce the topic to some polite drawing-room conversation and send all the ladies into a mass fit of the vapors.

Nor could he feel quite comfortable to find her one morning tête-à-tête with Julia, describing in the most graphic detail one of her three experiences as assistant to the local midwife. And she an unmarried young lady of gentle birth! Had she stopped the moment the door opened to admit him, he might have felt some confidence that she would not dream of talking of such things in polite society. But after flashing him a smile and uttering what sounded to him like a distinctly absentminded greeting, she had continued the completely unexpurgated account. He had almost had a fit of the vapors himself!

No, he definitely could not expect the coming few weeks to be tranquil, Lord Kincade decided. "Uneventful" was perhaps a better word. He might hope that what remained of his betrothal would proceed uneventfully.

And so he conveyed his betrothed and her sister, Hetty, Arthur, Judith, Sir Phillip Corbett, and Colonel Appleby to the theater six days after his betrothal in a more cheerful frame of mind than he would have expected the week before, and settled them in his private box. They were to watch Edmund Kean in *The Merchant of Venice*.

Daisy too was feeling pleased with life. With far less time and trouble than she had expected, she seemed to have settled Rose's future. Although Rose had met other gentlemen during the week, half a dozen of whom would be calling and generally dancing attendance on her with the smallest encouragement, a doting Daisy thought, Sir Phillip Corbett seemed to have established his claim without delay. He had spent some time

with Rose, even if only for a five-minute conversation on Bond
Street, every day since the first ball they had attended. He
seemed perfect in every way for Rose. Apart from having rank
and wealth, he was handsome, charming, and well connected.

"I should not be surprised if Sir Phillip will be declaring
himself before many more weeks have passed," she had said
to Rose just that afternoon.

Rose—dear Rose—had looked startled. She was far too
modest to realize what effect she had on gentlemen. "But we
met just a week ago," she had said. "We scarce know each
other, Daisy."

"But what a splendid match it would be," Daisy had said.
"All would seem worthwhile, Rose, if only you could make
such an advantageous connection. All the work of the last few
years, all the opposition I had to fight in order to bring you
here, all the problems of leaving Mama alone to cope with
running Primrose Park, the setback we had when we arrived
here to find Aunt Pickering gone, that ridiculous situation that
forced me to become betrothed to his lordship—it will all seem
so worthwhile, Rose, if I can only see you benefit from it. I
love you so very much. I want more than anything to see you
well-married."

Rose had stared at her mutely, and Daisy had hugged her and
smiled at her and almost shed tears over her, she had felt so
happy.

And now here they were at the theater and Rose looked a
perfect picture dressed in green, and Sir Phillip was obviously
drinking in the sight of her. And how very fortunate they were,
Daisy thought, to have met Lord Kincade so opportunely on
the road to London and to have been able to secure an introduction to his family. She liked them so very well. Lady Hetty
was a dear, and had made no fuss and shown no regret at having
taken them in even the morning after the disaster of that first
ball.

She also liked Lady Julia very well indeed. It was true that
she visited daily because she knew that that lady was dreadfully
bored as well as physically uncomfortable, though she still held
to the ridiculous notion that it was not at all the thing to go
outside to get some fresh air and exercise. But she went from

inclination too. She could talk to Lady Julia, and listen too. Daisy had had no close female friend since Prissy Hanover had married five years before and moved away from home. She suspected that she and Lady Julia could become fast friends.

And Judith interested her. She was certainly pleased that she and Rose were friends. And Arthur Fairhaven, of course, was an angel. Altogether, she thought with a feeling that was almost a pang of regret, as she smiled at her betrothed and seated herself in his box, arranging her gold-colored gown carefully about her as she did so, they would have been a lovely family to marry into.

There was his lordship, of course. And she really would not enjoy being married to him, even if at this late date she should ever begin to change her mind and think about marriage. She had always thought that she would not be able to bear being married to a man she could easily dominate—and that meant every man she had met so far in her life, Papa included. But she did not think she would be able to endure one who was so stubborn about getting his own way, either.

All that ridiculous fuss about carrying her about when her ankle had been sprained, even when she was already able to put her foot to the ground without screaming. Every time she had explained to him, using perfectly reasonable and logical arguments, that she did not need to be carried about like a sack of meal, he had merely sat and sulked while she talked, refusing to be drawn into argument, refusing to accept her way, until in the end she had had to give in to him, just because he was acting like a big spoiled child and it was not worth making a huge issue out of something so unimportant.

She could think of nothing more mortifying than having to be carried wherever she went. Especially when the carrier was a tall and handsome gentleman who had kissed her and held her close in an attempt to protect her honor once upon a time and whose physical closeness now awoke uncomfortable and totally unwelcome memories and sensations.

"Has no one ever told all those gentlemen in the pit that it is rude to stare so openly through their quizzing glasses?" Daisy asked Lord Kincade.

"Doubtless their mothers did or their nurses when they were

still in the nursery," he said. "But perhaps no one since then. And not you either, Daisy," he added hurriedly, having a sudden nightmarish mental vision of Daisy standing in his box and wagging a finger at all the bucks below while instructing them to put away their glasses and watch their manners. "It would not be at all the ladylike thing to do. Try to feel honored that they are interested enough to look at you."

"Oh, they are not looking at me," she said, smiling at him. "Why would they care to look at me? They are looking at Lady Judith and Rose."

"Then perhaps I should get to my feet and upbraid them for their lack of taste," he said. "You are looking remarkably pretty tonight."

Daisy laughed merrily. "I think," she said, lowering her voice and leaning confidentially toward him, "that your sister is beginning to look more favorably on the colonel. And Sir Phillip is very taken with Rose. That is obvious at a glance. Is not everything working out splendidly?"

"Quite so," he said, "and if we make just the smallest effort, I am sure we can persuade ourselves that we are entirely responsible for such a happy turn of events. It matters not at all, of course, that Corbett and your sister have been acquainted for only a week and that Appleby is twelve years Judith's senior."

"Well, of course not," Daisy agreed. "I am glad you see things my way. Have you seen Mr. Kean act before? I am looking forward dreadfully to seeing him. I do not know this particular play. Is it worth watching?"

Daisy was answering her own questions a short while later. After exclaiming with delight at the great actor's first appearance on stage, she settled her arms on the velvet rest before her and appeared to go into a trance. Lord Kincade watched her in some amusement. It took someone of the caliber of Edmund Kean, clearly, to silence Miss Daisy Morrison.

And indeed she did look remarkably pretty, her cheeks flushed with pleasure, her eyes bright, her lips parted slightly. He wondered again, as he had done during other unguarded moments, what her hair would look like loosened from the braids. He imagined it down over her small rounded breasts,

her slender body, her slim arms on which she leaned her weight.
He imagined it spread on a pillow, his hands in it and his face
breathing in the scent of it. His eyes moved down her body,
and in imagination he caressed her naked flesh with his hands
and felt her slender curves with the length of his own body,
pressed her against a mattress with his weight. And . . .

And he was letting a very superior performance of a Shakespeare play pass him by. And having very carnal and very school-
boyish thoughts about the woman he was gazing at. He had had
her all but mounted in his imagination. Daisy Morrison. Good
God! They would be carting him off to Bedlam before the spring
was out if he did not take care.

"Oh!" Daisy looked around at him suddenly, her expression
indignant, so that Lord Kincade thought for one dazed moment
that she had somehow observed his eyes unclothing her and read
his mind putting her to bed beneath him. "How very obnoxious
that Antonio is and Bassanio and their friends. I look forward
to seeing Shylock vindicated at the end of this play."

"Er, Shylock is the villain of the play," he whispered as she
turned to face the stage again.

"Oh, what nonsense," she said, turning large eyes on him
again. "If someone called me dog and spit in my beard—not
that I have a beard, of course, because I am not a man—I would
think twice about giving him a loan too. They will come to grief
before the end, mark my word."

Lord Kincade smiled quietly to himself as Daisy became
absorbed in the action again. Only his betrothed could ever
conceive such a ridiculous notion.

Judith and Rose sat with their heads together during part of
the interval while Sir Phillip and Arthur took themselves off
to visit acquaintances in other boxes and Colonel Appleby
chatted with Lady Hetty and Lord Kincade. Daisy uncharacter-
istically was still gazing at the empty stage, apparently oblivious
to the conversation.

"He wrote to me again today," Judith said, "and he loves
me as much as ever. He says he cannot endure being parted
from me for much longer."

"Should he not just go to your brother openly if he feels so?"

Rose asked doubtfully. "Or better still, to your papa in Bath? I cannot understand the necessity of all the secrecy."

"But he knows that Giles and Papa would reject his suit," Judith said. "He is a reformed man, you know, but he will readily admit that he has lived a wild youth. The worst of it is that he has squandered all his own money, even though now he would know how to use it wisely. He does not mind that for himself, for he says that he can exist on very little, but of course he knows that Giles and Papa will not want to see him allied to me. And it hurts him to know that he would not be able to support me in the manner to which I am accustomed."

"Are you quite sure that he would not squander your fortune too?" Rose asked. "I do think you are far better-off with the colonel, Judith. He is an exceedingly amiable man."

"I like him," Judith admitted. "And twelve years is not an impossible gap in age, is it? Papa is ten years older than Mama, but one would scarcely know. They are excessively fond of each other. But it is dreadful to have on one's conscience the breaking of another's heart. And that is what I will do to Lord Powers if I desert him now."

Rose stared at her friend for a moment. "But you cannot have a proper relationship if you merely pity him," she said.

"He is such a very sad character," Judith said with a sigh. "His father the marquess will not help him out, though he is fabulously wealthy, according to Lord Powers. Not that Lord Powers wishes help from his father anyway. He says he does not deserve it. Oh, Rose, he is so noble! He wants to arrange to meet me the night we go to Vauxhall. He says that if I can seem to be compromised, Papa will be forced to let me marry him and we will not have to elope either. How can I possibly say no?"

"How can you possibly say yes?" Rose asked, squeezing her friend's hand.

They were interrupted at that moment by the return of Arthur to the box. He smiled at both of them. "This looks like a very private conversation," he said. "May I break in on it?"

He sat talking to Rose for the minutes that remained before the play resumed, while Judith was drawn into the conversation of the main group.

"Are you enjoying the play?" he asked with a smile.

"Yes, indeed I am," Rose said. "It brings alive the text I labored over in the schoolroom."

"At home?" he said. "Or did you go away to school?"

Rose shook her head. "Papa never sent us," she said. "But I was glad. I never wanted to leave home."

"Did you not?" he said. "I often think that young boys and girls are sometimes wrenched from their parents at far too young an age. And now, do you like to be away from home?"

"Yes," Rose said. "Daisy has worked hard to be able to bring me here. I am privileged to have a Season. To see and be a part of all this. And I have to find a rich and distinguished husband, for Daisy's sake."

He raised his eyebrows and looked at her gently. Rose had two spots of color high on her cheekbones. "For your sister's sake?" he said. "Not for your own?"

Rose, gazing back into his eyes, looked for a moment as if she were drowning. "I had never thought of it," she said. "I want to marry. I want a husband and a family. I want a home of my own. But I had always thought of accepting a man I found amiable. Someone I could be comfortable with. I knew I was being brought here to meet gentlemen. But I did not know until today that I was under an obligation."

Why was she saying this to him? Rose wondered. Because he was a clergyman perhaps, and one instinctively felt it safe to confide in a man of the cloth? But she had never confided in the rector at home.

"I cannot believe that you are under any obligation," he said gently, laying a hand over hers for a brief moment. "My dear, your sister is the kindest of ladies and lives only for your happiness. I cannot be mistaken, surely."

"No, you are not," she said. "Daisy is the very best of sisters. I love her more dearly than anyone else in the world. She has sacrificed so much, worked so hard for me. Now I must make her happy."

"Yes," he said with a smile, "you are exactly right. You must make your sister happy. But I think—forgive me for criticizing you—that you do not know what will make her so. Your happiness will make her happy, my dear. She thinks you will be happy with a distinguished and fashionable gentleman. And perhaps she is right. But he must be a man of your own choosing. If you marry someone merely to please her, then you will end up making her the most miserable of ladies. Because she will live to see you unhappy. Come, smile at me. Rose.''

She was looking at him, her eyes suspiciously bright, when it became evident that the play was about to resume. Rose smiled at Sir Phillip, who took his place beside her again.

Daisy, meanwhile, who had been so rapt in the first half of the play that she could not force herself to concentrate on or participate in the conversation during the interval, missed the first five minutes of the second half of the play because her mind had been quite unwittingly distracted by something even more absorbing. She now had to grapple with a new problem. How was she to rescue Lady Judith from the scheming clutches of Lord Powers at Vauxhall?

Colonel Appleby departed with Judith and Arthur as soon as the farce at the end of the play was over. Sir Phillip Corbett escorted Lady Hetty and Rose to Lord Kincade's carriage. The viscount himself and Daisy were almost the last to leave the theater, as Lord Doncaster had strolled over to their box to pay his compliments and apologize for not doing so earlier.

''I had to call on my grandmother and my aunt during the interval,'' he said. ''Veritable dragons, the pair of them. I would never have heard the end of it if I had failed to put in an appearance in their box. Nor would my mother.''

Daisy was still disturbed over the unfair ending of the play and amused Lord Doncaster to no small degree by indignantly berating William Shakespeare for writing such a very stupid play.

''For one expects the bad characters to come to grief at the end,'' she said, ''and the downtrodden to be vindicated. I do not say that Shylock was right to demand his pound of flesh even after Portia had pleaded so eloquently for him to show mercy. But I can understand his need for revenge, and I really do not think those other characters should have prospered as they did.''

''What an interesting point of view,'' Lord Doncaster said

with a grin for Daisy and a wink for his friend. "I do not believe anyone else in England would dare criticize the great bard, Miss Morrison. I do believe it might be a capital offense, you know."

"What nonsense!" Daisy said, laughing nevertheless when she realized that she was being teased. "I do not like the play, I must confess, though I did think Mr. Kean quite splendid."

The theater was almost deserted by the time the three of them emerged onto the pavement to find Lord Kincade's carriage awaiting them. Daisy, her arm linked through the viscount's, gazed about her while he said a final good night to his friend.

And then she was marching purposefully away to her right, realizing only when she was already in motion that she had no umbrella or parasol or even reticule in her grasp. But she did not slacken her pace.

Lord Kincade, too startled to react for a few moments, gazed after her, saw the object of her mission, understood all too clearly, and tore after her. Lord Doncaster, an interested spectator, heard a muttered "I'll wring her neck!" as he watched his friend depart.

Daisy was bearing down on a street prostitute, whose arm was in the ungentle grasp of an elegant gentleman and who was obviously in the middle of a heated argument with him.

12

"He was not willing to pay her what she asked," Daisy was explaining to a fascinated Lady Hetty and an interested Rose in the carriage on the way home from the theater. "And he was trying to drag her off by force. It was most ungentlemanly of him, especially when it seemed perfectly clear that he could afford her price."

"My dear," Lady Hetty said faintly, "it is as well to ignore such sordid matters, pretend that one sees nothing. Such creatures are beneath our contempt and deserve whatever happens to them."

"Oh, no," Rose said, turning eyes full of concern on her hostess. "Almost all of them are poor unfortunates, you know, who have been forced into their way of life by the necessity to survive."

Lady Hetty patted her knee. "You sound just like Arthur, my dear Rose," she said. "And I am sure you are right. My words were without feeling, were they not? But we can do nothing, you see. Perhaps Arthur can do a little because he is a man, and a clergyman too. But ladies must keep clear of such matters."

"Well," Daisy said, "I certainly gave that particular gentleman the length of my tongue. He took himself off in high dudgeon, and the girl was saved from him."

"For which favor she will doubtless be eternally thankful." Lord Kincade spoke from behind his hand, which was spread over his face, his thumb and forefinger pressing his temples as if he had a massive headache. His eyes were closed. "She lost a lucrative customer."

"It is a good thing that you knew the gentleman," Daisy said, looking at him, "and that there were a few other people passing on the other side of the street. I had the feeling he was about to cut up nasty."

Lord Kincade did not change his position. "Doubtless the black umbrella would have made him take to his heels without further ado if only you had had it with you," he said.

"Yes," Daisy agreed. "But I would not think of taking it with me to the theater." She added, frowning, as Lord Kincade finally looked up at her in disbelief, "Besides, it would have been inside the carriage, and I would not have had the time or forethought to grab it."

Lord Kincade resumed his private meditation as Daisy continued to regale the two ladies opposite her with her opinion of gentlemen who thought they could treat females in any way they pleased merely because they had been created with superior physical strength.

"Hetty," Lord Kincade said when they had arrived at the house in Hanover Square and a footman was already handing Rose out, "I wish to speak with Daisy for a few minutes. Alone."

"Of course, Giles," Lady Hetty said, sounding almost relieved. "Here? Would you be more comfortable in the house? I will have candles lit in the salon while Rose and I retire to my sitting room for a cup of chocolate."

He nodded and vaulted out of the carriage after her before turning to hand out his betrothed.

Daisy turned to him as she entered the salon, smiling warmly. "How kind it was of you to come after me," she said. "I do thank you, though I could have handled the situation perfectly well on my own."

"I did not follow you out of kindness, Daisy," he said. "I did so out of desperation. And if you knew what danger your neck was in of being snapped off your shoulders, you would not be standing there now smiling at me as if I were your best friend in all the world."

Her smile did not falter. "I do not believe he would have actually become violent," she said. "After all, he was a gentleman, I suppose."

"I was not talking of Fotheringham," Lord Kincade said.

"Oh." Daisy seemed lost for words for the moment.

"Daisy," he said, stepping closer, "you must stop these zealous crusades of yours. Maybe, just maybe, they are acceptable in the country. Here they are not. I turn hot and cold when I think of how the *ton* is going to react to the delightful news that Miss Daisy Morrison rushed to the rescue of a whore plying her trade outside the theater. And by noon tomorrow I will wager that there will not be a single member who will not know. Not to mention all their servants belowstairs."

"But why should that fact upset me?" Daisy asked. "I have no wish to be conspicuous or to be talked of, but if I must be both, then I am glad it is because I was defending one of the downtrodden."

"What you did, Daisy, was deprive the poor girl of a night's earnings," Lord Kincade said, glaring down at her and feeling his temper tauten despite his resolve to remain cool. "She is probably swilling gin at a grog shop at this very moment raining down curses on your head."

"I did not do what I did in order to be thanked," Daisy said. "She was being cheated. And she was being abused. If she had been a lady, every man on the street would have rushed to her defense long before I even noticed her."

Lord Kincade took a deep breath and let it out slowly. "There is truth in what you say," he said. "Doubtless Arthur will applaud your actions when he hears of them. Perhaps it is a good thing he is not of the Roman persuasion. He would be applying to Rome to have you canonized. But all that is beside the point, Daisy. The main point is that what you did was dangerous. Highly dangerous."

"I think not," Daisy said. "In my experience I have found that bullies invariably back down if one confronts them boldly."

"There are exceptions to every rule," Lord Kincade said. "What if the thugs who were working me over at the Golden Eagle had turned on you and decided to disarm you and punish you? You would very probably have been killed, Daisy. And gentlemen can behave in a very ungentlemanly way when being deprived of a night's sport, if you will pardon my plain speaking. And street prostitutes very rarely work alone. Those who protect them and take most of their earnings and see to it that they do not retire from their profession until no man can be enticed any longer to pay for their services will not take kindly to an interfering, misguided, crusading lady cutting into their profits." His voice had risen. He was glaring. He closed his mouth and held on to his control.

"Perhaps you would have been killed if I had not come to your aid," Daisy said. Somehow her voice sounded less assured than usual. "Or at least you would have been badly hurt. Perhaps that girl tonight would have been beaten or used and underpaid if I had not gone to her aid. How can I watch people wantonly hurting others and walk on by as if I did not know that someone was suffering within reach of me?"

Lord Kincade sighed. "Daisy," he said, "what am I to do with you? I pass by entirely all the arguments I meant to use on you about the spectacle you are making of yourself, the embarrassment you are causing others by your very publicly unorthodox behavior. Instead, you have turned the tables on me and given me a lesson in compassion. But you must not. You must not involve yourself any longer in potentially dangerous situations. Leave them to me, will you? Call on me when you see someone in need of help. Will you promise me?"

"How can I?" she said after a moment's thought. "How can I ask you to do what I do not have the courage to do myself? Besides, you are not always with me."

"This is not a question of courage," he said, "but of strength. No one in his right mind would deny your courage, Daisy. You must promise me. I am your betrothed. I owe you my protection."

"No, you are not," she said. "Not really."

Lord Kincade looked steadily into her eyes. "Yes, I am," he said. "It may be a temporary betrothal that we have contracted, Daisy, but it is a real one. Until you tell me that it is at an end, I am your betrothed. And I do not want to have to start chaining you to my wrist in order that I will feel a warning tug when you are tearing off on one of your saving missions. Promise me now.''

"Well," Daisy said, "I will promise to call on your help whenever I can. Will that do?''

"I suppose it will have to," he said, "though I have the feeling that you have promised nothing whatsoever.''

"You really need not concern yourself about me," Daisy said kindly, as if she were consoling a child. "I am five-and-twenty and well able to look after myself. I have never come to harm yet.''

"Yes, but I *am* concerned about you," Lord Kincade said with a frown. "One of these days you are going to go just too far. I just hope I am close enough to save you.''

"How kind you are," Daisy said, her smile returning.

"Kind!" he said, exasperated. He lifted his hands and set them on her shoulders. He moved them until they were circling her neck loosely. "I might just give in to temptation one of these days, Daisy, and squeeze. I will thereby release myself and the world of the necessity of wondering what your next scrape is likely to be.''

Daisy smiled dazzlingly. "What a good thing it is, then," she said, "that you have to put up with me for only another few weeks.''

"Yes, isn't it?" he agreed fervently, and lowered his head and kissed her. And lifted it, looked her fiercely in the eye, muttered, "But you might be the death of me long before that, Daisy Morrison," wrapped his arms around her, and kissed her again.

And, yes, he thought before conscious thought receded and totally irrational impulse took its place, the fates had dealt him a cruel hand when they had decided to house Daisy in such a delectable little package and when they had brought her running with her nightgown and her greased face and her umbrella into a certain stableyard on a certain fateful morning. Very cruel indeed.

But she felt very good, very right, arched into his body, warm and yielding, small and softly feminine. Her slim thighs felt good pressed against his. Her breasts were firm and fit comfortably into his hands, which fondled them through the thin silk of her gown. Her mouth was warm and inviting against his tongue. Her hands both soothed and excited as they feathered over his face and ears and lost themselves in his hair.

And here he was again, he realized, thought returning altogether too soon and far too late, making hot love to Daisy Morrison despite the fact that they were both still on their feet and fully clothed. A deal hotter than his imagined bedding of her had been at the theater a few hours before. And what was he to do about it now? he thought, uncupping her breasts and sliding his hands around to a more chaste position at her back and withdrawing his tongue into his own mouth, where it definitely belonged. What was he going to say to her when he had the courage to lift his mouth away from hers?

"They used to burn people for witchcraft," he said. "It is not fair. Now I have to put my own soul in jeopardy by disposing of you myself."

Daisy seemed to realize that her hands were still twined in his hair. She removed them and set them on his shoulders for lack of any other resting place, since he still held her against him. She swallowed awkwardly and noisily and said nothing. She merely turned an interesting shade of scarlet.

"What?" he said. "Have I found the key to the mystery? Can I silence you and paralyze you with a kiss? Perhaps I should do so far more often."

"What nonsense!" Daisy said feebly. "I cannot think what you are about unless you mean to comfort me after the danger you supposed I was in."

"Oh, yes," he said. "That was a very paternal and comforting embrace, Daisy Morrison, was it not? I had better take my leave before Hetty comes storming in here demanding that I marry you without further delay. We would be leg-shackled for life. Would not that be a shocking and mutual nightmare?"

"Yes indeed," Daisy said with spirit, pressing her hands against his shoulders and pushing herself away from his circling arms. "I could not endure being married and always having a man caution me and coddle me and force me into making promises that I have no wish to make or intention of keeping. And I could not endure having to be embraced whenever he took a notion to do it either. I like to belong to myself, and one does not quite belong to oneself when kissing. I don't like it.''

"Good," he said. "You made a tolerable effort to hide your disgust a few moments ago, though, I must say. And now we really must part, having at last found a topic on which we can agree. I shall say good night before we spoil this atmosphere of amity by quarreling again. Good night, Daisy.''

"Good night, my lord,'' she said.

"Giles," he said. "Call me Giles, since we are betrothed.''

"No, we are not," she said.

"Yes, we are.''

"No, we are not, Giles," she said firmly.

And Lord Kincade, not feeling it necessary to have the last word, smiled grimly, turned, and strode from the room.

"I am very thankful I declined the honor of being your sparring partner this morning, Giles," Lord Doncaster said cheerfully, lounging at his ease while he watched his friend change his shirt preparatory to leaving Jackson's Boxing Saloon for White's. "I am not sure I have as much blood to spare as poor Brown.''

"A nose bleeding always looks worse than it is," Lord Kincade said.

"As I see it," his friend said, "blood is blood, no matter what part of the body it is spurting from. One consolation for old Brown is that if he chooses to walk out at night for the next week, he will not have to hire a torchbearer to go ahead of him. He will carry his own beacon on his face.''

"Perhaps now he will learn to keep up his guard instead of lowering his fists so that he can mince around in that ridiculous dancing routine," Lord Kincade said.

"My, my," said Lord Doncaster, "you are in a foul mood this morning. Upset over the little Miss Morrison, are you, Giles?" He grinned. "I hope you did not rip up at her too severely after you had taken her home. She was rather magnificent, I thought.''

"Magnificent!" Lord Kincade threw him a look of disgust. "I just wished the earth could have opened at my feet and a friendly devil beckoned me with his pitchfork. I would have gladly jumped in.''

Lord Doncaster laughed. ''She is priceless, Giles,'' he said. ''I envy you more than I can say. The main reason I have not considered marriage seriously yet is that I cannot contemplate the boredom. With Miss Morrison you will not know a dull moment.''

''Exactly what I am afraid of,'' Lord Kincade said, pulling on his coat as if he had a quarrel with it and reaching vengefully for his hat.

''I thought''—Lord Doncaster laughed again as he followed his friend out onto the street—''I really thought she was set upon rescuing poor Fotheringham from the clutches of a whore. But I might have known better. It is just like your little Miss Morrison to champion the whore. Did she really ask Foth where his manners were to treat a lady so? Or did my ears deceive me over the distance?''

''If you don't mind, Peter,'' Lord Kincade said, ''I would prefer to forget the episode—at least for as long as it takes us to walk to White's. Since it was the talk of Jackson's this morning, I suppose it is too much to hope that it will not also be the principal topic of conversation at White's.''

''Just look at it this way,'' Lord Doncaster said cheerfully. ''If you are embarrassed, Giles, imagine how Foth must be feeling.''

''It doesn't bear contemplation, does it?'' Lord Kincade said, looking somewhat cheered. ''Do you think I can expect a challenge, Peter? He might prove to be my savior at that—put a bullet between my eyes and save me from having to live through anything like this ever again. Drat the woman. I will surely strangle her one of these days.''

If only he had not kissed her, he thought. And then he thought with some relief, with enormous relief, that at least no one else knew about that except Daisy. It would be the final humiliation. His fiancée had done something almost unspeakably vulgar and unladylike. He had taken her home to reprimand her. Very few would blame him if he had beaten her, even though she was not yet his wife—and never would be, thank the good Lord. And what had he done? He had kissed her!

It was that fact probably more than any other that accounted for his vicious mood that morning. And he had been rather unfair to Brown. They had been only in a sparring bout after all, not a serious fight. And the poor man might as well have shouted out, ''Come and hit me,'' for all the defense he had put up at that particular moment when Lord Kincade's fist had collided with his nose. He might have waited until Brown had stopped his dancing and raised his fists again.

It was shameful and humiliating to admit to himself that he found Daisy Morrison almost irresistibly attractive. He undoubtedly wanted to take down her hair, unclothe her, lay her down, and make thorough love to her—in that order. He had forced himself to admit as much the night before after he had got himself unsatisfactorily drunk alone at home, hurled his empty glass into the fireplace, and spent all of ten minutes picking up every single shard of glass so that the servants would not know that he had had a fit of temper.

How could one find such a woman even physically appealing? She was like a nightmare come to life to dog his footsteps wherever he went. He had even found himself the night before in the fog of his inebriety considering entering the foreign service and taking himself off to India for the rest of his life, unless there turned out to be somewhere farther away where he might go, and for a longer period of time.

And then her wide and warm smile had intruded on the fog, and her slender, supple body and the smell of her hair and the remembered feeling of her breasts in his hands and a thousand and one other tantalizing little details, all of which had made him ache to hold her again and had rekindled his self-hatred and sent him to hunt in renewed despair for the empty brandy decanter.

And drat the woman, she had not even had the decency or the good sense to push him away after he had first put his lips to hers and smack his face hard enough to shake his brain cells back into reasonable order. She had put herself against him with a shocking lack of modesty—but why would one expect such a ladylike attribute as modesty from Daisy Morrison anyway?— and allowed his hands to wander at will. And she had opened her mouth at the first tentative request of his tongue, and after he had accepted the invitation, she had done wonderfully erotic things to it that one would expect only a practiced courtesan to be experienced at.

Yes, Daisy Morrison had wanted him quite as much as he had wanted her. Say what she might about her age and her spinster status, she had wanted—and been quite willing to receive—a great deal more than she had got the night before. The wanton hussy. The baggage.

"Did you know that the Marquess of Chalcott is so far in debt that he is like to lose everything, including his liberty?" Lord Kincade asked his friend suddenly.

"Eh?" Lord Doncaster had been deep in contemplation of two young ladies walking along the street ahead of them. "Chalcott? Don't even know him, Giles. Nobody does, as far as I know."

"Powers' father," Lord Kincade said.

"Ah." Lord Doncaster looked interested. "And so he is. So it would be of concern to you. Where did you hear such a thing? The man is such a recluse, one forgets he so much as exists."

"I have a servant on staff who has been a thief, a pickpocket, and doubtless a dozen other things that I would not care to know of," Lord Kincade said. "One of Arthur's protégés. A thoroughly useful man, though I don't believe my stables have suffered unduly from his absence in the past week."

"Ah," Lord Doncaster said. "And there is a point to this undoubtedly interesting but apparently useless piece of information, Giles?"

"At least one of the men who tried to make pulp out of me on the road to Bath is the marquess's servant and runs errands from papa to son," Lord Kincade said.

"You know, Giles," his friend said, looking at him in some admiration, "you are a gifted storyteller. One would be twitching at the corners of the page if you were a book. As it is, all I want to do is grab you by the shirt points and shake firmly."

"Powers' need for a wealthy wife becomes more obvious, does it not?" Lord Kincade said. "And a good deal more desperate. And sinister."

Lord Doncaster raised his eyebrows. "They did not want the earl your father back from Bath, then," he said, "to make your sister less accessible for elopement or seduction? Powers is a nasty customer, by the sound of it—not just unprincipled, as we thought."

"And perhaps not even Powers or not solely Powers," Lord Kincade said. "The marquess apparently likes to go abroad in order to feed his obsession with card playing. He travels forth incognito, according to the inestimable Baker. The man has been given another day free of the stables to find out what our reclusive marquess looks like and possibly also what kind of female he favors."

"What was the name of the man you played cards with?" Lord Doncaster asked.

"Martin, or so he said," the viscount replied. "And the female had hair as red as Brown's face looked half an hour ago."

"Interesting," Lord Doncaster said. "You have missed your vocation, my lad. You should be with the Bow Street Runners."

They ran into Arthur as they were on their way into White's. He was on his way out.

"You are going in the wrong direction, Arthur," Lord Doncaster said. "Come and have luncheon with us."

"I will," Arthur said, "since I do not know where else to look, and it is pointless to wander aimlessly all over London. I have been looking for Ambrose."

"Julia?" Lord Kincade said sharply.

"Quite all right," Arthur said with a smile. "She was just having false labor pains this morning and was feeling a little sorry for herself. I undertook to find Ambrose if I could."

"She was having what?" Lord Kincade handed his hat and his cane to the doorman and frowned at his brother.

"False labor pains," Arthur said. "Not the real ones. Daisy assured Julia that that was all they were, and sure enough, she had no more in the hour we were there."

"*Daisy* assured Julia?" Lord Kincade asked faintly.

"Oh, is it all right with you, Giles?" his brother asked. "She said we were to call her that."

"Has the world gone mad?" Lord Kincade asked of no one

in particular. "Was the physician not summoned? I suppose Daisy would deliver the child too if the false labor led to a false birth?"

Arthur smiled again. "I sometimes think you are as nervous as poor Ambrose, Giles," he said. "There is nothing at all to worry about. I am quite confident that Daisy knows what she is talking about. And she says that Julia need not expect to be brought to bed for several more days yet."

Lord Kincade could think of no reply more eloquent than a snort.

Lord Doncaster coughed. "Er, might one be permitted to change the subject, considering our surroundings?" he asked. "What do you think of the estimable Miss Morrison's exploits of last evening, Arthur, my boy?"

"How splendid she is," Arthur said, his face beaming with pleasure. "I never knew a lady with more courage. You must be very proud of her, Giles."

"Perhaps it is as well that you phrased that as a statement rather than as a question, Arthur," his brother said, laying a hand on his shoulder. "Let us go in search of food. It seems to me, if I am not mistaken, that I went without breakfast this morning."

13

"He kissed me!" Judith made the announcement in a hissing whisper to her very best friend as they huddled against a bookshelf in Hookham's library, supposedly choosing books. Daisy was away at the other side of the room, reading a newspaper. Her life was always too full of practical concerns to allow her to indulge frequently in novel reading. She never had progressed beyond page one of *Robinson Crusoe*.

Rose regarded her friend, saucer-eyed. "Did he?" she whispered back rather unnecessarily.

"We drove back from the theater," Judith said, "and Arthur went inside, leaving the door open, and the footman was busy taking his cloak and hat, and the colonel took me by both hands and kissed me. *On the lips*!"

"Did he?" Rose asked again. "And did you mind, Judith?"

"It was divine!" Judith clasped her hands to her bosom. "He merely touched his lips to mine, you know, and squeezed my hands, but I liked it quite as much as the time when Lord Powers took me right into his arms and kissed me hard. Indeed, he even caused me to cut my own mouth on my teeth."

"I have never been kissed," Rose said, somewhat wistfully. "And do you now love the colonel, Judith? And are you going to tell Lord Powers that you no longer wish to communicate with him?"

Judith, who had been looking a little dewy-eyed, looked stricken suddenly. "I don't know how I can," she said. "He does love me so. How can I hurt him to the extent of telling him that I love another? Besides, I am not even sure that I love the colonel. I just think that perhaps I might come to do so.''

''But, Judith,'' Rose said, ''can he really love you if he wanted you to elope with him, and if he writes to you daily even when he knows that his lordship has strictly forbidden you to receive his letters, and if he now wants to compromise you so that your papa will be forced to agree to a marriage? I don't think that is love, for love is unselfish, and such behavior is quite the opposite.''

Judith sighed. ''I do like having you for a friend, Rose,'' she said. ''You are able to put into words thoughts that float around in my mind and will not form themselves into clear ideas. At the same time, you disturb me, for you force me into making decisions, and I have never had to make my own decisions. Someone has always done it for me. I will have to decide before the night of Vauxhall, won't I? Four days!''

Rose squeezed her arm and looked halfheartedly along the bookshelf.

''And do you love Sir Phillip?'' Judith whispered. ''Perhaps he will kiss you at Vauxhall. That is a splendid place to be kissed.'' She giggled, clapped a hand over her mouth, and glanced about her self-consciously.

''He is very charming,'' Rose said. ''I like him.''

Judith pulled a face. ''That sounds like very faint praise,'' she said. ''But do you not think him very handsome, Rose? The more I see him, the more I think that auburn hair on men is not so unattractive, after all.''

''Yes, he is handsome,'' Rose said. ''Daisy thinks he will offer for me before the Season is out. Do you think it likely?''

''Very,'' her friend assured her. ''He has taken marked notice of you and has not looked at another lady since he set eyes on you, I think. You will accept him? Lady Rose Corbett. It sounds impressive.''

''Daisy has her heart set on my making a brilliant match,'' Rose said. ''I cannot disappoint Daisy. She has worked so hard so that she might provide the best for me.''

Judith stared. ''But Daisy would not want you unhappy,'' she said. ''And you would be unhappy with Sir Phillip, wouldn't you? You strange girl! I could name half a dozen others who would kill for the chance you have.''

Rose smiled. "I do like him," she said. "Perhaps I will grow to love him, like you with the colonel.''

"Get him to kiss you at Vauxhall," Judith said wisely, "and then you will know.''

Daisy had read the whole of the front page of the newspaper. At least her eyes had moved over every single word written there, and she felt satisfied that she now knew all the latest news.

She hoped Julia had been able to fall asleep as she had planned to do after they had left her. The poor lady was finding these last few weeks of her confinement particularly irksome. She had complained, she had said that morning, when the baby was high beneath her bosom because she could not bend. Yet now that the baby was low, she could scarcely sit.

If only their society were not so ridiculously prudish about pregnancy and birth, Daisy thought, ladies would know a great deal more about them and not be near as fretful with their first child. For no matter what discomfort went before, and no matter how much pain accompanied the birthing process, the actual birth, the moment when all the discomfort and pain translated themselves into a curled-up, squawking red bundle of humanity, the mother became joy personified. And a year or two or at the most three later, she would be at it again whether her husband had insisted or not.

Daisy had seen it three separate times. And those were the only occasions in the last five years or more when she had somewhat regretted her spinster state. She thought she might have liked to go through that discomfort, to carry a man's child and her own inside her for nine months. But Daisy would not be content to hide from the world as soon as it became obvious to the eye what she was about. She would want the world to see how proudly she carried her burden.

And she would have rather liked to go through the pain of childbirth so that she would be all the more aware of the miracle of birth at the end of it all. What a pinnacle of human bliss it would be, she had thought on those occasions when she had held another woman's newborn infant, to hold her own, to put it to her breast, to try to recognize herself and her man in the suckling babe.

Daisy was not a sentimental soul, but everyone is human and entitled to some human weakness, she had consoled herself on those three occasions when for days afterward she had ached for the experience of motherhood. But it was not for her. She was far too busy mothering the people around her whose biological mothers had completed the birthing process years before.

But because the library was hushed and she was comfortable and a little tired after an almost sleepless night and unusually isolated behind her newspaper, Daisy's thoughts strayed from Julia's plight and put herself in the same case.

She too was within a few days of having her first child. The child was low and heavy and huge in her womb, and she was excited and impatient for him to be out of there so that she could see him and hold him and put him into his father's arms. But Giles was not like the elusive Ambrose, whom she had never met and who was so dreadfully frightened of what he was putting his wife through that he had to flee the house each day.

No, Giles sat beside her, his arm comfortingly about her, her weary head nestled on his shoulder. He was kissing her forehead, her nose, her cheeks, her lips, and assuring her when his lips were not so occupied that of course it would not matter if the child were a daughter. All that mattered was that it was their child and that it had been conceived out of love. And all that mattered was that she not have to suffer too much pain bringing it into the world.

And his hand moved gently and soothingly over her swollen abdomen so that the child wriggled inside her, and he laughed. And she told him, turning her face into his neck, that she did not care how much pain there was, that she would endure ten times as much as what the worst might be so that she could be the mother of his child, and that she would do it half a dozen more times too if he did not mind dreadfully the mother of his younger children being in her thirties when she did it.

She was about to go into labor with a raging blizzard performing its worst outside the house so that Giles would have to deliver their child while she gasped out calm and lucid instructions between her pains.

"Daisy? It's time England had another war, I see, so that the news would not put you to sleep."

It was not quite the same tender, solicitous voice as that of the man who had been about to bring his own son into the world, but it was unmistakably Lord Kincade's nevertheless. Daisy jumped, let out a snort of a snore, and dropped the paper, which went rustling to the floor as she lunged at it in an ineffectual attempt to keep it within her grasp.

"Oh," she said, "did you have to pop up over the top of the paper like that? You startled me. I was deep in concentration."

Lord Kincade passed a hand over his eyes as two separate voices hissed, "Sh!"

"How foolish of me," he muttered, "to expect you to open your eyes, smile sweetly, and whisper an afternoon greeting. I suppose you were dreaming of attacking dragons or rescuing a beleaguered army from annihilation by the enemy?"

"No," she whispered, shuffling the pages of the newspaper and slapping at them to get them into order again while Lord Kincade closed his eyes once more and grimaced. "How foolish it would be to indulge in silly daydreams like that. I was not sleeping, you know."

"I am not sure I do know," he murmured. "But this is not the place to begin an argument, and I do not have the energy today to participate in a was-wasn't-was-wasn't type of discussion. Come and have an ice with us. I see that Arthur and Peter have asked Judith and your sister already."

Daisy looked up and smiled at the two gentlemen who were standing near the door with Rose and Judith. Lord Kincade took the large and untidy bundle of paper from her hands and folded it neatly, efficiently, and almost silently.

The conversation outside the library turned inevitably to Daisy's exploits of the night before. Lord Doncaster congratulated her with a twinkle in his eye and a wink for Arthur. Arthur, of course, had already expressed his admiration that morning at his sister's.

"I have never seen Fotheringham back off from any opponent," Lord Doncaster said. "But I will swear that his knees were knocking together when he saw you coming, Miss Morrison, and his teeth chattering like Spanish castanets by the time you had finished with him."

Daisy laughed gaily. "I believe you exaggerate, sir," she said. "I would say his teeth were more probably gnashing with rage."

"It was excessively brave of you to do such a thing anyway, Daisy," Arthur said, smiling gently at her. "I wish I had been there too so that I could have ensured that the poor girl was not hurt and did not need further help."

"Doubtless she did," Lord Doncaster said, "but not the kind you would have been prepared to give, Arthur."

He won a pointed glare from Lord Kincade and had the grace to look sheepish.

Daisy, walking along at Lord Kincade's side, her arm linked through his, was feeling even more sheepish. He felt and looked alarmingly real: large and tall, with firmly muscled arm, and very fashionably dressed, and of course impossibly handsome with that blond hair that gleamed even brighter than Rose's. It was mortifying to remember the images she had had of him—and herself—just a few minutes before: his child huge inside her, his hands about to receive the baby she delivered.

Gracious heavens! And she was not at all sure that he had not peered over that newspaper and seen it all. She had the uncomfortable feeling that he knew very well what she had been dreaming and that that knowledge was responsible for the hardened muscles of his arm, his disinclination to talk to her, and his bad mood.

And having resolved to put her dream from her, and convinced herself that he could not possibly know, she found herself remembering the very real experience of being in his embrace the night before. If that had not happened, she would have slept properly during the night and then she would not so easily have fallen into that silly trance at the library.

Good heavens, she thought, glancing at him out of the corner of her eye, she knew exactly what every part of that splendid body felt like—through his clothing, anyway. Every part! She felt herself flushing and hoped he would not look down or the others around until she had banished such memories and resumed her more normal and sensible self. And she knew how silky that thick blond hair felt. And she knew what he tasted like.

Not at all the thoughts for a twenty-five-year-old spinster, she thought, squaring her shoulders and smiling brightly at nothing at all.

"You are either an actress working up the courage to step out on stage, or a boxer about to step into the ring, or a queen about to walk out onto the scaffold in order to set her neck on the chopping block," Lord Kincade said without looking down at her. "Am I permitted to know which, Daisy?"

"You seem to be in a bad mood," she said, "and I did not wish to disturb you by talking. So I was thinking."

"What?" he said. "Me in a bad mood? What a ridiculous notion. Why should I be in a bad mood? I am merely the laughingstock today because my betrothed chose to become public champion of Drury Lane prostitutes last night. And Fotheringham has barricaded himself inside his rooms and declares that he will never come out again. Nothing at all to upset the calm geniality of my nature, Daisy."

"I am glad Mr. Fotheringham feels ashamed of himself," Daisy said. "I hope he learns a lesson from this. As for you, Giles, I do not see why you should be the laughingstock when all I did was defend a poor girl from attack by a brute. And besides, why should you be ridiculed? I am the one who did it. I am the one people should laugh at. And if they did, I should not care a fig."

Fortunately for Lord Kincade's temper, which was already hanging on a thin thread, they arrived at the confectioner's at that moment and conversation became general as they all sat at the same table.

Rose and Arthur had continued to talk about the happenings of the night before.

"I admire Daisy too," she said. "And I know that what she did was very brave. But it was so very foolhardy too. I am always terrified for her. She does things like that without any thought to her own safety."

He smiled down at her and patted her hand. "You need have

no fear, I think," he said. "Daisy has a strong sense of what is right and wrong, and she is the sort of person who must act on what she sees. I believe that such people are protected. By God, you see. And Giles is to be her husband. He will look after her. He used to fight my battles when we were boys until he realized that it was not because I was thin and puny that I would not fight but because I did not believe in fighting. I am afraid I had to knock him down once—I took him quite by surprise or I would never have succeeded—in order to prove my point." He laughed.

Rose laughed too, up into his face, which was very far above her own. "Did you mean it," she asked, "when you said that you would have helped that girl last night? And you a clergyman?"

He raised his eyebrows. "But of course," he said, "and *because* I am a clergyman, or at least because I am the kind of person who has become a clergyman. It is with such people that my mission lies. The poorest of the poor. The poor are not just those without money, you know. They are those who have had no chance of acquiring any of life's riches—good homes, loving parents, exposure to nature and gentle living, knowledge of the beauties of life. I could go on and on. These pros—these girls are very poor indeed. It is they who need the love of God more than anyone."

"Oh," Rose said, "then I wish you had still been with us last night. You could have talked to her and she would have been very happy and reformed her way of life."

Arthur smiled gently. "Unfortunately it is not as simple as that," he said. "Not nearly. I know many men like myself who have despaired of ever making even the smallest difference to those whose poverty extends to the heart and the mind. But one has to remember how small and insignificant one is and how great God is. One has to have faith and keep on working and loving. The parable of the mustard seed is my favorite, you know."

"How fortunate your parishioners are going to be," Rose said admiringly, "to have a real man of God living among them."

Arthur laughed. "I am merely a very average man and

average Christian and average clergyman,'' he said. He added ruefully, ''The only thing that is not average about me is my height. Ah, here we are. I am glad you mentioned this morning that you were going to the library after luncheon. A man feels foolish coming for an ice unless he has a lady with him.''

On the same afternoon—indeed, at the very time that Lord Kincade was watching his betrothed eat her ice, and thinking how annoyingly pretty she looked laughing at some teasing remark Lord Doncaster had made, and wondering if they would be able to sit there for all of half an hour without her finding something she might do to attract the attention of the whole of London their way—on the same afternoon a gentleman who had at least once called himself Mr. Martin put aside his cards without apology to his redheaded companion and turned to greet his son.

''Ah, Basil,'' he said, beginning to drum his fingers slowly on the edge of the table, ''you make yourself quite the stranger. How goes the siege?''

''Growing somewhat cool,'' Lord Powers said. ''But I think the time is right. The brother's suspicions have been lulled and the little chit's appetite kept panting.''

The Marquess of Chalcott laced his plump fingers together. ''Yes, the time is right,'' he said. ''And the time is urgent. I was cheated out of a bundle again last night. When a man's fortunes turn for the worse, there seems to be no turning them around again. But this will serve.''

''The arrival of Miss Morrison on the scene has been fortunate,'' Lord Powers said with an arctic smile. ''She has kept Kincade's attention distracted. She displayed all her considerable vulgarity again last night by attacking Fothering-ham when he was soliciting a street prostitute. Kincade had to step in to smooth out the situation.''

The marquess's shoulders shook with quiet laughter. ''I still fail to understand why you will not go after one of the Morrison females,'' he said. ''Each one of them is ten times as rich as the Fairhaven chit, I daresay.''

''But the younger one is sharp,'' Lord Powers said. ''She was onto my game the very first time I talked to her. I could tell. Besides, she is altogether too close to my little Judith. I cannot afford to have each discover that I am wooing the other. And as for the other sister, I think I prefer to keep my distance. As much as anything, I don't believe any fortune would quite compensate for being landed with her for a lifetime.''

"You lack spirit, Basil," the marquess said. "If I were only younger and more in health, now, I could enjoy the taming of that particular female." He glanced sidelong at the redheaded female, and his shoulders shook again. "But to the point. Everything is arranged?''

"I have her eating out of my hand," Lord Powers said. "She will meet me in Vauxhall, never fear. Then it will merely be to whisk her away, drive her about in a carriage for an hour or so before returning her there or to her home, make sure that her absence is noted by a large-enough number of people, and the deed is done. Neither Kincade nor the earl himself will be able to save her reputation except by marrying her to me.''

"Far too risky," the marquess said. "Any brother with a moderately active brain would be able to think of a reason for the girl's absence for an hour or so. She has to be missing for the whole of the night. And her reputation must not be merely tarnished. It must be ruined. You will bring her here. I shall arrange to be absent, of course. And you must seduce her, Basil. Force her, if necessary." He laughed softly again. "I envy you. You have told me that she is pretty? How fortunate for you that on this occasion beauty and fortune go hand in hand.''

Lord Powers nodded. "Yes," he said. "I like the idea. There will doubtless be tears and pleadings, but what does the chit have to complain about, after all? She fancies herself in love with me. And she will be marrying a title, and an even more illustrious one to follow when you decide to take yourself off.''

The marquess laughed heartily and looked at his mistress until she joined him in his mirth. "I plan to keep you waiting a while for that, boy," he said. "Just a little while yet, Basil.''

Lord Kincade and Daisy were walking home, having watched Lord Doncaster stride off on his way to another appointment and Arthur drive away in the carriage with Judith and Rose. They had promised to set Rose down at Hanover Square.

"Well, Daisy," he said, "your sister seems to have settled quite happily into London life. I am pleased with the friendship between her and Judith. Judith needs steadying, and it is so difficult for an older brother or sister to do it. From us any advice is seen as interference."

"Yes," Daisy said happily, "I am pleased for Rose too. And I am in hopes that Sir Phillip will declare himself soon. It will be such a splendid match for Rose. I am so happy for her. And as soon as her betrothal has been safely announced, we can put an end to ours."

"Not too hastily," he said. "I must forbid you to end our betrothal before you leave London, Daisy. And the matter is not even open for discussion. Your sister would suffer if you were still in town and under the shadow of scandal over a broken engagement. And my sister would suffer. Julia, I mean. She is very fond of you, and she is in a very delicate state of health at the moment—mental as well as physical. No, I am sorry, but you and I will have to put up with each other for a while longer yet."

"Well," Daisy said, "I daresay Sir Phillip will not speak up for a week or so yet, and by that time Julia's confinement will be over. And once that is so, she will be able to countenance any disappointment beyond the nursery. Besides, once the baby is born, her husband will doubtless forgive himself and come home again."

Lord Kincade laughed and looked down at her in some surprise. "You have not even met Ambrose, have you?" he said. "You have just analyzed him to perfection. Poor Ambrose."

"I wonder," Daisy said. "Was he christened 'Poorambrose'? I should say 'poor Julia' was more to the point. But then men tend to have many weaknesses. Women have to learn to put up with them because women are far stronger."

Lord Kincade looked down at her sidelong. "I refuse to be drawn, Daisy," he said. "I absolutely refuse to be drawn. Good heavens, do you think that women are the stronger sex merely because they suffer childbirth?"

"No," Daisy said. "Not just that. There is men's embarrassment about being observed in the middle of a public spectacle, for example, especially when it might seem that a lady led them into it.''

Lord Kincade had still not turned his head, but his eyes were sharp on her. ''Witch!'' he said. ''I have been drawn, haven't I? Be very, very thankful, Daisy Morrison, that you do not have to spend the rest of your life with me. I can assure you that it might prove to be a very short one.''

She smiled dazzlingly up at him. ''Perhaps I would be glad to die young if the alternative were to spend the rest of my life with you, Giles,'' she said. ''Have you thought of that?''

Lord Kincade turned to look down at her with narrowed eyes. And since they were at the foot of the steps leading up to the house on Hanover Square, and since he did not intend to go inside with her, having sent a message with Judith that he would be calling on Julia forthwith, and since he wasn't thinking particularly rationally, he took her by the shoulders, bent his head, kissed her thoroughly on the lips, and bade her a good day.

14

It was the following day that Daisy conceived her plan. It was true that she did not enter into it with a great deal of thought. Thought and logic were not her strong points. But by the end of the day instinct and chance and sheer ingenuity had all contrived together to give her a definite, or almost definite, scheme.

It had all started two evenings before when she had overheard, quite by accident, part of the conversation between Rose and Judith at the theater. Judith, the silly girl, was still in communication with Lord Powers. And it was perfectly clear to Daisy that he was trying to trap her into marriage. It was equally clear that Judith was flattered by his apparent devotion but that her feelings were not deeply involved.

Lord Powers was planning to do something on the night they were all going to Vauxhall. He was planning to compromise Judith so that her father would be forced to allow her to marry the man. And Judith, it seemed, was too dazzled by the romance and intrigue of the situation to resist it.

The problem for Daisy was how she was going to prevent such a disaster from occurring. She had rejected the idea of taking Judith aside and having a good talk with her. Young people can be remarkably stubborn when dealing with their elders, she knew. Her advice would probably only stir Judith on to do something that she did not really want to do in the first place. And she rejected the idea of confiding in Giles. She

did not think that tact was one of his strengths. He would
undoubtedly lock Judith up again and take other drastic measures
that would result only in a hardening of his sister's resolve to
defy him.

She thought of talking to Julia about the matter but did not
want to add any worries to her friend under present circumstances. But the subject was brought to her mind again when
the two of them were sitting and talking during the morning
while Arthur took the two girls to see the Tower of London.

"I do believe a serious romance is developing between Judith
and Colonel Appleby," Julia said.

"He has been attentive to her," Daisy said. "He is certainly
a distinguished-looking gentleman."

Julia sighed. "I have met him only once," she said, "and
that not recently. I would have taken a closer look if I had known
that one day he would be interested in my sister. But I am
pleased. I have heard good things about him. Giles says he
distinguished himself at Waterloo last year and in Spain before
that. Indeed, he has remarkably high rank for a man so young.
Mostly, though, I am pleased because I have been worried that
Judith might never grow up and settle down. And of course there
has been that dreadful business with Lord Powers."

"That is all over?" Daisy asked.

"Well." Julia hesitated. "I believe there are still some letters
going back and forth, and that is always a potentially dangerous
situation. But I think Judith's ardor has cooled. I hope that if
I ignore the letters and Giles is sensible enough to leave matters
well enough alone, the whole situation will sort itself out. And
I really believe that she is growing fond of the colonel."

"That is good," Daisy said with a smile, and changed the
subject.

She thought of her problem again when at a musical evening
that night at Mrs. Sayer's with Lady Hetty, Rose, and Sir Phillip
Corbett. Lord Kincade had another engagement. Daisy, looking
about her while a soprano with an alarmingly piercing voice
sang an aria replete with sinuous trills and soaring crescendos,
saw that Lord Powers was also present.

And since she was not particularly enamored of the music
and could not merely get up and walk away and had nothing

else to do with her mind, she continued to gaze at him until he looked up, caught her eye, and inclined his head. Daisy smiled dazzlingly, the plan beginning to form.

Perhaps Lord Powers was a little surprised when he rose to stretch at the end of the aria during the break before the baritone began his repertoire, to find as he looked around him for an acquaintance with whom to while away the time that Daisy was at his elbow, apparently similarly employed. Perhaps he noticed nothing strange about the situation at all.

"Good evening, ma'am," he said with a slight bow.

Daisy smiled dazzlingly again. "It is disconcerting, is it not," she said, "to be at a gathering like this and to find that one knows scarcely anyone?" Such an attitude, of course, did not explain why she would have left her own party under such circumstances.

Lord Powers, glancing almost absentmindedly down into her face, seemed suddenly arrested by something he saw there. He smiled. "Perhaps we should join forces, Miss Morrison," he said. "Shall we go in search of some lemonade, and you shall tell me what you made of that last performance?"

Daisy took his proffered arm and looked up at him with wide-eyed gratitude. "I was rather wishing I had wads of cotton with which to stuff my ears," she said. "But perhaps you enjoyed the performance, sir?"

Lord Powers laughed and squeezed her arm against his side briefly. "My sentiments exactly, ma'am," he said.

And he found for the following ten minutes that Miss Daisy Morrison was an excessively amiable young lady who made conversation very easy by talking on and on herself. And it seemed that her favorite topic of conversation was her deceased papa and all his prosperous coal mines and all the jewels he had loved to buy for his three women, especially his elder daughter, on whom he doted—not that he did not love her mama and her younger sister, of course—and all the money he had left them, though to her pained embarrassment he had left her the lion's share of his fortune.

"We did not dare bring too much with us to town, of course," Daisy confided, fingering the pearls at her neck, "for fear of highwaymen. We brought only one servant with us. And indeed it was as well that we had taken such a precaution, for we were witnesses to the cowardly attack on Lord Kincade on the way here, and who knows but what we would not have been victims too if our carriage had been loaded down with even one-tenth of all our jewels.''

"Just so," Lord Powers murmured, fascinated.

"But perhaps I bore you?" Daisy said, wide and innocent eyes gazing up into his. She bit her lip. "Lord Kincade says I talk altogether too much about myself and my jewels and my fortune. But you see, I was so very fond of poor Papa, and that is all I have left of him. I would give it all up if I could just have one hour with Papa again. But Lord Kincade does not understand that. He does not have a great deal of sensibility.'' Daisy had to be content with the pathos of her words. She found that she could not squeeze a single tear anywhere near the vicinity of her eyes.

Lord Powers covered her hand with his. "I have wondered about your betrothal," he said, all tender concern. "It was forced upon you, rather, was it not? And I am afraid that I was partly responsible, for had I not tried to humor Lady Judith by giving her a few minutes of my time at the Riplinger ball, you would not have been downstairs to take Kincade out of the way and become compromised yourself.''

"But if I was able to prevent trouble between you and his lordship," Daisy said, "then the sacrifice was worthwhile, my lord, no matter how painful that sacrifice has been.'' She smiled bravely.

Daisy considered it wise at the end of the ten minutes to decline an invitation to sit beside Lord Powers for the rest of the concert. It was true that even seated beside Lady Hetty, she was unable to let loose the whoops of laughter that threatened to disgrace her, but she felt that her acting skills had been stretched to the limit for one evening. She had, however, somehow managed to work into the conversation the seemingly irrelevant and quite untrue detail that she liked to walk in the park early each morning with only a maid for company. In the solitude of such surroundings she was able to remember more clearly her beloved papa.

That night, while Daisy lay awake, three pillows piled beneath her and her hands clasped behind her head, her papa acquired two—she gradually whittled down the number from five—diamond mines in South America and a gold mine somewhere in Africa. Daisy was not strong on geography—she hoped that there were such mines in those particular places. Although the mines had been sold for a large profit years before, she and Rose and her mama still possessed ten—was that an appropriate number?—gold bars each.

And her papa had given her on her twenty-first birthday—Daisy thought rather guiltily of the modest pearl necklace lying in a drawer across the room—a diamond so large and so flawless that all the diamond merchants he had consulted had been unable to put a price on it. There were also, of course, all the other diamonds—mere baubles—that had been made into necklaces and brooches and rings, probably with gold from the African mine.

Daisy shifted her position and threw one pillow on the floor beside the bed. The reason she was five-and-twenty and still unmarried was that she was always so afraid that the gentlemen who showed interest in her were mere fortune-hunters. How could she be sure of their intentions when her fortune would probably buy England twice over and the diamond would doubtless buy Wales and Scotland and Ireland ten times over to go along with it? She frowned. Was she exaggerating too much? A few tears would serve her purpose very well at that point. Daisy concentrated very hard, contorting her face, screwing up her eyes. Well, the words would have to suffice.

And now she had been forced into a betrothal with a near stranger. How could she know that in addition to being humorless and bad-tempered, he was not also a fortune-hunter? Her situation was truly tragic. Her aunt and her dear uncle were in Paris—and of course her beloved papa was dead—and dear Rose was so young and there was no one whose opinion she could trust. No one except . . . unless . . . Oh, those tears would be desperately needed.

Daisy yawned until her jaws cracked. Should she add a grandfather who owned a cotton mill in the north of England? Two? Five? No, better not to stretch the credibility of her story too far.

Giles had kissed her again that morning, on the cheek. He

had come into Julia's sitting room when she was still there, bent to kiss his sister, hesitated, and then crossed the room to kiss her too. It was getting to be a habit. A very silly habit, considering that they were starting to get a little on each other's nerves, and considering that they had no intention of continuing their betrothal into the summer anyway. She must tell him the next time he came at her with the obvious intention of embracing her that she would really rather he didn't.

Daisy yawned again, aloud and at great and satisfying length. Now, where had she been? Ah, yes. She was stretched out in bed, in a sweat-soaked bed, her lips raw with the effort of not screaming aloud and alarming Giles, who needed to remain calm. She had sent him to boil water, but he would be back soon to hold her hand and murmur soothing words to her. The wind howled outside and the sleet beat against the windowpanes. She thought her waters had probably broken. Her pains were coming thick and fast.

Daisy moved her hands from behind her head and spread them on her very flat abdomen. She smiled as Giles gently kissed her forehead and smoothed back her hair. Some minutes before their child was born, she slid into a peaceful sleep.

Rose was disappointed the following morning after making the journey alone to Lady Julia's, apart from a maid, to find that her friend as well as her sister had deserted her. Judith, it seemed, had gone out shopping with Lord Kincade.

Arthur was with Julia, rubbing her back while she had her eyes closed, whether with weariness or in ecstasy, it was not immediately apparent to Rose.

"I do beg your pardon," she said. "I did not mean to disturb you. But I decided, when I was told that Judith is out, to pay my respects to you, ma'am."

Julia smiled and moved away from her brother. "Do come and sit down," she said. "Poor Arthur will be as glad as I when this child is born. Is Daisy not with you today?"

Rose frowned. "She went walking in the park," she said, "because it is such a lovely morning." She glanced doubtfully at the heavy clouds that were visible beyond the windows of the sitting room, as the other two did also. "And she declined company because it was too cold. Sometimes I find Daisy hard to understand."

"We all need to be alone at times," Arthur said gently. "I am sure Daisy does too. She certainly takes a great deal of responsibility on her own shoulders. Sometimes she must need to be just with herself."

"Yes," Rose said doubtfully before turning to Julia and inquiring politely after her health. But it was clear that that lady was indeed weary and out of spirits. After a decent few minutes had passed, Rose got to her feet again to take her leave.

"I will accompany you, if I may," Arthur said. "Would you care to dismiss your maid and your carriage and walk home, since it is such a lovely morning although rather cold?" He smiled.

"Yes, please," Rose said, "if it is not out of your way, sir."

Soon they were strolling along, Rose's arm drawn through Arthur's, and agreeing that it was neither a lovely day nor particularly cold.

"Did you enjoy the concert last evening?" Arthur asked.

"Yes, it was pleasant," Rose said. And then in a rush, "Oh, not really very much. But I must confess to preferring a musical evening at home when the neighbors play the pianoforte and the violin and sing and sometimes make mistakes or do not sound quite as they ought. I am very silly, and I would not tell Daisy, who was in transports of delight when we returned home."

"But you may tell me," Arthur said, patting her hand. "You are too kind to hurt your sister by telling the truth, but you may pour out your heart to me."

"Oh," Rose said, "that must be burdensome for you, sir. It will be burdensome when you have half the people in your parish coming to confide in you."

"No, no," he said. "It is a great privilege to find oneself trusted enough that people will confide their deepest thoughts to one. And a great honor. People need to be able to tell the plain truth to at least one other person. And sometimes God is not quite enough, because when one talks to God, it perhaps seems that one is talking to oneself. It is wonderful indeed to stand in the place of God for a short time."

Rose smiled at him. "What a lovely idea," she said. "And to whom do you talk, Reverend Fairhaven?"

He smiled back at her and said nothing for a long moment. "I don't know," he said at last.

"You said everybody has the need," Rose said. "Do you not? Is there not someone very close and special to whom you can confide your thoughts and problems?"

"I had not thought about it," he said after a pause. "Perhaps I was wrong. Perhaps not everybody needs a father confessor."

"Are you completely happy, then?" Rose asked. "Is there nothing that irks you? Nothing that frustrates you?"

"Oh, yes," he said. "There are a number of things. Many things. I have always been gentle Arthur, everyone's favorite. It is wonderful to be the darling of one's family, the one no one ever upbraids or speaks sharply to or treats unfairly. It is also unspeakably annoying. Everyone looks conscious if they slip and use an obscenity in my hearing or speak on a topic that they think my ears too innocent to hear. And they all think it wonderfully sweet and typical of me to become a clergyman and to refuse the portion that my father wanted to give me. They picture me, I do believe, smiling beatifically at the poor and patting them on the head and winning instant conversion."

Rose was gazing up at him, her eyes wide with amazement.

"They do not know," he said, "the squalor, the tough mental attitudes, the evil, the ridicule, the raw exposure to the most basic and sordid elements of life that are my daily portion. They do not know that my joy comes from doing our Lord's work in a very small, sometimes invisible way, from planting the mustard seed. They do not know. They see only gentle, innocent Arthur. And how can I tell them? How can I ruin the joy they have in their image of me?"

Rose swallowed. "I am sorry," she said. "I have seen you that way too. And liked you a great deal. Now I admire you very much more. And, yes, you are right. It is a privilege, is it not?"

He looked down at her and flushed. "Forgive me," he said, his voice full of remorse. "Do forgive me, Miss Morrison. I have never said that to anyone before. Indeed, I did not even know that that resentment was in me. How ungrateful I am. I have the best and most loving of families.''

"As do I," said Rose. "And so we can understand each other in our reluctance to do anything that might hurt them.''

"But we must be true to ourselves too, dear," he said, laying a hand over hers again for a brief moment. "I hurt my father by rejecting his desire to provide for me. I know I did, but I had to do it because I could not have lived with myself if I had not become what I have become. You must be careful, Rose, that you do not lose yourself in your eagerness to make your sister happy. My father would have been unhappy to see me fretting in the life of an idle gentleman. Now, a few years after our arguments, he delights in seeing me as a gentle, harmless clergyman." He smiled. "Daisy will be happy in a few years' time to see you contented, whatever it is that you will find to bring you happiness.''

"Yes," Rose said. "Yes. It is just so hard now. Daisy has had this dream for me for a long time.''

"Here we are at Hetty's already," Arthur said in some surprise. "Did you steer us here, Miss Morrison? I have not even been conscious of the streets we have walked along.''

"Neither have I," Rose said.

"Well, then," he said, "we must have been guided. I will not come inside or Hetty will be wanting me to stay for luncheon. And I have a busy afternoon planned. I will see you tomorrow at Julia's, I daresay.''

"Yes," Rose said.

"Good day to you, then, my father confessor," Arthur said with a smile as he bent to kiss her gently on the cheek, just as he was accustomed to do with Julia and Judith. He looked surprised after he had done it.

It would be hard to say whether Rose or Arthur was blushing the redder as she climbed the steps to the front door and he turned back to the gateway.

Lord Kincade helped Judith choose a new fan and paid for it, though she insisted that their father had left her quite enough pin money. He suggested that they go to Gunter's for an ice.

"What? Twice in as many days, Giles?" she said, turning a delighted face up to his.

"I need to talk to you," he said.

"Oh." Her smile faded. "You are going to play the substitute father again just when I thought you had left off being so stuffy. I wish Papa would come home to be my father. I would far prefer you as a brother, Giles. I always loved you dearly when you were merely my brother."

"Yes, well," he said, "I have discovered that being a parent is no unalloyed delight, Jude. I think I will put off being a father to an almost grown-up lady for at least twenty years, thank you. But it is not a scold I am going to give, so you may plan to enjoy your ice."

Judith smiled at him and linked her arm through his, clutching the package containing her new fan in her free hand. "I always like to walk with you, Giles," she said. "You are so very tall and handsome. I like to watch other ladies who do not know you are my brother look at me with envy."

"Wretch!" he said. "There are doubtless as many men who would like to be in my place right now."

Judith laughed. "Are you going to marry Daisy soon?" she asked. "I do hope so. She is a great deal of fun. Do you love her dreadfully, Giles?"

"Can one love dreadfully?" he asked. "But perhaps it is the best description of all for my feelings about Daisy. And what about you, Jude? Do you have any feelings for Colonel Appleby?"

He was seating her at a table in Gunter's. Judith looked up at him in some surprise. "I like him," she said. "He has a great deal of character."

"Hardly surprising in one who has distinguished himself so well in battle," Lord Kincade said. "He is offering for you, you know."

Judith turned pink. "No, I do not know," she said.

"He came to me yesterday," Lord Kincade said, "to ask if I thought it would be quite inappropriate for him to post down to Bath to talk to Papa."

Judith's jaw had dropped. "What did you say?" she asked, and waited impatiently while her brother ordered their ices.

"I said I thought it quite appropriate," he said, "though I could not speak for you. But he decided that he would speak with Papa before making his offer to you. I believe he has left already."

Judith stared.

"How do you feel about it?" he asked.

"He wants to marry me?" Judith said. "But he is a hero!"

"I suppose heroes can fall in love as well as be heroic," Lord Kincade said with a grin. "Do you love him, Jude? Or feel any affection for him? Or is it unfair of me to ask?"

"I think I do," she said. "I think I do, Giles. I am not quite sure yet. I . . ."

"Powers?" he said tentatively, and watched her color up.

"He thinks I love him," she said in a small voice, "and he loves me dreadfully, Giles. And he wants me to meet him at Vauxhall and stay with him for a time so that Papa will be forced to let me marry him." The words came rushing from her mouth.

Lord Kincade watched her grimly. "Can't you see, Jude," he said, "that it is your fortune he is after? Love? That man does not know the meaning of the word."

"But he is reformed," Judith said, tears in her eyes. "And I don't want to hurt him, Giles. I have been so thoughtless."

"Listen, Jude," her brother said, "your Lord Powers and his father between them love you so much that they saw to it that I did not reach Bath two weeks ago. And if Daisy had not intervened, they would have seen to it that I was otherwise unable to interfere with their plans for you too."

Judith looked stricken. "It is not true," she said. "Oh, it is not true, Giles. His father does not even like him. He is as rich as Croesus and will not even help his own son."

"The marquess is so far in debt," Lord Kincade said, "that he is like to spend his future years in debtors' prison, Jude, unless the family fortunes are somehow restored. Marriage to an heiress is the quickest and surest way of doing that."

Judith stared at him and then at her ice, which she had been eating without even realizing the fact. "I don't know what to believe," she said, "or what to do."

"Leave it to me," her brother said. "Just leave it all to me, Jude, will you?"

"You will not hurt him?" she asked.

Lord Kincade hesitated. "Not unless I have to," he promised. "Jude, tell me you will have nothing more to do with him. I don't want to watch you like a jailer or distrust you. Yet I must, if I think that a misguided sense of obligation might put you in that man's clutches for the rest of your life. Can you reassure me?"

"I shall write to him today," Judith told her ice, "and tell him that I cannot love him and cannot marry him and must release him from all obligation to me."

"And if he answers, Jude?"

"Then I shall read his letter," she said. "But I will have nothing more to do with him after that, Giles."

"Good girl," he said, reaching across the table to squeeze her hand. "You have made a decision worthy of the girl I have watched grow into womanhood for the last few years."

"Flatterer!" she said, looking up at him through her lashes, pleased.

15

The morning after the concert Daisy chose to walk early in the park, declining all company except that of a maid. Rain kept her at home the next day, though she was back for more exercise and more fresh air the day after, the same day as had been appointed for the visit to Vauxhall.

On the first morning she acquired an aged and infirm aunt in Scotland, widowed and without child, very rich, of course, and equally inevitably holding Daisy in deep affection. Daisy was not at all sure that the aunt would not will her fortune to all of her three surviving relatives: Daisy, Rose, and their mother. But Mama was quite convinced that all would be left to Daisy. Not that she wished the aunt to pass on soon, of course, and not that she was greedy for the fortune, considering the fact that her own was large enough to keep her in considerable luxury for the rest of her life. But, still, it was pleasant to know oneself loved.

Daisy had still not mastered the trick of producing excess water from her eyes, but she had learned the almost equally satisfactory trick of dabbing a lace handkerchief against her nose and sniffing delicately.

On the second morning, the rainy one, Judith received a reply to her letter, in which Lord Powers expressed his deep sorrow at her decision to see him no more, swore his undying love and devotion, and chivalrously renounced all claim to her affections, since that appeared to be her wish. He remained et cetera, et cetera before affixing his signature with a flourish.

On the third morning, the day of the Vauxhall visit, Daisy asked advice of the gentleman she had coincidentally met in the park twice within a week. Not that she usually asked advice of anyone, being a woman of independent character. But sometimes the burdens of life bore down on one's shoulders so that one felt almost bowed to the ground.

"Would it be very improper," she concluded, "and very wrong of me to end my betrothal, do you think?" But her kid gloves covered her mouth almost before the words had escaped it and she gazed in dismay up at Lord Powers. "Oh, my lord," she almost whispered, "please disregard those words. I have no right to ask such a thing of a virtual stranger. You have been so kind to me that I sometimes forget that in fact you are scarcely more than that."

Lord Powers stopped walking and turned to her, deep concern in his eyes. He took the hand closer to him in one of his and covered it with the other. "Indeed, my dear ma'am," he said, "I am more honored than I can say to find that you trust me so. And I beg you not to concern yourself about the burden you have put upon me. It is a sweet burden when it comes from a lady whose esteem it is an honor to cultivate."

Daisy allowed her eyes to drop to his chin and then bravely forced them to look into his again. She applied just a touch of pressure to the hand beneath her own.

"Your betrothal has been a mistake?" he asked gently. "I own I am not altogether surprised, ma'am. The Fairhavens are all high in the instep. For all that he must covet your wealth, I will wager that it weighs heavily with Kincade to know that your father was in trade. Indeed, I would not for the world distress you, but I heard him say as much in White's a mere few days ago."

Daisy gulped. "Oh," she said, reaching with her free hand for her lace handkerchief.

"Break your engagement," Lord Powers said with fierce impulse. "Oh, ma'am, I have said nothing in the past few days because I have felt it dishonorable to do so. But I would lay all my devotion, all my love at your feet. And I can see now that you are unhappy. Allow me to be of service to you. End this betrothal, which is no less than an insult to you. And allow me to protect you from all gossip and scandal. Marry me, and I will take you away from here.''

"Oh, my lord,'' Daisy said. "I am overwhelmed. I am speechless. I could not possibly so impose upon your good nature.''

"Good nature!'' he cried, possessing himself of her other hand and holding both against his coat. "I am confoundedly selfish, ma'am. I see the chance of gaining what in the past days I have dreamed of and convinced myself is far beyond my reach. I see the chance of winning your esteem and—dare I hope?— your love. There will be those, of course, and many of them, who will say that I too am merely interested in your fortune, but I will trust to your better judgment of me to perceive the truth. I wish you might be penniless so that you would know the purity of my devotion to your person.''

"Oh, my lord,'' Daisy said. "But, no, it cannot be. The scandal would be too great. For you as well as for me.'' She laughed a little shakily. "You have given me a glimpse of heaven, sir, but we are on earth. It is impossible. I must ask you to release my hands.'' But she leaned forward and rested her forehead very briefly against those hands and his.

"Do you think I care,'' he asked fiercely, "what the world says about me? I would gladly exchange my reputation and even my honor, ma'am, for your love and—oh, happiness beyond imagining—your hand in marriage. But of course, your honor must be protected from permanent taint. Let me think for a moment.''

Daisy obediently gave him that moment, hanging her head and making no attempt to force him to grant her request to release her hands.

"You said you are going to Vauxhall tonight?'' Lord Powers asked at last.

Daisy looked up at him, hope in her eyes, and nodded. She could not recall telling him any such thing.

"Very well, then,'' he said, pressing her hands closer to his heart. "You must meet me there. It must appear that you have wandered away by accident rather than by design. And I shall take you away for an hour or two—not long enough to completely destroy your honor, ma'am, but long enough that your reputation will be called into question and Lord Kincade made anxious to be rid of you. All the blame will be on me, of course. You will receive a great deal of sympathy, but all the highest sticklers will agree that it is only fitting that you marry me.''

''But''—Daisy looked earnestly up into his eyes and moved a step closer—''you will be seen as a rogue, my lord. Perhaps his lordship will even challenge you to a duel. I cannot ask such a thing of you.''

He laughed softly down at her before releasing her hands suddenly and taking a step back as a maid walking a dog almost as large as herself came into view at the end of the path they were standing on. ''I am known as a rogue anyway, Miss Morrison,'' he said, drawing her arm within his and beginning to walk again. ''I am afraid I have lived a wild life. But it is amazing how love can smite one quite unawares and transform one. One more wild deed, ma'am—I shall kidnap you for an hour this evening—and then a lifetime of love and service to the lady of my dreams.'' He squeezed her arm against his side and smiled warmly down into her eyes.

Daisy found it as impossible to induce a blush as to force tears. She contented herself with a worshipful look and a murmured ''Oh, my lord!''

Daisy's own maid, who had been sent on a shopping errand for the second morning that week, also appeared a few minutes later, but not before a time and a place for a rendezvous that evening had been set. Altogether, Daisy decided as she walked briskly home a few paces ahead of Penny, life had been made a great deal safer for that silly Judith, who surely had not realized in how much danger she had placed her virtue and her happiness.

Lord Kincade was dressing for dinner and feeling remarkably cheerful, too cheerful, he thought with a frown as his valet finally succeeded in tying his neckcloth to the satisfaction of both. For the best part of a week life had been relatively free of problems. And embarrassment.

Judith had been true to her word and written to Powers after their talk at Gunter's. She had received and read his reply the following day, and had shown it to him when he called to see Julia. She had even smiled rather ruefully when he had suggested that Powers' easy capitulation must mean that he had another poor rich innocent on a string. And he believed that the affair—if it could be called that—really was at an end.

Judith had been quiet and biddable ever since, driving out only once with Rose and Arthur and once with him. Although she had attended a ball two evenings before and had smiled and danced the night away, she had taken a different partner for each set and had not seemed to favor any one of them. She seemed preoccupied. and Lord Kincade rather hoped that it was Colonel Appleby who was causing the somewhat absentminded expression, so uncharacteristic of his younger sister.

The colonel was coming to dinner, as were Daisy, Hetty, Rose, Arthur, Judith, and Peter. Daisy had suggested the day before that he not invite Sir Phillip Corbett.

"What?" he had said. "You have failed to net him, Daisy? I am amazed that you have given in without a fight. And yet I see no visible bruises."

"Oh," she had said, coloring up prettily, "he offered for her, you know. He came to speak to me yesterday and asked if he should write to Mama or go and visit her. But I said no, that Mama would be delighted with anyone that Rose and I approved of. I sent him to talk to Rose."

He had raised his eyebrows and grinned at her before turning to concentrate on the tricky business of guiding his phaeton through the park gates while someone in a curricle was trying to come at a gallop in the opposite direction. "Never tell me that Rose has rejected the brilliant suitor you cultivated for her," he had said when he was able.

"Well, she did," Daisy had admitted. "And can you imagine anything more silly? I found her in tears afterward and quite inconsolable for all of ten minutes. I thought Sir Phillip must have insulted her dreadfully and was all prepared to go running after him with my umbrella. But the silly girl was crying because she thought she had let me down."

"And she had not?" he had asked.

"Well, what do I have to say to the matter?" Daisy had said. "I am not the one who would have to spend my life with him.

It seems that Rose cannot feel enough affection for him to wish to marry him. If I had only known that, I would not have been pushing them together at every turn. But the foolish child has been trying desperately to develop an affection for him because she thought her refusal would grieve me.''

''So, Daisy,'' Lord Kincade had said, ''you have to begin all over again. Perhaps we can invite any stray dukes or marquesses we happen to find at Vauxhall tomorrow to join us in our box. They are all bound to be young and handsome and rich, you know. It is an essential qualification for such high rank.''

''Oh, what nonsense!'' she had said before laughing gaily. ''But you are quite right. We must begin again. Rose surprised me, though, by telling me that she does not want anyone grand or anyone who will be always wanting to live in London or at one of the spas. She wants to live in the country, she says, and lead a quiet, comfortable life. How strange! I never thought to ask her before we came to London. Not that she could have made an informed decision at that time, of course, having never been in town to know how well she would like it. I think perhaps it will be wise for me to let Rose choose whom she wants to show interest in. Do you not agree?''

''Decidedly,'' he had said, smiling down at her before being alerted by her suddenly fixed stare and change of expression.

''Stop!'' she had commanded, and the phaeton had swayed alarmingly as she had tried to jump to her feet and he had had to calm the horses with one hand while his other was busy holding her down in her seat.

''No, Daisy, I absolutely will not,'' he had said firmly. ''There are at least half a dozen gentlemen rushing to the rescue of the poor girl. I am sure that her dress will be ruined after getting itself caught so firmly in the wheel of that carriage, but perhaps the sensation she has created will be compensation enough. She certainly does not need your assistance, my dear, when she has six—no, seven—men to choose among.''

''You are quite right,'' she had said, relaxing in her seat again. ''Poor girl. She was doubtless not looking where she was going and did not realize how close she was to the passing carriages.

Now she will be embarrassed to have drawn attention to herself. Poor girl.''

Lord Kincade had grinned, partly in relief. A mere week or so before and he would not have reacted in time to prevent Daisy from vaulting out of the very high seat of the phaeton, doubtless giving a few dozen people in the vicinity a delightfully shocking display of legs and ankles and petticoats in the process.

"Do you realize that Rose's very single state forces us into an extended betrothal?" he had asked, wondering why the thought amused rather than exasperated him. "Perhaps she will decide to go to her grave as an octogenarian old maid. Have you thought of that? This could be the longest betrothal in history, Daisy.''

"Oh, nonsense!" she had said. "We will end it when the Season is over whether Rose has a beau or not. Indeed, we might as well do so right now. I am sure everyone has forgotten that silly kiss in the Riplinger salon."

"Ah, but I have not," Lord Kincade had said. "And you have wounded me beyond all bearing, Daisy. I have kissed a number of females in my time and received not a few compliments on my expertise, as well as one or two stinging slaps at my presumption. But never have my kisses been called silly before.''

She had looked at him, startled, before giving vent to such a merry peal of laughter that Lord Kincade could have wished that he had chosen to say what he had, if at all, in some place other than the middle of Rotten Row at five o'clock of the afternoon.

And so, Lord Kincade thought, allowing his valet to help him on with his tight-fitting evening coat of dark-green velvet, the days had gone by with remarkable ease. He could trust Judith, he felt. Indeed, it seemed altogether likely that the colonel would choose that very evening to declare himself and Judith to accept him. And he could almost believe that Daisy had settled down to town life and knew now just how to comport himself in order not to draw attention either to herself or to him.

Almost! But perhaps not quite. He would always feel like a coiled spring when Daisy was close by. One never knew when

she was likely to charge off on some self-appointed and quite
unnecessary crusade. He was going to have to be especially
watchful at Vauxhall. It was a place of unusual revelry, a place
for high and low born, a place for romance and intrigue and
plain enjoyment. It could be a veritable paradise for someone
like Daisy—not that there was anyone else like Daisy. She would
doubtless see a dozen injustices to be put instantly right. He
must stay very close to her.

And that would not be quite the death sentence he would have
found it a week and more before. It was true that his opinion
of Daisy Morrison had not changed. She was an independent,
managing, interfering, impulsive, and downright irritating
baggage. And life was going to be indescribably tranquil again
at the end of the Season when he was finally rid of her. But
for all that, he was finding her amusing. One never knew quite
what she might say or do in a given situation, and he could enjoy
the surprise, provided it was not one of her famous disasters.

He found her sense of humor refreshing. She did not mind
laughing at her own expense. And she certainly did not try to
guard her dignity by tittering and simpering behind a hand.
Daisy Morrison threw back her head and laughed out her amusement for the whole world to hear no matter where she was or
who present. And she always succeeded in looking quite
impossibly pretty when she was doing so. And yet there was
nothing posed or self-conscious in any of her words or actions
or gestures. She seemed to have no conception whatsoever of
her own attractions.

And he was attracted. He found himself, at first unconsciously
and then quite deliberately, touching her whenever he could do
so without being too obvious. And he was always pleased if
she was at Julia's when he made his daily calls, for then he had
an excuse to kiss her as he kissed his sister. He would like to
have one more opportunity to kiss her properly before their
betrothal came to an end. He would have to be careful not to
go too far, of course. It would not do to find that he was honor-
bound after all to insist upon marriage. But just once more to
hold her slim and supple form fully against him, to possess
himself of her mouth instead of merely pecking her on the cheek.

Once more to feel her response. Because she did respond to him. She was as attracted to him as he to her.

Perhaps that night at Vauxhall, he thought, realizing suddenly that he must have been staring into the mirror and smoothing the lace of his cuffs over his hands for several minutes. He looked around him rather consciously, but remembered in some relief that he had already dismissed his valet. He got to his feet and went downstairs to await the arrival of his guests.

They would approach Vauxhall Gardens by water, Lord Kincade announced, since it was far more enchanting, if more inconvenient, to do so than to cross the river by carriage on the new iron bridge.

It was doubtful that Judith and Rose would have noticed if they had been lifted into a hot-air balloon and conveyed to the pleasure gardens that way. They had had their heads together whenever they could snatch a moment of privacy since they had arrived at Lord Kincade's for dinner.

"He was back this morning," Judith had said when they had retired for a few moments after dinner. "He must have flown like the wind to Bath and back again. And he came this afternoon far too soon after luncheon for a normal call."

"And?" Rose had prompted.

Judith's eyes had become dreamy. "And he said . . . Oh, he said such wonderful things, Rose. I cannot tell you, truly I can't. His words would sound silly if said aloud now."

"And you accepted him?" Rose had asked eagerly.

"No." Judith had looked stricken for a moment. "But I did not say no either. I just could not bring myself to say either. I was in love with Lord Powers just a few weeks ago, and now I love the colonel. How can I trust my feelings, Rose? I am so fickle. But this has crept up on me unawares. There has not been the romance that there was with Lord Powers, and no intrigue. But, oh, I do love him. I do. I want to say yes."

"And you still have the chance?" Rose had asked.

"Oh, yes," Judith had assured her. "He took my hand and told me with the greatest show of kindness that he would not rush me, that he would wait and ask me again. Oh, Rose, I do love him so. Does he not have quite splendid looks? And have you noticed the trick his eyes have of crinkling in the corners when he smiles? And his military bearing? And I think it matters not at all that he is twelve years my senior.''

And when they had climbed into the boat and begun the crossing, Judith remembered that her friend had had a less happy experience in the last two days. She squeezed her hand. ''Have you felt any regret about rejecting Sir Phillip?'' she asked. ''He is so very handsome, Rose, and was so very attentive.''

But Rose assured her that she felt only relief that she had been able to put an end to the unwelcome courtship before she could hurt the gentleman too greatly. ''For he is very charming and kind,'' she said.

Lord Kincade took Daisy's arm firmly through his when they entered the gardens, and listened indulgently to her exclamations of delight. A beautiful evening had brought out revelers by the score. And he had chosen a night when there was to be dancing and fireworks, always more popular occasions than those evenings when there were concerts.

He looked down at her as they approached the tiered boxes, one of which he had hired for the night. ''It is all rather splendid, Daisy, is it not?'' he said. ''One cannot come to London, you know, and not spend at least one night at Vauxhall.''

''It is like a fairy tale,'' she said, clinging obediently to his arm and walking with a spring in her step.

But she had been unusually quiet during dinner and the journey to Vauxhall. Suspiciously quiet. And quite unnaturally docile. If one did not know better, one would assume that Daisy was a perfectly normal young lady of the *ton*. Unfortunately, or perhaps fortunately, he knew Daisy Morrison better than to think that for a moment. Considerably better. He imprisoned her arm more firmly against his side.

Daisy was looking about her, trying to envision the route Lord Powers had described to her so that she would not miss their rendezvous later. She thought she would be able to find the spot. But just a few details teased at her mind. Daisy was not a creature of forethought. She could act with great resolution when an urgent situation presented itself to her. She was not a very effective planner.

Exactly how was her plan going to secure Judith's safety for all time? She was almost convinced that she had ensnared Lord Powers in the last few days with her tales of wealth, real and pretended. But could she be quite sure? What if he were as good an actor as she hoped she was? And what if he was a man who hedged his bets? What if he had assignations to meet both her and Judith at Vauxhall? And what if his meeting with Judith was to precede his meeting with her? There was only one solution to that particular problem: she would have to keep her eye on Judith for every moment that ensued before it was time to effect her own disappearance.

And how long must she stay with Lord Powers? Her own desire would be to meet him, laugh in his face, spit in his eye, or preferably punch him in the eye if she had the chance—and return to her party with an account of all that had happened in the last several days. The news would be painful and humiliating for Judith, it was true, but Daisy thought that only so could she show the girl beyond all doubt just what her beloved Lord Powers was really like.

But would such a brief meeting be enough? Would she be believed? Would she have to drive around with him for an hour, as he had suggested, so that her absence would be noted and her explanation of that absence seem more credible? But how could she support the thought of driving in a closed carriage with Lord Powers for an hour? What on earth would she talk about for that long? Would she have to invent an uncle in Ireland and a godfather in Wales?

One idea that she was toying with was to listen to Lord Powers' proposal again, cry a little, or rather dab at her nose and sniff a little, hesitate, gaze meltingly at him, allow him a kiss . . . No, not that! Even the idea of saving Judith could not induce her to make that sacrifice. She would ask him to call on her the following morning for her answer. And she would have them lined up—Judith, Giles, and anyone else who cared to enjoy the show—listening to the man as he repeated his vows of undying devotion and as she, at last, and with enormous satisfaction, unleashed on him the full force of her true sentiments.

It was a very satisfactory idea—the best, she thought. But of

course, she would then have to keep Judith under watch for the
rest of the evening in case Lord Powers decided that a bird in
the hand was worth a little more than a better-feathered one
in the bush.

And so Daisy allowed Lord Kincade to seat her close beside
him in their box, danced with him, talked with him, smiled at
him, warmed to his closeness, thought absently how she would
enjoy stealing down one of the shaded paths with him until
they were quite alone with the night and the darkness and
the music and each other, and scarcely took her eyes from
Judith.

Lord Kincade, after a waltz during which he had drawn Daisy
rather closer than he would have dared to do in a ballroom,
and held her firmly with a hand at the small of her back, and
breathed in the scent of her hair, and gazed down at her pretty,
bright-eyed face, also felt the urge, even the need, to take his
betrothed onto one of those more secluded paths. Yet, when
he suggested almost against her ear that they walk for a while,
she glanced hastily about her, said no, she would prefer to return
to their box, and then grabbed his arm more tightly and said
yes, indeed it would be delightful to walk.

Yet she proceeded to confound his intentions and frustrate
his desires not a little by quickening her pace, dragging him
in her wake, and hailing Judith and Colonel Appleby, who were
ahead of them. She had about as much sensibility as a boulder,
Lord Kincade thought, trying not to grind his teeth quite audibly.
It was perfectly clear to him that Appleby had been about the
same sort of not quite proper business as he had been contemplating. And Judith did not look altogether pleased to glance
back over her shoulder and find a brother wearing a wide and
artificial smile walking along behind her, almost close enough
to breathe down her neck.

He felt that old familiar urge to feel Daisy's neck between
his two hands.

The two couples strolled on, conversing amiably about
nothing in particular, while at least three of them, Lord Kincade
thought, were doubtless dreaming of how they might have been
using their time to better advantage. He felt progressively less

charitable toward the fourth, who chattered brightly on and seemed neither to know nor to care that she might have been deep in a very improper and satisfactory embrace with him by that time.

16

Rose felt sad about Sir Phillip, for she knew that her rejection of his offer had disappointed him, and she liked him. However, it was a relief to be free again, and to know that she had not hurt Daisy as much as she had feared to do. Although the future did not look particularly bright, consisting as it must of a return home during the summer and probably marriage to one of the local gentry whom she had known all her life, she felt more relaxed on this evening at Lord Kincade's and at Vauxhall than she had felt since before she had left home with Daisy. She was with her sister and the people who had become her friends since her arrival in London, and she was happy.

She was happy dancing with Lord Doncaster, who kept her amused with a constant stream of teasing remarks and amusing comments on the people surrounding them. And she was happy dancing with Arthur, though by no stretch of the imagination could he be called skilled at that pursuit.

She liked Arthur a great deal. He was a kind gentleman, a dear friend, the brother she had never had. And something more too. She had looked on him somewhat differently since that morning when he had revealed to her such an unexpected inner glimpse of himself. She would not have suspected that behind the very genuine kindness and sweetness and gentleness there was a certain toughness and a very human resentment of those who saw the surface and not the soul of the man.

Of course it made sense, Rose had realized in the days since that revelation. No man who was nothing but gentle could hope to penetrate the evil and the corruption that poverty and deprivation had ingrained in the people among whom he worked. Such a man would be laughed out of the slums, if he were allowed out at all. And such a man would crumble under the impossibility of his task or be embittered by repeated rejection. Only a man who was very tough inside could maintain his sweetness and his commitment to love against such odds.

Arthur smiled ruefully at Rose after apologizing for the third time for his poor dancing skills. He glanced at his brother and the colonel, both of whom were performing the steps and guiding their partners as if they had been born to the task. "I think I am more skilled at walking than dancing, Miss Morrison," he said. "Would you care to walk?"

"I would love to, sir," she said, taking his offered arm. "This place is so very lovely. The lanterns in the trees make it seem an enchanted land. I wonder if it looks quite ordinary by daylight?"

"The best thing to do," Arthur said, "is not to come here by day to find out. Some truths are best not known. Let us enjoy the night and keep the memories unspoiled afterward."

"A very sensible idea," Rose said, laughing.

They strolled along the main path, looking up at the lanterns, trying to name all the colors and shades of colors they could see in the swaying beams and interminglings of light around them and in the lighter and darker shadows.

"Tell me about the parish to which you will be going," Rose said.

"It is beautiful," he said. "A picturesque village in the Cotswolds. And a small cottage of my own near the church, with a lovely garden that must have been the pride and joy of my predecessor or his wife. Only yesterday I decided finally that I would go there."

Rose looked her inquiry. "I thought it had all been settled long ago," she said.

"Oh, it was," he agreed. "But since coming here to spend the spring with Giles, I have seen the extent of the poverty, the extent of the need here, and I have thought that perhaps it is selfish to settle in my peaceful Cotswolds village."

He led her without thought off the main path to sit on a wooden bench half-hidden among some of the deeper shadows.

"But I realized only yesterday," he said, "that it would be far more selfish to stay here. I have felt no calling to be here in London. If I stayed, it would be only because I feel that I could be important here, that I am needed here, that I do not trust anyone else, even God, to do the work. My calling is to parish duties, where my name will never be famous for spectacular service to the poor." He smiled. "But there will be poor enough to serve wherever I go. Our Lord himself said that we would always have the poor with us."

Rose smiled at him. "The people in your Cotswold village are fortunate," she said.

"And you," he said. "Have you made any decisions about your future? I notice that Sir Phillip is not here this evening."

"I rejected his offer two days ago," Rose said. "I was sorry, for he is a pleasant gentleman and deserves better than rejection. But he also deserves the undivided affection of the woman he will marry, and I could not give him that."

"You have done what is right," he said. He took her hand in his and ran his thumb along the length of her fingers. They sat in silence for several minutes, watching the revelers walk past on the main path, some in noisy gaiety, others in quieter conversation.

"Life in the country can be very dull," Arthur said, "after this. Very few entertainments, little that is fashionable, very few people of one's own class and background."

"Only close friends and a warm sense of community and all the loveliness of nature and the changing seasons," Rose said.

He closed his hand around hers and squeezed it. "Ah, yes," he said. "It makes town life sound insufferably dull, does it not?"

"Yes," Rose said, her eyes on his long-fingered hand closed around hers.

"But you have grown up in a grand house with a wealthy father," he said. "Life in a cottage would be far more restricting."

"Papa was very rich, but we lived frugally," Rose said. She smiled fleetingly up at him. "There are those who would say that Papa was miserly. Your cottage sounds lovely. Is the garden very full of flowers? Are there roses?''

"Dozens, I believe," he said. "To match your name."

Rose smiled at his hand.

"Perhaps you would like some time," Arthur said after a pause. "To think about it."

Rose shook her head.

"One would like to be able to offer the world and the universe to one's loved one," he said.

"I think that is what you have to offer," Rose said in such a small voice that he had to bend his head closer to hear what she said.

"I have always prided myself on my independence," Arthur said. "I have known myself loved by a great many people, but I have thought that I needed no one but God. And now I see that in that too I have been guilty of pride. We need to depend on others. We need to be vulnerable. You have become very indispensable to me, my little friend."

"Have I?" Rose looked up at him, the faint light from the main path revealing the brightness of her eyes. "Have I really, Arthur? I thought you so complete in yourself. I thought it presumptuous to imagine that you might ever need me."

"You have become my friend during the past week," he said. "The only one I have ever had really. I have always been so careful not to disappoint those who have been my friends. But I have shown you my weaknesses, my dear, my pride, my tendency to trust in my own powers more than in my Lord's. And I feel stronger for having done so."

"I am glad," Rose said, gazing up into his face.

"But I want to be more than your friend," he said. "I must be more if I am to ask you to share my life. I want to be your lover, Rose. I have never been anyone's lover, either—you see how poor my experience of life has been? I have no idea how to make a woman happy, how to show my love. But I want to be your lover."

"I have never been anyone's lover either," Rose said. "But I will give you my heart and my self and my lifelong devotion, Arthur." She lifted his hand and laid it against her cheek. "I love you, you see."

He smiled suddenly. "This is very nearly a public place," he said, "and we are not even quite betrothed, are we, since I have not spoken yet with either your mother or your sister and indeed have not said the words, 'Will you marry me?' But I must kiss you, Rose. May I kiss you?"

She smiled impishly back at him. "I was just wondering if you were something of a slow top," she said.

She was on her feet suddenly, being kissed quite thoroughly enough to answer her doubts by her very tall lover, her head tipped back over his arm.

"Now," he said breathlessly when they were finished, bending in order to bring his forehead against hers, "that is acceptable behavior in a clergyman only if the lady is his betrothed. You had better save me from everlasting fire, Rose, by marrying me. Will you?"

"A foolish question, sir," Rose said, turning her head so that she could kiss his mouth again. "I do not allow any man but my betrothed to kiss me, you know. That was my first kiss, Arthur, and more lovely than I imagined it could be. Yes, I will marry you. Of course I will. Kiss me again?"

Arthur spent all of five minutes obliging his newly betrothed.

By a little before midnight, a little before the fireworks display was to begin, Judith was beginning to look somewhat out of sorts. She had danced with the colonel, with Lord Doncaster, with a couple of other acquaintances from adjoining boxes; she had walked twice with the colonel; and she had sat in their box, eating ham and bread rolls and drinking wine.

All very satisfactory, one might think. But how could one relax and enjoy oneself, and—more to the point—how could one invite the kisses of the gentleman one was realizing more and more each moment that one loved when every time one turned one's head one's brother was there smiling sheepishly at one? Poor Daisy, Judith thought when she was inclined to spare sympathy for anyone but her own poor self. Daisy should be enjoying her first visit to Vauxhall, but instead she was being dragged around by Giles, who clearly did not trust his younger sister's word, given in a burst of affection and confidence earlier in the week.

Judith turned on her brother finally when Lord Doncaster was dancing with Rose and the colonel with Hetty, and Arthur had taken himself off to speak with some acquaintances, who looked like shady characters if she had ever seen any. Daisy was sitting at Giles' other side, watching the world go by.

"This is insufferable," Judith hissed. "I wonder you did not just attach my wrist to yours by a chain, Giles, and be done with it. I hate you!"

"What is this?" Lord Kincade asked in surprise.

"Don't act innocent!" his sister said, her dark eyes blazing into his. "You have followed me everywhere tonight. Not only have you not let me out of your sight, you have not let me out of your reach. I thought you trusted me."

"And so I do, Jude," he said in some amazement. "I have not been following you. It is just that Daisy looks for company and has grown fond of you. You wish for a few moments alone? With Appleby, I assume? You shall have them, my dear. We will occupy ourselves alone or with other company for a short while, will we not, Daisy?"

And he realized immediately the fatal mistake he had made, as soon as he turned and smiled at empty air suspended above the equally empty chair beside him. For the first time all evening he had not held Daisy's arm imprisoned against his side. And sure enough, she had probably spotted some poor courtesan fleeing along the path, flirting her fan at a panting pursuer, and Daisy had gone crusading off to rescue her. And there she went, almost out of sight already, for all the world like a naughty child escaping its nurse.

Lord Kincade uttered a series of oaths, did not pause to apologize for the abuse to his sister's ears, and raced off after his betrothed. This time, he thought as he shouldered and elbowed his way past the press of people in his path and tried not to lose sight of the fleeing figure in white lace ahead of him. This time when he caught up to her and extricated her from whatever embarrassing predicament she had got herself into, she would not escape with a polite scolding. Or with a blistering from his tongue. This time he would surely give her a thorough walloping or—or something, anyway.

Lord Kincade lost precious moments of time when he missed

Daisy suddenly on the path ahead of him and had to decide which of two paths, one bearing to the left and one to the right, she had taken. But a pair of lovers blocked the one to the left, he saw as soon as he turned into it. He headed down the path to the right.

The sound of voices halted him before he saw her. How would the couple she had come upon greet her arrival? he wondered. He imagined that the man, whoever he was, might well cut up rough. Such a dark path was not likely to have been chosen by a pair merely intent on snatching a light kiss. He might help Daisy better by not rushing ahead too precipitately himself. He crept quietly forward, keeping behind the trunks of trees, though the darkness itself was an effective screen.

Yet, when he came within sight of Daisy, it was to find that she had only one companion, if one discounted the much larger individual who was himself hidden behind a tree. And if his eyes did not deceive him, Lord Kincade thought, squinting in an attempt to accustom his sight to the darkness and if his ears did not deceive him, Daisy's companion was Lord Powers.

"Yes, of course I came," Daisy was saying. "Did you think I would not?"

"Ah," Powers said, taking her hands and holding them against his coat, "I feared perhaps you would lose your trust in me, my dear. You have to be very brave to put your reputation in jeopardy thus in order to free yourself from an unwelcome betrothal."

Lord Kincade gripped the trunk against which he was leaning.

"How could I lack courage," Daisy said, "when I saw that I was fleeing to you, my lord? But for all that, I am not courageous. I am taking the coward's way out, allowing you to blacken your name because I do not wish to be known as a woman who willingly ends her betrothal. I will not have it that way, sir. I have come to tell you that I shall hold my head high and do this the proper way."

"My dear?" Lord Powers said, while Lord Kincade clamped his teeth so tightly together that he might have expected them all to crack had he been free to contemplate the danger. "It must not be. I will not have you spoken of disparagingly."

"And I will not have you wrongfully accused," she said. "I

want you to come to Hanover Square tomorrow. And there I want us to make a public declaration of our betrothal for Lady Hetty and my sister to hear. And may his lordship rot in hell.''

His lordship regarded her neck from behind his tree with more deadly intent than ever before.

Lord Powers lifted one of Daisy's hands to his lips. ''Bravo, my dear,'' he said. ''And now, shall we go to my carriage? It is all ready for our little ride.''

''No,'' Daisy said. ''It is quite unnecessary, sir, and will only add scandal to the ending of my betrothal. You must be patient and come to me tomorrow morning.''

''Ah,'' he said, lifting the other hand to his lips, ''but patience is not my strong suit, my dear. Just a very short ride?''

''None at all,'' Daisy said briskly, trying to withdraw her hands from his.

''But I must insist,'' Lord Powers said, refusing to relinquish his hold on her.

''You must unhand me immediately, sir,'' Daisy said, ''or I will think you no gentleman. I will think that perhaps you, like all the rest, are interested only in my fortune.''

''You will think what you will, my dear,'' Lord Powers said. ''But I am not fool enough to let you go until I have some positive assurance that you will be mine. You see how desperate is my love for you?''

''Or for my fortune,'' Daisy said tartly. ''Unhand me, sir, this instant.''

Lord Powers laughed low. ''You are almost magnificent when you are angry,'' he said. ''Come, let us not quarrel. My carriage awaits. And so does my coachman.''

''Oh,'' Daisy said, turning toward the giant of a man who had just stepped from behind a tree and stood silently in front of it with folded arms. ''I have met you before, if I am not mistaken. In the stableyard of the Golden Eagle Inn. And on Bond Street, though you were uncivil enough to run away when I approached.''

Lord Kincade was torn between his desire to rush to her rescue and his certain knowledge that he would be of little help if he emerged from his hiding place at just that moment. He would be no better than Daisy Morrison herself, he thought somewhat uncharitably before focusing all his attention on the scene developing in front of him.

"Come, my dear," Lord Powers said, a hand firmly against the small of Daisy's back.

"I am not going one step with you, sir," Daisy said. "You may go to hell alone or in company with your coachman for all I care."

Lord Powers tutted. "Such sentiments from a lady," he said. "Enough talking. You will come quietly, my dear, or by force. The choice is yours."

His final word ended on something of a grunt as one of Daisy's fists connected with his stomach and the other bounced rather harmlessly off his jaw. The next moment she was engulfed in the giant man's black cloak, lifted unceremoniously from her feet, and borne kicking away under his arm.

"Take her! I will join you later," Lord Powers managed to hiss after his father's servant as a human cannonball launched itself at his midriff and deprived him far more effectively of breath than Daisy's fist had done a moment before.

Daisy, struggling in vain inside a moving coach to free herself of the foul-smelling cloak or blanket or whatever it was that covered her from head to knees, and from the bonds that held her wrists behind her and her ankles immobile, wondered why she was alone. That bully who had carried her away from Vauxhall was evidently driving. She would like just one chance to remove the yellow teeth that remained in one half of his mouth, and she envied the person unknown who had already performed that office for the other half.

But where was Lord Powers? Was she to be driven around for an hour alone like this, half-suffocated, fully blind, the circulation in her feet and hands cut to the point of total numbness? And no one on whom to vent her anger? Or was she being taken somewhere? And where was that? And what of Judith? Was she being similarly abused? Was Lord Powers himself racing toward the Scottish border with the foolish girl?

Perhaps she should have told Lord Kincade, after all, and enlisted his help, was Daisy's final thought before the carriage jolting to a stop hurled her to the floor, where she lay, kicking and struggling quite uselessly until she felt herself being hauled out as if she were a sack of meal and hurled over someone's shoulder. The breath went from Daisy's body in a *whoosh* and she struggled to regain it.

When she finally came right side up again, she found her feet on firm ground, and to her great relief hands undid the bonds around her ankles, lifted away the heavy cloak, and released her wrists. She turned to face her grinning assailant.

"You coward and bully!" she scolded. "Are you capable of attacking only females, my man, or gentlemen when you have two other bullies to hold his arms for you?"

The servant continued to grin.

"Never tell me," she said, "that whoever deprived you of half your teeth also had the good sense to remove your tongue. Doubtless the world has been deprived of a great orator. I demand that you let me go immediately. Where am I, anyway?"

In a well-appointed if shabby bedchamber, anyway, she could see at a glance as the silent giant gathered up his cloak and his scarves and took himself out of the room without having the courtesy to answer any of her queries. She heard the sound of a key turning at the other side of the door. And an inspection of the window at the other side of the room revealed, as Daisy expected, that a jump to the ground would mean certain suicide.

Not that she had any intention of jumping even if the window were ten inches from the ground and a fleet-footed hunter ready saddled were tethered there waiting for her. She had some business to conclude with Lord Powers when he deigned to put in an appearance, and he would not find her reluctant to face the confrontation.

However, Daisy thought, looking about her as she rubbed her hands together, shook them vigorously in the air, and tried to ignore the severe pins and needles that shot through them and her feet as the blood resumed its normal course through her body, he would not find her unprepared and unarmed this time. Not by any means. If her fists were not sufficient to do more than make his speech a little breathless, then she would arm herself with some more lethal weapon. She mourned the absence of her father's black umbrella for one moment, but she did not have it—indeed she would have looked quite conspicuous walking into Vauxhall with it tucked beneath her arm—so there was no point in wasting energy lamenting her lack.

There was, of course, no convenient pistol or knife lying on the washstand or in any of the drawers. Indeed, she found after a swift and determined search, there seemed to be nothing at all that would assist her in running through a man's body or smashing his skull to smithereens. Even the candles were balanced on saucers instead of being fastened into tall silver candlesticks as they ought to have been if this were any sort of respectable establishment.

Daisy was about to conclude that she would have to rely upon her less-than-effective fists when she knelt down to peer underneath the bed and espied the china chamberpot. Not a thoroughly orthodox weapon, she thought, dragging it out, weighing it in her hands, and finding it was of a quite satisfactory weight. But it might do. The only trouble was that with her height and the weight of the chamberpot, she would find it difficult to hold it high enough for it to have built up any speed by the time it collided with the top of a tall gentleman's head.

It took Daisy all of ten exhausting minutes to drag the washstand inch by inch across the room and behind the door. Yes, she thought, lifting her skirts around her thighs and clambering on top of the stand after first placing the chamberpot on it, this would do quite nicely. She lifted the pot with effort above her head, imagined the door opening, swung downward, and decided that Lord Powers might well see stars before hitting the floor when he came for her. Or if the half-toothed giant was the first in, then it would not matter greatly. She owed him a headache too.

Daisy sat on the edge of the washstand and wrapped her arms around herself. It was chilly in the bedchamber with nothing to do but wait. She contemplated dragging some of the blankets from the bed, but decided that it was better to keep herself alert and unencumbered by unnecessary coverings.

She was almost despairing of anyone's visiting her that night when she heard footsteps approaching the door. By the time she heard the key being fitted into the lock, Daisy was poised atop the washstand, the chamberpot hovering at the extremities of her stretched arms, a look of murderous determination in her eyes.

And then the door swung open and someone stepped inside. Daisy took a deep breath, shut her eyes tightly, and struck downward with all the weight of the chamberpot and her own meager strength behind it.

Someone grunted and fell to the floor an instant before Daisy's ears were assailed by the tinkling sounds of smashed china.

17

Lord Powers was neither undergrown nor unfit. It took Lord Kincade several minutes of sustained, determined effort before he bent panting over his victim in the darkness, a fistful of ruined neckcloth in his hand.

"Where has your henchman taken her, Powers?" he demanded of the dazed and bloody face below him.

"I've no idea and would not tell you if I did," Lord Powers muttered, fingering his upper lip with a hand that seemed not to be sure that it was moving in the right direction and looking rather as if he were seeing stars above the treetops. But his eyes focused a moment later on the fist poised above him and in line with his already broken nose. "To my father's house," he said. And eyeing the fist, which had not moved, "It is true, Kincade."

"And who might I expect to find there in ambush?" Lord Kincade asked, tightening his grip on the neckcloth.

Lord Powers' eyes appeared to be rolling in his head. "No one," he said. "M'father's gone away for the night and all the servants given the night off."

"So it was to be seduction full and complete," Lord Kincade said before altering the direction of his fist sufficiently to bring it crashing down onto his adversary's jaw and releasing him into unconsciousness.

Lord Kincade jumped to his feet and hovered uncertainly for a moment, looking down at the figure at his feet, glancing off in the direction the giant had taken with Daisy and back toward the main path and the boxes. He stooped down at last, dragged off Lord Powers' Hessians, peeled off his silk stockings, secured his ankles with one and his wrists with the other, looping it first around a treetrunk, and rushed off in the direction of the main path and the lights.

Several heads turned at the strange, disheveled, wild-eyed, bloody-nosed gentleman who tore past them all, and even more turned a few minutes later when he dashed back the same way with two other gentlemen in hot pursuit, one remarkably tall and slender, the other tall and muscular and of a distinctly military bearing.

"Yes, yes, you go, Giles," Arthur urged his brother as soon as they came across the still-unconscious figure tied to the tree. "Go and rescue Daisy. We will see to it that Powers is well-looked-after for the rest of the night."

Colonel Appleby was already grappling with the stocking that had been knotted around the tree and glancing with grim disgust at the prone, blood-smeared form of Lord Powers. "It is my guess that you have dealt him a sleeping potion that will last through the night, Kincade," he said, though only Arthur heard him.

Lord Kincade was already off through the trees, in search of his carriage and his pistol inside it, and leaving with his coachman the ticklish problem of conveying his passengers home with one horse too few.

One part of Powers' story seemed to be correct, anyway, Lord Kincade thought more than half an hour later as he approached with caution the dark grounds and house close to the River Thames that he had never entered before. There seemed to be no one there. The house was in darkness except for one room upstairs and one downstairs, next to the main doors.

The servant, the one who had carried Daisy off and the one who had tried to reduce him to pulp a few weeks before on the road to Bath, confirmed the fact a few minutes later as he gazed in some terror down the barrel of the viscount's pistol. There was no one in the house or anywhere else on the grounds except him and the young lady upstairs.

The man obligingly handed over the key to the young lady's room and preceded Lord Kincade to the kitchens, where he was locked inside the stout pantry. As the viscount said, having satisfied himself that no one except perhaps a circus artist would be able to get himself out of that particular prison in fewer than twenty years, the man would not starve while he waited for rescue. It irked him not to be able to set down his pistol and put to the test the question of who could reduce whom to pulp in a fair fight, but under the present circumstances, he did not feel that he could afford the luxury of possibly losing.

It was not difficult to locate Daisy's room. He remembered the position of the only room abovestairs that was lighted, and indeed, as he walked upstairs with a single candle in his hand, there was only one door that had a slit of light beneath it. And he found to his relief and satisfaction that the key fit into the lock without any trouble and turned easily.

Lord Kincade opened the door and stepped inside the room. And found himself a moment later on his hands and knees on the floor, a shower of china pieces tinkling around him, pain shooting through his shoulder, and a string of unthinkable oaths proceeding from his mouth.

"Devil take it!" he concluded mildly, addressing the floor a few inches from his nose and not bothering to look up. "I should be locked up for a blithering idiot. Why would I not have known to wave a white flag through the doorway on a fifty-foot pole? Why would I even have expected to find you cowering at the other side of the room, awaiting your fate in terror like any other decent woman?"

He rose to his knees and looked around him when there was no answer. Daisy was poised on top of a washstand behind the door, her hands covering her mouth, two large horrified eyes regarding him over the top of them.

"What in thunder are you doing up there, Daisy?" he asked, his hand going to his shoulder. "No, don't answer. You are doubtless learning to fly. And I should be thanking Providence that your aim was not all it should be, or perhaps I would be learning to fly by now too, or to stoke furnaces, depending on which place I would have ended up in. Have you turned to stone, girl? Get down from there at once."

"Oh," she said, not removing her hands, "I might have killed you."

"You might indeed," he said, looking down at the ruined china at his feet. "What was it? Some priceless ornament?"

"A ch—" Daisy gulped. "A chamberpot."

"A what?" Lord Kincade said, looking down again. "Empty, I hope."

"Oh yes." Daisy's shoulders began to shake.

"Oh, don't cry," Lord Kincade said, his voice softening. He reached up his arms for her and winced. "Don't cry, Daisy. It is all over now. You are safe."

But when he took her by the waist and lifted her down, it was to find her helpless with laughter. " 'A what?' " she said, pokering up and doing a tolerable imitation of his look of horror. " 'Empty, I hope.' " She dissolved into giggles again.

Lord Kincade ground his teeth, took the key from the keyhole, shut the door firmly, locked it from the inside, and dropped the key into his pocket.

"Now, my girl," he said grimly, "an explanation. Why did I find you in Powers' arms in Vauxhall?"

She sobered immediately. "Judith," she said, looking wildly at him. "Is Judith safe? Has Lord Powers run off with her?"

"With Judith?" he said, frowning. "Of course not. Judith put an end to that affair days ago. And he did not argue. He must have another wealthy . . ." He stopped and scratched his head. "Daisy, what in the name of all that is wonderful have you been up to?" he asked. "Have you been on a crusade to save Judith from a fate worse than death, to be followed by a marriage worse than death?"

"Have I succeeded?" she asked eagerly. "Have I saved your sister from that worm?"

He shook his head and stared down at her. "Daisy Morrison," he said, exasperation in his voice, "what am I going to do with you? Yes, you succeeded."

She clasped her hands to her bosom and beamed at him. "Where did the bruises and the blood come from?" she asked.

"From Powers' fists and my nose, I would imagine," he said, fumbling in his pocket for a handkerchief.

Daisy took it from him and dabbed at the dried blood. She lifted the handkerchief to her mouth, stopped, told him to stick out his tongue, moistened the linen, and cleaned off the blood to her satisfaction. Then she smiled and put the handkerchief back in his pocket.

Lord Kincade watched her all the while. "You did this for my sister," he said. "Did you not realize what might have happened to you, Daisy? You would not have left this room with your virtue intact."

"Oh, nonsense!" she said. "I can look after myself."

"Daisy," he said, taking her hands in his, "what am I to do with you? I think I had better marry you."

"No, no," she said, smiling warmly back at him, "there is no need. You really do not owe me anything. I did it because I like Judith and strongly dislike that toad."

"I would be doing the world a favor," he said. "And besides, only if I am your husband will I feel justified in giving you a good walloping one of these days. Daisy, I could shake you until your teeth rattle in your head. You might have been ravished, you foolish, impulsive, utterly brainless little innocent." He took her by the shoulders and did shake her two or three times.

"I will break off our betrothal immediately," she said kindly. "I see that I upset you. And though you have no cause to worry about me at all, I can understand that as a gentleman you feel responsible for my safety as long as you are sort of betrothed to me. Well, sir"—she smiled warmly up at him—"you may consider yourself free."

He shook his head and held her at arm's length. "I should be feeling like a condemned man who has been granted a reprieve as the noose is being settled over his head," he said. "The trouble is that I have grown accustomed to worrying about you. And I think perhaps I would worry more if I were not close to you and did not know what folly you were up to. I think I had better keep you near enough to be able to rush to the rescue in time. Will you marry me, Daisy?"

"Oh, how very kind you are," she said, patting the front of his waistcoat with both hands and leaving them there to pursue the absorbing task of twisting one of his silver buttons. "But you really must not worry about me, you know. You would not wish to be married to me. I would not be at all biddable."

"I know," he said, finding a spot beneath her ear so

fascinating that he had to bend his head to kiss it. "But the trouble is, Daisy, that I am thinking perhaps I would find life dull with a biddable wife."

"You must not think so," she said. "And you must not be blinded by your gratitude over what I have been able to do for Judith." He was nuzzling her earlobe, an activity that seemed to be responsible for the fact that her toes were curling themselves up inside her dancing slippers.

"I am not grateful," he said. "In fact, I think I might still wring your neck over that particular folly. But I think I will have to marry you in order to see your hair down. I have wanted to see it without the braids since I first set eyes on you."

His mouth had found the pulse at the base of her throat. Daisy felt her knees weakening. "What a silly reason for wanting to marry me," she said. "All you have to do is ask. Shall I take it down now?"

"Yes, please," he said. His mouth was feathering kisses along her bare shoulder.

"You had better put this in your pocket, then," Daisy said, coloring up and handing him one silver button. "I am afraid it came off."

"Daisy," Lord Kincade said, standing back from her as her hands deftly unpinned her braids and then unraveled them, one by one, "you are a walking disaster."

"No, no," she said, her hands going to the second braid. "It is just that your tailor did not sew it on firmly enough. Why did you lock the door from the inside?"

"There is no one in the house," he said, "except for a certain giant with half a mouthful of yellow teeth, which are probably busy at present eating the marquess out of house and home. And no one is like to be here until morning. But there is no harm in being doubly sure. I think I intend to make love to you."

"Do you?" she said, dropping her hands and giving her head a vigorous shake. "There. Is it not ridiculous? My big vanity. Mama and Papa have always tried to bully me to have it cut, but I have been mulish and refused."

"Thank heaven for stubborn women," Lord Kincade said fervently, lifting a hand to touch the fair waves that cascaded down her back to her bottom. "You are beautiful, Daisy. Will you marry me?"

"Silly," she said with a bright smile. "It is just the hair. But it is rather splendid, is it not?"

"I think I love you," he said.

"Oh, nonsense," said Daisy. "You do not."

"You are right," he said, twining his hands through her hair and around her waist and drawing her against him. "I don't *think* I love you at all. I do love you. Will you marry me, Daisy?"

The look she gave him was very strange. He hardly recognized her. She looked lost and uncertain suddenly. "You can't love me," she said. "I am a twenty-five-year-old spinster and I am loud and managing. I am unfeminine."

"Lord help me if you were feminine, then," Lord Kincade said, his mouth touching hers as he spoke. "I am burning up with desire for you as it is, Daisy Morrison, and eyeing that bed behind you with a lecherous eye. Make love with me. Marry me. Preferably in that order, love. I can't wait. Though I will if it is what you wish."

Daisy was still not herself. She hid her face against his neckcloth. "Make love to me, then," she said, "and get this silly nonsense out of your system. And then you can take me back home and I can pack to return to the country."

A very firm hand beneath her chin forced her face up and her eyes to meet his. They were angry. "Do you think it is lust only?" he said. "Do you think I can bed you and go on my way satisfied? You are in my blood, Daisy, in my soul, in my heart. I will never be free of you, and now at last, and totally to my surprise, I know that I will never want to be. You will be the torment of my life and my everlasting joy. You will promise to marry me before I take you anywhere near the bed. Daisy, what on earth is happening? You are not crying, are you?"

"Ye-e-e-es," Daisy wailed inelegantly. "Gi-i-i-iles." He was holding her head against his shoulder. She gulped noisily. "Make love to me, then. Marry me. But promise me, oh, please promise me that you will not always give in to me. I will try to dominate you, you know, and I will hate it when you will not allow me to. And I will hate you if you do.''

''I shall beat you once a week,'' he said soothingly. ''Shall we agree to Tuesday mornings? Will you marry me, Daisy?''

''Ye-e-es,'' she said on a leftover sob, and fumbled around in his pocket until she had found his handkerchief. She blew her nose loudly. ''Are you really going to make love to me, Giles? I think I would like that, though I own to being very nervous. I have never done it before, you know. Oh, of course you know that, or guess it anyway. Oh, what are you doing? Are you going to undress me? I could probably do it more quickly myself, but it feels good to have you do it. Are there not a lot of buttons down the back of my dress? I always think it foolish, when one's arms do not bend that way. Why not put the buttons at the front? But perhaps they would look ugly there and spoil the fall of a gown. Shall I undress you? These are splendid buttons on your waistcoat. I am sorry I pulled off the one.''

Lord Kincade covered her mouth with his at that moment while his hands slipped beneath her gown and shift at the shoulders and slid them downward. ''You can prattle on in a moment, love,'' he said against her mouth. He was propelling her backward and lifted her onto the bed after peeling back the blankets. ''I find it strangely arousing. Just let me kiss you for a while first.''

''I did not expect to have all my clothes removed,'' Daisy said considerably later when she had her mouth to herself again, her lover's being occupied elsewhere. ''It is shocking, really, is it not? I am sure I should not allow it. Oh, yes, Giles. Touch me there. Oh, yes. You are very beautiful. I knew you were, even with your clothes on. But you are even more beautiful with them off. Why are you laughing? Have I said something funny? Oh, dear, Giles, my teeth are chattering. But I am not at all cold.''

His face, full of laughter and passion, was poised above hers. ''I wonder if you will run out of bedtime conversation after forty or fifty years,'' he said. ''I hope not, Daisy. I do hope not.''

''Giles,'' she said. ''oh, Giles, you really do not want to be marrying me, you know. Oh, this is going to hurt, is it not?

But you must not be afraid that I will scream. I will bite my lips and not do so, I promise. I do wish my teeth would stop chattering. Oh! Oh, Giles, I think I have wanted you to do this to me since I first saw you standing below my window at the Golden Eagle. I saw red when those bullies . . . Ohhhh!''

Daisy chattered on while Lord Kincade moved in her and loved her and while she opened to him and loved him in return, but it is doubtful that anyone was listening since there was no one else closer than the pantry downstairs and certainly the two occupants of the bed were too intent on each other's pleasure and their own to listen to anything as mundane as a monologue.

''What on earth was that ghastly oily mess on your face in the stableyard?'' Lord Kincade asked sleepily many minutes later as he lay beside his betrothed, his arm beneath her head.

Daisy frowned and thought awhile, her own descent into sleep halted. ''It must have been lemon oil,'' she said. ''For my freckles, you know. I should use it every day, but I seem to forget most of the time.''

''Thank heaven for forgetful minds,'' Lord Kincade said. ''I doubt if oil would ever be effective to get rid of your freckles, Daisy, but I can tell you that it would soon effectively mask them. They would be scarcely visible beneath the spots. I forbid you ever to use the stuff again. Understood?''

''Yes, my lord,'' Daisy said meekly.

She was grinning impishly, her eyes closed, when he looked across at her.

''Tuesday mornings,'' he reminded her, closing his own eyes and wriggling into a more comfortable position. ''And perhaps Friday afternoons too.''

''Yes, my lord,'' she said. ''I will try to deserve them.''

''Sleep!'' he commanded. ''It is what is done after lovemaking. I will be waking you up soon enough anyway. We must be mad making love and sleeping like this in enemy territory. We are definite cases for Bedlam, Daisy-Morrison-soon-to-be-Fairhaven.''

They slept.

Lady Hetty was pacing the floor of her drawing room, her son Humphrey sprawled asleep in a chair by the fire, when Lord

Kincade returned with Daisy only just before dawn the following morning.

"You are safe, my dear!" she said, holding out both hands to Daisy and kissing her on the cheek. "Whatever happened? We heard only the most garbled account from the colonel, who came back again after you had gone rushing off looking like a madman, Giles, to entrust us to poor Lord Doncaster's care. Is it true that you were kidnapped by a monster, Daisy, and Lord Powers responsible?"

Daisy said that yes, indeed, it was true, but that no harm was done, as Lord Kincade had come after her and rescued her. Not that she had been in any danger anyway because that man had behaved in such an ungentlemanly way that he had got her temper up. She had agreed before the ride home in a borrowed carriage to say nothing about the chamberpot. But where was Rose? She had expected her sister to be up and worried about her.

"Oh, it is Julia," Lady Hetty said, her hands flying to her mouth. "I meant to tell you as soon as you came in, Giles. She has been brought to bed. Rose went to be with Judith."

"I am coming with you," Daisy announced before her betrothed could even open his mouth. "And this is not one of those occasions when you may forbid me to be dominating, Giles. Let me come."

"If you would just stop arguing with yourself," he said, "we could be on our way. I don't think the dear marquess will mind if we borrow his carriage and horses for one more short journey."

"I knew it would happen today or tomorrow," Daisy said as he guided her out of the house, "or I suppose I mean yesterday and today, it already being tomorrow. I was right, you see."

"So you were," Lord Kincade said, vaulting into the carriage after her, closing the door before a hastily summoned Gerry could do it for him, and kissing her squarely on the mouth. "I was rather busy driving this carriage home, my love. We have lost time to make up for."

"Yes, Giles," Daisy said meekly.

All was confusion when they arrived at Julia's house. Judith and Rose were seated together, a little apart from the rest of the company, looking flushed and anxious and pleased with themselves all at once. The Earl and Countess of Atherby had arrived sooner than expected late the previous evening and were anxiously awaiting the arrival of their first grandchild and the return of their two sons, who had apparently gone tearing off on some hair-raising adventure that no one could make much sense of.

Colonel Appleby had arrived moments before Lord Kincade and Daisy and was trying to clarify those events to people who were more intent on plying him with questions than listening for answers. Arthur was still absent.

And in the midst of them all was a huge mountain of a man, all muscle and scarcely an ounce of fat, who had been reduced to wild-eyed, trembling jitters by the fact that his beloved wife was giving birth to their child abovestairs and there was nothing in this world that he could do to help her. Daisy had not met the elusive Ambrose before. His wiry dark hair looked rather as if someone had dragged him through a hedgerow and back, she thought.

And then everyone—except the oblivious Ambrose—spotted her and Lord Kincade and plied them with questions that they might have had answered minutes before by Colonel Appleby.

"Well, I am safe," Daisy announced after the tale had been told quite satisfactorily, apart from the fact that the long period of time that had elapsed between Lord Kincade's leaving Vauxhall and their return home had not been accounted for. "And all is well that ends well. I think it is time you presented me to your mama and papa, Giles." She flushed.

"So it is," he said, "especially since you are to be their daughter within a few days."

There was a renewed buzz of excitement.

"I am?" Daisy asked.

"Certainly," he said. "I am going in search of a special license as soon as the hour is a little more decent."

"And where is Arthur?" Daisy asked Colonel Appleby. "And what has happened to Lord Powers?"

Colonel Appleby scratched his head and looked somewhat apprehensively at Lord Kincade. "The reverend is escorting

him to Dover," he said. "He seemed to think Powers would
be safer on the continent for the next year or so. I think he was
afraid that you might kill the man, Kincade."

"Damnation!" Lord Kincade said before looking his apology
to his mother. "I had not nearly finished with him."

"If it is any consolation," the colonel said, "the reverend
popped him a good one when he said something disrespectful
about Miss Morrison."

"Arthur?" Judith said in disbelief. "Arthur hit Lord Powers?
Impossible! Arthur could not harm a flea."

"Oh, I am glad!" Rose cried, her hands clasped to her bosom,
a flush high on her cheekbones. "It is just the sort of thing he
would do." And then she flushed a brighter red when all eyes
turned her way.

Fortunately for Rose, the housekeeper came bustling in at that
moment, full of importance and suppressed excitement, to ask
Ambrose to accompany her upstairs.

"The child?" the countess said, jumping to her feet.

The housekeeper clasped her hands in front of her and nodded.

"And Julia?" the countess asked.

"Tired, my lady," the housekeeper said, "and wanting her
husband."

Ambrose sighed and fainted.

"Oh, goodness gracious me," Daisy said, kneeling down
beside him and chafing his hands. "It has all been too much
for him. Grab that tablecloth, Giles, and fan his face with it.
He will soon be over the shock. Poor gentleman. It is hard for
large, strong men to stand by and see their wives go through
the discomforts of childbirth. You see, he is stirring already."

The countess had left the room. The earl was staring down
at Daisy with fascination. Judith, looking thoroughly pleased with
life and remarkably unconcerned over the fate of her erstwhile
lover, was standing at the other side of the room, both her hands
in the colonel's. Rose sat, still flushed, her eyes dreamy.

"Come on, sir," Daisy said to a blank-eyed Ambrose, "it
is time you aroused yourself. Julia is waiting for you, as is your
child. And gracious heaven, we do not even know if it is a son
or daughter. You should have been with her for the birth, you

know. That way you would not have to pace down here imagining all sorts of horrors.''

''Hush, Daisy,'' Lord Kincade said, noting that his brother-in-law's color was changing from white to pale green. ''Come on, old chap. Up you get. Fatherhood is making you weak.''

Ambrose managed to stagger to his feet and out through the door.

Daisy gazed fondly after him. ''When our children are born, Giles,'' she said for all the room to hear, ''I want you there to witness all the pain and blood and mess. And to share all the wonder. I hope it will be soon. Oh, I do hope so. I am five-and-twenty already, and I want us to have children. Perhaps in nine months' time, do you think?''

Lord Kincade met his father's eyes across her head, and the earl raised one expressive eyebrow. The viscount grimaced and passed a hand over his eyes. ''Tuesday mornings, Daisy,'' he muttered, ''and definitely Friday afternoons. And probably Sunday evenings too.''

SIGNET REGENCY ROMANCE
COMING IN OCTOBER 1989

Anita Mills
Newmarket Match

Leigh Haskell
The Paragon Bride

Sandra Heath
The Pilfered Plume